BOOK 3 OF
THE YELLOW HOODS

ALL THE KING'S-MEN

D0191149

AN EMERGENT STEAMPUNK SERIES
BY ADAM DREECE

ADZO Publishing Inc.
Calgary, Canada

ADZO Publishing Inc.
Calgary, Alberta, Canada
www.adzopublishing.com

Printed in Canada, United States, and China

This is a work of fiction. Names, characters, places, and incidents are a product of the author's imagination. Locales and public names are sometimes used for atmospheric purposes. Any resemblance to actual people, living or dead, or to businesses, companies, events, institutions, or locales is completely coincidental.

Library and Archives Canada Cataloguing in Publication

Dreece, Adam, 1972-, author
  All the king's-men / by Adam Dreece.

(Book 3 of the Yellow Hoods : an emergent steampunk series)
Issued in print and electronic formats.
ISBN 978-0-9881013-6-4 (pbk.).--ISBN 978-0-9881013-7-1 (pdf)

 I. Title. II. Series: Dreece, Adam, 1972- Yellow Hoods ; bk. 3

   PS8607.R39A64 2015   jC813'.6   C2015-901435-2
                                         C2015-901436-0

1 2 3 4 5 6 7 8 9 5/19/15 71,157

DEDICATION

To my daughter who is my muse,

To my wife who is my rock in the windstorm,

To my sons who reignite my imagination every day,

and

To the incredible people who have become fans of the books and encourage me to keep going...

You are too numerous to mention, but you are

"All The Awesome."

EORTHE

Cartographer: Driss of Zouak, 1793
Created at the behest of the Council of Southern Kingdoms

CHAPTERS

CHAPTER ONE

HEAD AND HEART

"I'm coming with you," said Richy adamantly. "Bakon and you are family to me. I'm coming."

Egelina-Marie smiled proudly at the yellow-cloaked young man. It seemed like an eternity ago that he'd come running up to her in a flash of yellow on her first day of guard patrol. He'd been so nervous and desperate when he'd asked for her and the sergeant's help to save Nikolas Klaus. Her smile grew as she remembered taking the leap of faith to follow him, and how her superior threatened to shoot her for it.

That scared boy, who had quickly become a haunted teen, now stood before her as a young man of conviction. His electric blue, almond-shaped eyes and yellow, hooded cloak contrasted sharply with the old brown ledger under his arm and the Ginger Lady's decrepit house behind him.

Egelina-Marie stared at the ledger. How could so much ill have come from such an old thing so quickly, she wondered. "I can't begin to imagine what that moment was like for you."

Richy folded his shoulders in and tucked his head down, as if bracing himself against the icy-cold truth that threatened to hit him again. "It…" He paused, lost for a moment. "I'm glad Bakon was there."

"I should have been there, too," Eg replied. "I can't —"

"Honestly," interrupted Richy, an awkward expression on his face. "I think it was easier for me to just be with Bakon. To have him be the one to tell me that ten years ago I was sold to the Ginger Lady, to help me understand that for two months I lived in a place like that... it made it easier for me to hear it from him. Is that wrong?"

Egelina-Marie gave him a hug and kissed him on the forehead. His words lightened her emotional burden. "Did you have any sense from him what he was thinking? That he suspected that maybe he and his brothers were in those ledgers somewhere?"

A look of guilty disappointment stared back at her as she released him from the hug. "I couldn't think straight. He was my anchor. I—"

"Hey," she said, wiping the fledgling tears from her eyes. "You are amazing. Don't forget that. I don't know what I would have done in your situation." She'd seen something in Bakon's eyes when she'd arrived with his brothers to pick up him and Richy. She should have suspected something when he'd insisted on catching up with them, rather than leaving with them immediately for Mineau. She was disappointed in herself for letting the man she loved run into the arms of his greatest insecurity alone.

A gunshot startled Egelina-Marie back to the present.

"What was that?" asked Richy.

Eg scanned the forest and clearing, finding nothing. Remembering a trick her father had taught her, she closed her eyes and turned her head slowly, trying to remember where the sound had come from.

Another shot rang out and Egelina-Marie pointed sharply. "There," she said, opening her eyes. "I'd guess that it's at least two parties shooting at each other. We need to check it out."

"Are you sure?" said Richy, willing to back her, but nervous.

"For all we know, this whole area is about to get overwhelmed with more foreign soldiers. Richy, can you find us a ladder to a canopy bridge to take us toward the shots?"

"Yeah, I'm on it," he replied, pulling his hood down and running off to study the surrounding trees in detail.

Egelina-Marie quickly walked her horse over to a tree and tied it up. She freed the repeating rifle from its saddle strapping and checked it: there were only two shots left. "Richy?" she called out, glancing around.

"Over here!" he yelled, a surprising distance away.

As she approached the tree, she marveled at how

hard it was to see the ladder carved into the large tree's trunk, even up close. The bark had regrown over it perfectly, and though it had clearly been used recently, it looked perfectly natural.

When she arrived at the top, Richy pulled one of the two levers and a walkway expanded out from their tree through the canopy to another tree in the direction Eg had requested.

"Are your shock—" she started to ask.

"Charged and ready," said Richy, smiling and tapping the hidden pockets of his cloak. "Let's find out what's going on."

Eg stopped herself for a moment. "What did you do with the ledger?"

"I dropped it by my sail-cart," replied Richy. "Why?"

"Don't bring it with us when we go, okay? I don't want any part of this cursed place coming with us."

Richy nodded. He could see something in her face, and felt the same way.

Two shots snapped the air in rapid succession.

"Let's go," commanded Eg.

A minute later, as they were halfway across a second canopy bridge, they caught sight of the scene. A wounded soldier was stumbling through the forest, clutching his right side. Two other soldiers were chasing him with their rifles drawn, all of them dressed like the ones they had encountered earlier in the day.

"There," said Egelina-Marie, taking the rifle off her back and going down on one knee. "Are you sure no one can see us up here?"

Richy nodded. "Even if they knew what they were looking for, they'd have a hard time finding us."

"Good," she replied. "Now we just need to figure out what's going on. I wish we were closer."

The wounded soldier slumped against a tree a hundred yards away. He gestured feebly, yelling something at the other two.

"Hmm," said Egelina-Marie, squinting and trying to glean any detail that she could.

"Should I get closer? I think there's another bridge right over them," said Richy, eager to help.

Eg leaned against the metal, crisscross-barred side of the walkway. "Those riflemen are reloading." She put her rifle back up against her shoulder and got into position. "We're going to have to guess. What's that expression? The enemy of my enemy is my friend?"

Richy raised an eyebrow and smirked. "Doesn't your dad say that the enemy of my enemy is my next enemy?"

Egelina-Marie chuckled. "He does. He's never wrong on that either." She paused as she drafted a plan. "Okay, when I shoot, I want you to get as close to their position as possible. That wounded guy's arm just slumped, so I'm guessing we won't have a lot of time to get to him."

"Ready," said Richy.

Taking a well-practiced, calming breath, Eg thought back to her earliest days, when she would borrow one of her father's rifles without permission and slink off into the forest to shoot targets. Every type of rifle had its own personality, and not having fired this type before, she knew she had at most one chance to learn how to use it before needing to fire its last shot perfectly.

Richy jumped as Eg fired. The shot just missed one of the riflemen's legs.

"Okay, so it fires low and to the left," she said, cranking the side of the rifle to prepare it for its next shot. She glanced in Richy's direction and saw the canopy bridge over the action expanding out.

The two riflemen started to argue, and one pulled a pistol on the other. "Woo," said Eg to herself. "These guys are some really nasty pargos." Steadying her hand, she pulled the trigger and nothing happened. "Jammed!"

Eg caught the glint of something falling from the trees, and smiled as both riflemen flailed about while the shock-sticks made their presence known.

She scrambled over to Richy's position, and they descended together.

"Who are you?" asked the wounded soldier as they approached him. His face was pasty white and his uniform jacket was soaked in blood.

Egelina-Marie kneeled down beside him and studied his jacket. "We're the guys who just saved you. Who are you? What are you doing here?"

He shook his head. "Doesn't matter."

"What?" said Richy, trying to make sense of why the soldier was giving up. "You're going to be all good soon, right, Eg?"

Egelina-Marie and the soldier stared at him, letting him in on the reality of the situation.

Knowing they didn't have much time, Eg turned back to the soldier and said, "We're from Minette. We saw some soldiers like you earlier today. Why were you running?"

"Mineau?" said the soldier, blinking, his eyes going wide with each painful breath.

"Close enough," said Eg, opening his jacket and wrinkling her face as she saw the extent of his wounds.

"I'm sorry," he said, gulping for air.

"Eg, do something!" said Richy, his eyes welling up.

A moment later, the soldier's face went slack.

Egelina-Marie bowed her head and closed his eyes with her hand. After whispering a few words on the wind, Eg saw the expression on Richy's face. She knew that expression all too well.

"Richy? Are you okay?" she asked, walking over to him and rubbing his shoulder.

"Yeah," he said, retrieving his dropped shock-sticks.

"What do we do now?" he asked, still half-dazed.

"We get back to my horse and your sail-cart."

"We're going after Bakon, right?" he asked hopefully.

"I... I need to think," replied Egelina-Marie, a sadness creeping across her face.

———————

"Egelina-Marie, you are not going out with those friends of yours without this backpack!" thundered Lieutenant Gabriel Archambault to his fifteen-year-old daughter. His huge right hand pointed at the leather backpack he'd prepared for her. He looked like an average father in his brown pantaloons, beige knee-high socks, jerkin, and white shirt.

The ponytailed Egelina-Marie glared at him, arms crossed, her brown eyes narrowed. She was the spitting image of her father, just smaller and female. She had his eyes and was similarly dressed. "Papa, it's heavy! You can't expect me to carry that much!"

Gabriel rolled his eyes. "That's because it has two days of food and water, and proper supplies! You can't expect it to weigh nothing."

Egelina-Marie leaned forward. "I don't need that! I'm just going into the forest for a couple of hours with some friends! We aren't going to sleep in the forest overnight or anything. I'll be home before the sun goes down. Anyway, none of the other parents are making their kids take anything like that. I'll look like an idiot."

Gabriel leaned in and put his meaty hands on his hips. "If I wanted you to look like an idiot, I'd use more imagination than giving you a backpack!"

Victoria slipped into the room. "He wanted you to

wear a winter coat. I told him it's only September!" she said as she vanished again.

Egelina-Marie scowled at the bedroom door as it closed.

"No!" said Egelina-Marie, turning back to her father.

Gabriel rubbed his famously huge, black-and-gray moustache and paced about, his eyes locked on his daughter.

He could see Egelina-Marie was ready for a fight. He also knew that was the last thing the two of them needed. Gabriel had promised Victoria that he'd handle this in a way that she'd approve of.

He walked around the table, and pulled out a chair. "Sit," he commanded, pointing. Egelina-Marie intensified her glare and folded her arms more tightly.

Gabriel took a deep breath and stared at the well-worn wooden floor. He tapped the back of the chair as he thought. "Sit. Please," he asked nicely.

After some hesitation, Egelina-Marie slowly made her way to the old wooden chair. Gabriel noticed a slight wobble in the chair as she sat, and had half a mind to go get some tools and have Egelina-Marie help him repair it, as she usually did, but he stopped himself. He wasn't going to allow himself to escape from the situation. He needed to bridge the gap that had been growing between them lately.

Gabriel sat down and tried not to glare at his daughter over the backpack. "There are a couple of rules..."

Egelina-Marie scoffed and started to get up.

"No, listen," said Gabriel firmly, but without raising his voice. His daughter sat back down, folded her arms, and leaned back.

Gabriel fumbled with his fingers and glanced around the kitchen. "When I was your age, I had an uncle go missing in the Red Forest. He was—"

"I know, he got lost and died," said Egelina-Marie rudely. She stared at her dad, and recognized for the first time that he was making a serious effort. "Sorry, Papa."

Gabriel nodded and continued. "My uncle Jacques was a strong and very capable man, but arrogant. He'd been a Procession Scout for the Frelish royals for years. Always out there, hundreds of yards ahead of wherever the royal family was traveling to, checking for enemies and whatnot. There'd never been a single incident when he'd been on duty. A year after he'd retired because of his eyesight, one of the young Frelish princes was kidnapped and taken into the Red Forest."

Egelina-Marie unfolded her arms and straightened up. She sighed. She'd heard this before, but could tell her father wasn't saying it simply to wear her down.

Gabriel smiled sadly. "Now, as it happened, Jacques had been traveling along the road with his younger brother—my father—and a few neighbors that day. Jacques was in his late forties, the oldest of the group by a few years.

"They came upon a royal carriage that had been attacked. The two guards had been shot and the little prince had been kidnapped. The new procession scout had missed signs that my uncle felt were obvious. Jacques took the kidnapping personally. He yelled at the incompetent entourage to the point where they were ready to shoot him, and they would have, if it weren't for the royal family asking him to help.

"The prince was only two years old. Jacques had been there at the boy's naming ceremony, and thought of him as the child he'd never had. He missed that job terribly, as it had done more than pay him handsomely—it had filled him with purpose."

Gabriel smiled a little as his daughter leaned forward, planting her elbows on the table.

"Jacques took a pistol and sword, and ran off into the forest. He figured that the kidnapper couldn't have been more than fifteen minutes ahead of him. Plus, given they were carrying a child, I assume Jacques figured he would catch up to them in no time.

"The last time my father told me this story, he mentioned how oddly insistent Jacques had been about the route they took and the time of day they left."

Egelina-Marie scratched her head. This was notably different than the version she remembered.

Gabriel leaned in a bit more. "After bandaging the guards and making sure the royal family was okay, my father and a friend went into the Red Forest after Jacques.

"They made sure to be careful, marking trees as they went. At the first hint of the sun going down, they followed the trail they'd marked back. The King had left riders waiting to take them back to the kingdom for commendations. They weren't able to return to the forest until two days later."

"Why didn't the King care more about the baby?" asked Egelina-Marie.

Gabriel stopped and smiled proudly. She was a sharp one. "I… I don't know. It is odd, isn't it? It troubled my father too. The whole story never sat well with him," said Gabriel, rubbing his chin and thinking like the investigator that he was. "Did you know it was a king's advisor who recommended to my father that we move here a few years later? He said that the people here were special, and needed people like my father to protect them. That's why, I suppose, I followed in my father's footsteps. There's something about this place," Gabriel glanced about, "something special. I've never been able to put my finger on it."

"What happened when they went back for Uncle Jacques?" asked Egelina-Marie, intrigued.

Gabriel's face darkened. "When they finally found Jacques, he'd died of thirst. He'd fallen off a blind cliff into a dried riverbed, and broken both of his legs. He'd dug a hole in the dirt, about two feet deep, searching for water.

"My father said the lesson was always think first, and

never go anywhere unprepared. It's served me well, and I want you to understand that nature seems wonderful and kind, but it isn't. There are also dire lynx and other predators out there."

Egelina-Marie rolled her eyes. "Dire lynx? Why not just say dragons?" Seeing the response her dad was preparing play out on his face as his eyes furrowed and his jaw tensed, she quickly added, "But I get your point." She slouched in her chair and poked at the backpack.

Standing up, Egelina-Marie slung the backpack over her shoulder and paused. Then she walked around the table and gave her father a hug. He was an enormous man whose moustache occupied almost half his face at times.

"I love you, Egelina-Marie," said Gabriel, his eyes misting up.

"I love you, too, Papa. Thanks for the story. I'll always remember to think before I do something like Uncle Jacques, okay?"

Gabriel gave his daughter a kiss and watched her walk to the door and pause.

"Did they ever find the baby?" she asked, her face bracing for the answer.

With a heavy sigh, he replied, "No. The King, from what I heard, pretended like he'd never had the boy. He removed all paintings of him, took his name off the official ledgers, and so on. For all intents and purposes, the boy never existed."

Egelina-Marie wondered if there was some poor soul out there, unaware of who he really was, wondering why he felt like a third wheel in whatever world surrounded him.

Smiling at her father, she walked out the door.

Gabriel stood there, thinking, after the door closed. A few minutes later, Victoria came out from the bedroom and cuddled right up to him. "Now that makes me proud enough to make you some pudding." She poked him in the belly.

"You know, I don't think I need any right now."

"Who are you, and what have you done with my husband? Because I'll help you hide the body," whispered Victoria, laughing.

———————

A flash of light caught Egelina-Marie's attention. She turned to notice Richy practicing with his shock-sticks.

"What are you doing?" she asked, curious.

Richy stopped and pulled back his hood. "Oh, you're back," he said, smiling. "You were quiet for a long time, and so I thought I'd practice a bit. I didn't know what else to do."

Egelina-Marie frowned. "Was I really thinking that long?" She remembered them getting back to the Ginger Lady's house, but it seemed like it was only a moment ago.

"I'm not sure. Long enough for me to get bored," Richy replied.

"Do you practice a lot?" she wondered.

"Usually every morning with Tee and Elly. We started doing that about a month ago, or at least I found out about it a month ago. It's kind of weird doing it without them." Richy put his unarmed shock-sticks back into the hidden pockets of his yellow cloak.

Egelina-Marie untied her horse and walked it over to him. "Richy... we can't go after Bakon without help."

Richy deflated. "I kind of figured you were going to say that."

She lifted his chin and smiled into his eyes. "We have no food, no water, no firearms and almost no money. We have no idea what we're heading into or which of the two cities he went to, if that's where he even went. Never mind that the soldier was sorry about something, and my gut is screaming that we've got to find out what it is."

Richy nodded in understanding, a small smile on his face.

"What?" she asked, trying to make sense of his reaction.

"You sounded like your father for a second there. He said things like that when we were hunting for the Red Hoods, the day we met Franklin."

"You seem to know a lot about what my father says," she retorted.

"Yeah, well, he says interesting things."

Egelina-Marie grinned and messed his hair. "Let's go

get the others, and then we'll head out after Bakon together. He's a big boy; he'll be okay," she said hopefully.

As she mounted and slowly turned her horse to point westward, she stared longingly over her shoulder. As the horse started to saunter forward, she was hoping to see a sign that would tell her to go with her heart.

CHAPTER TWO

CHILDHOOD'S END

"Soldiers. Lots of them," said Tee, returning to her grandfather's hidden downstairs study. She pulled her hood back, revealing her black eye and shoulder-length, dark brown hair. Adrenaline had vanquished any signs of fatigue or injury from the battle earlier in the day.

Elly came up right behind Tee. "I spotted some going around to the back of the house."

"Do you think they are the same ones that took Anciano Klaus?" asked Mounira.

"No," said Christina sharply. "They'd already know the house. These are a different group, of that I'm certain." She couldn't imagine who they were working for, or what they knew about the house.

She closed her eyes and thought through its layout. She'd visited Nikolas many times over the years, but had never had to think about his house tactically. Given all the secrets that Nikolas had shared with her, and her with him, she'd never known he had a hidden study, let alone a huge secret lab. She was worried about what other secrets it housed.

Opening her eyes and glancing around the bookcase-lined room, she said, "Okay, I'm going to assume we're surrounded, and that they don't know about this room—at least, not yet." Her tone was that of an experienced leader.

Mounira walked over and took Christina's hand with her left, and only, hand. Christina smiled down at her little eleven-year-old sidekick.

Franklin stood at attention, several inches taller than everyone except Christina. He stared at her nervously. "Why don't we fight them?" he asked, aware that everyone knew he had no skills to support such an action. "You've got that gun and a shock-stick on your belt."

Christina shook her head. "We're in a small space, we don't know how many of them there are, we don't know who they are... no. We're at a tactical disadvantage. Remy would kill me if I died doing something like that."

"Who's Remy?" asked Mounira, frowning with curiosity.

"Later," replied Christina. "I need to think."

———————

As Nikolas' thick oak front door blew apart, a dozen soldiers flooded into his house, onto the landing, and up the stairs to the kitchen. With a few quick gestures, they spread out to the study on the left and the bedrooms on the right.

"This guy's got a lot of books," said one of the soldiers, glancing around the study. He moved his torch around, pushing back the night. "And a lot of stuff." He stared in disbelief at the two work tables, overstuffed bookcases, and piles of books and papers on the floor in heaps.

"Careful with that torch!" barked the captain from the landing. "We don't want this place going up in flames with us in it."

"No one over here, Captain," said a soldier returning from the bedrooms. "Walker's double-checking under the beds and closets."

"And you're not helping—why?" asked the captain, sending the soldier back. "Newbies." He rubbed his thick dark beard. "Keep an eye open. Look under and behind every piece of furniture. If there's someone here, we want them. If there are any brass tubes, you may just have found yourself an Abominator reward, so cough it up. You lunkers hear me?"

Several soldiers replied with eager yeses.

The captain took in his little theater of war. "Alright, you've got ten minutes to earn yourself an early Solstice bonus, so move with purpose."

Satisfied at the sounds of soldiers shifting furniture and things falling to the floor, the captain went up the landing stairs into the kitchen and noticed something affixed to the walls. "Hey, you bunch of lunkers! This place has candleholders on the walls. Probably has oil lamps, too. Let's get some light in this place. Come on! Use your heads!" He shook his head in irritation. Within a few minutes, the house was lit up so brightly that the soldiers and captain were squinting. "Okay, okay, enough! We don't want to burn the house down… yet," he said, waving off a soldier readying another oil lamp.

From the landing, a soldier made a startled noise.

"What is it, Grimes?" asked the captain.

"You're not going to believe this," said the young soldier nervously.

The captain raced down the steps. "You've got my attention, Grimes. What is it? All I see here is a door, stairs going up, and you squatting down like you lost your grandmother's wedding ring."

Grimes held his torch close to the floor and wall. "See how the stairs up to the kitchen have a shadow here? That's where you'd expect a shadow to be, right?"

"That's how light works, you —"

Pointing, Grimes quickly added, "But look here, this part of the wall… its shadow is in the wrong place. I tried to touch the wall, but it's like it's not there."

The captain stared carefully at the wall and the shadow. "You might have something." He reached his hand out, and it went through where the wall should have been. He laughed and slapped Grimes on the back. "It's a trompe-l'oeil! Never heard of one being in a house before. Huh, you learn something every day."

"A what?" said the confused soldier.

"It's a painted illusion, a trick for the eye. My father

used to be responsible for cleaning them in the palaces of Roja. He was the only one allowed to touch them." The captain closed his eyes and slowly slid his boot forward until he felt the edge, and then the step below. He banged his foot around. "You hear that? There are stairs going down." He grabbed Grimes by the neck and smiled at him fiendishly. "Good work, Sergeant."

The soldier grinned at the sudden field promotion.

"Now, get in there," said the captain, pointing at the wall. He raised his head and yelled, "You two, down here with us. The rest of you, the clock's ticking."

"Captain, there's a door down here," yelled Grimes from some distance away. "I hear something, too."

The captain led the other two soldiers down the stairs carefully. At the bottom they found Grimes, who was leaning against a door with blue light emanating from under it.

As they arrived beside him, Grimes said, "I heard voices and then a lot of weird sounds, like heavy metal moving."

"Okay," whispered the captain. "Pistols and swords at the ready. When I give the order, Sergeant, throw the door wide open. You two lunkers get in there and take them by surprise. Be careful. I'm told this Klaus guy is dangerous, so be prepared for anything."

The team nodded.

"Now."

As the door flew open, the soldiers flooded into the room, yelling.

The large room was lined with bookcases. There was a smoldering fire in the fireplace and two green books laying on the floor. It was otherwise empty, except for a rug, a worn couch, and a decorative chair with an ottoman.

"Where is everyone?" asked Grimes. "I really did hear voices."

The captain slapped Grimes upside the head. "I bet you heard voices, Corporal. Heard voices, my eye." He noticed one of his other soldiers turning around in a circle. "Is it time for dance lessons, Walker?"

The soldier stopped, a puzzled expression on his face. "Where's the light coming from? There are no shadows."

***

Christina stared up at the underside of the rug as it completed locking into place thirty feet above them. The elevator mechanism was impressive and she wished, once again, she had the time to figure out how it worked. Finally taking a breath, she put down the magnetic sticks she'd used to activate it. They'd barely made it out before the soldiers had burst in, and Christina knew it was probably just a matter of time before the men either figured another way to get down to the secret lab, or forced Christina and her team to leave it.

Tee, Elly, and Franklin stared in amazement at Nikolas' grand, secret laboratory. The lighting was the same omnipresent glow as in the study above. There were two workbenches nearby covered in geared machinery, and contraptions on the floor and hanging from the ceiling. Bookcases and wooden cabinets stood here and there, stuffed beyond capacity. Several corridors left the central area for parts yet unknown.

"I think we're okay for the moment," said Christina, sighing.

"The lab's even bigger than the house!" said Mounira excitedly to everyone, relieved she was finally allowed to speak.

"You've been down here before?" Tee asked Christina, surprised. She glanced down at the small painting of her Grandmama that she'd snatched off the mantel at the last minute, and wondered just how many secrets her family had. Her mother and father had certainly been filling her head with all sorts for months now.

"This is where we found the rocket-cart," said Christina, scrutinizing everything around them for its potential use, or a possible exit.

Tee frowned, feeling a bit left out.

"Well, the flying part," added Christina, spinning a finger in the air, "that's my invention. Well, was."

Elly took comfort in the continued surprise on Tee's face. They were in this ever-stranger world of the Tub and Fare together.

Franklin slowly absorbed the myriad machines and drawings around him. "This is beyond blooming marvelous. No wonder you didn't want to fight, Christina! Now, what are we going to build? A cannon maybe? Another flying machine? There's got to be a million things we could do to give those soldiers what for!"

Christina frowned at the girls, confused.

"He means kick their butts," said Elly. "We treat it like a speech impediment, him being Ingleash."

Mounira chuckled.

To Elly's surprise, Tee didn't react. The gloom that had enveloped her before had already returned.

"Ingleash expressions," said Christina, rolling her eyes. She wasn't particularly fond of the Ingleash to start with, but their expressions were something that made even less sense to her than their politics. "The plan is to grab what we can, find a way out of here, and make our way to Herve to get the steam engine plans. We're not going to fight."

As the rest nodded, Franklin shook his head. "Wait. Why would we run then? Let's just stay here until they're gone. We're safe down here."

"Because if I was them," said Christina, gazing up at the elevator mechanism, "I'd burn this place to the ground."

Everyone went silent.

Christina turned to Tee. "Do you recognize anything down here? An exit maybe? Last time, Mounira and I had to take the rocket-cart back up through the study, and trust me, it was crazy getting it up those stairs. I figure Nikolas has to have another way out of here."

Tee raised her eyes from the floor and nodded. "I'll see what I can find."

"Good," replied Christina.

Elly stared at Christina, bewildered. "Wait, how would Tee know anything about what's down here? Tee, come back here. That doesn't make any sense."

"I'm having a look around. I don't like the idea of burning to death," Tee retorted, her tone distant.

Elly couldn't decipher anything from Christina's steely expression. "Um, good point. Christina, I'm going to help her."

"Please. Let me know if you find anything," replied Christina, pushing her short, dark-blond hair back over her ears. There was something in Christina's voice that made Elly feel that she didn't expect the same results from her as from Tee.

Christina pointed at the prototype arm she and Mounira had discovered in the lab. "Start wrapping this stuff up," she said to Mounira. "Use the clothes from over there to make sure it can handle a couple of bumps, okay?"

Mounira saluted and got to work.

Christina studied Franklin, who seemed to be engrossed with something on the second workbench. "If we can use it, tell me."

Franklin shook his head, his eyes wide. "I don't even know what this is," he said, both impressed and troubled. He'd arrogantly always thought of his and his father's inventions as the pinnacle of scientific thought. At school, he'd deftly defeated almost every challenger. The few times he hadn't been top of the class, or won first prize at the biannual science competition, he'd found a way to make the person who had suffer. Part of him wished he didn't need such pettiness to fill the hole from loss, but his father had always laughed when he'd learned what Franklin had done, so he didn't see the harm.

Christina checked the contents of her and Tee's backpacks. There was very little of use. "Anything that can be helpful, let me know. Also, if you find any sacks or other backpacks, we need them. Tee's and mine are empty, but whatever we can carry out of here, the better. Assume we're not coming back."

Tee got a lump in her throat as she absorbed what Christina had said.

"I found some bandages and stuff," said Elly from somewhere in the lab.

"Let me see," said Tee, relieved for the distraction from her thoughts. She wandered over to Elly.

Tee inspected the bundle Elly had found. "Vinegar, knife, clean clothes, pins... Christina, we have one of my Granddad's traveling medical kits."

"Add it to your backpack, that could be vital," said

Christina.

"Your other grandfather is a doctor?" asked Elly, puzzled. "I thought he was a cook, you know, making muffins and stuff. A real baker."

"Yeah, well, he's good at a lot of things," replied Tee, walking away with the medical kit.

Elly glared at Tee. Never before had Tee done that to her. The only secrets Tee had ever kept from her were about the nature of her grandfather's inventions, and that was only until Tee's grandfather shared them outside his family. In most of those cases, Tee had hinted so much to Elly that when the invention was revealed, there wasn't much mystery left.

Franklin held the edges of one of the huge sheets of design plans. His mood had noticeably soured. Unable to contain himself, he asked Christina, "Is my father's steam engine a joke?"

Christina bristled at the question. Shaking her head, she replied sharply, "We don't have time for this."

Franklin snapped down the top of the sheet with a quick jerk, and glared at Christina. "I can barely figure out what this says, but I do get the distinct impression that if Mister Klaus was an adult intellect, my father was at best... Mounira!" Before Franklin knew it, he felt a sharp pain in his right shin. An angry Mounira had appeared out of nowhere.

"Oh, sorry. I didn't see you sitting there, being an idiot," said Mounira.

"Mounira," rebuked Christina, trying to sound as if she disapproved but unable to hide her smile.

The small Southerner nodded and went back to packing Christina's backpack.

Franklin's instincts told him there was something amiss. "You know what I'm talking about. Mister Klaus—Nikolas—has gone beyond my father's steam engine, or he's perfected it, or something. These drawings were for that rocket-cart thing, I'm sure of it. I can only figure out a couple of the encrypted words, but enough to suspect that even this small design went beyond my father's stupid steam engine. Why have my father risk his life, and mine, to have me come here with plans no one needed?" barked Franklin.

Christina slapped him, stunning everyone. "Grow up. You want to have a meltdown, do it later when we don't have a house full of soldiers trying to hunt us down. Right now, I've got a duty to get you all to safety, even you."

Franklin seethed, his eyes wide. He'd never been treated that way, never mind by a woman. He thought of the time that a girl, Amy, had earned the mathematics prize instead of him, and how he'd set things up so that she'd gotten ink all over her dress when she went to receive the award.

Pointing a finger sharply at Franklin, Christina continued. "You don't understand the importance of what your father's invented. It'll scale. It'll allow for bigger and better things to have been invented than anything before it! More importantly, the world's ready for it. Keep your insecurities in check or I'll check them for you. Got it?"

Franklin was about to retort, but Christina interrupted his thought with a renewed glare.

"Go see if there is any food or other supplies we could use," ordered Christina, taking the plans away from him and folding them up. She took solace in knowing that if Franklin tried to take anything from the lab, he only had his pants pockets and not a backpack to hide it in.

"I can't believe your Grandpapa had this place," said Elly, following Tee around.

"I know," replied Tee, her tone flat and distant.

"So you never knew about it?" asked Elly, fishing.

"No," replied Tee, studying the ceiling and then a wall.

"Not even a hint?" pushed Elly.

Tee stopped and rubbed part of a wall. "No. I always wondered where he did his real work, though. There were little things that I noticed, like when he'd been up all night, but his workbenches upstairs hadn't been touched." Tee stopped and thought for a moment. "Christina, there is another way out. A couple of months ago, my Grandpapa showed me a horseless cart. It wouldn't have fit through the doorway upstairs. He must have gotten it out somehow."

"You guys search for an exit," replied Christina. "I'll be back in a minute. There's something I need to check for."

Elly frowned, noting there was no surprise in Christina's voice. "What's a horseless cart?" she asked Tee, folding her arms. "When did he make it?"

"He showed it to me when LeLoup was in jail. It looked kind of like a normal cart you'd attach to a horse, but it moved on its own. He must have built it here, but how did he get it out?" she said, lost in thought as she studied each item they passed.

Elly bit her lip.

"There," said Tee, pointing to a picture on a wall. "That's the way out."

Elly studied Tee's face. There was no uncertainty present; it was as if Tee had just read a sign that said 'Exit'. She stared at the symbol Tee was focused on, and then it hit her. "Wait, isn't that the same as the one on the door to our treehouse?"

Tee shrugged.

"How long have you known what that means?" asked Elly angrily.

Tee gave Elly a blank stare, then turned and walked back to Christina.

"I found one of the two panels that we need to push to open the exit," reported Tee.

"Good work," said Christina, relieved.

Elly tapped Tee on the shoulder. "How do you know there's a second panel?"

Tee's eyes were cold, brown, and steely. Elly had never seen that withdrawn expression before, and it shook her deeply.

Franklin noticed Elly's expression and felt a bit of relief at not being the only one offside. He stopped himself from feeding the growing rift and trying to wedge himself between them, hoping to create a closer bond with one of them. Instead, he blurted out, "Before we leave, is there anything else we need to take from here? Something that can humiliate my father publicly perhaps?"

"Enough," snapped Christina. Slinging her half-full backpack over her shoulders, she followed Tee to the first panel. At the back of her mind, she kept expecting to hear an explosion and have the rug and its secret elevator come crashing down.

"Christina?" asked Tee.

Realizing she was staring at the ceiling, she turned to focus on Tee. "Do you think there's another way for them to get down here?" she asked.

"I don't know," replied Tee, shrugging.

"Really?" asked Elly, incredulous. "Are you sure? Because this is a matter of life and death."

Tee glared at Elly. "What are you talking about?"

Christina yelled, "Stop it! Look, we're all scared, so

let's focus on getting out of here."

Elly shook her fists and then stopped, fingers flaring out. "Never mind! You said you've never been here before, so you've never been here before. Though somehow, you knew exactly where the exit was and that there's another panel we need to find."

"Everyone, look for something with a picture of spring or coil that has two lines through it. That's going to be the other thing we need to unlock the secret door."

"No," said Franklin, playfully folding his arms.

Christina drooped. "Look, Franklin. We all need to—"

Franklin smiled smugly and pointed to the wall behind them. "It's right there. Behind you."

Tee pushed part of the picture around the shield in, then twisted the embossed shield to the right. She then ran over and pulled out the other panel a few inches.

"Listen!" said Mounira happily.

The sound of chains moving and clanking filled the room, and then a wall down the hall slid away, revealing a dark corridor. The cool, spring night air washed over them.

"Okay, wait here. Tee, crank a lantern," said Christina, pointing to one on a hook.

"Anyone else find it eerie how the light from the lab extends up to here and then just ends?" asked Mounira, standing where the wall had opened.

Elly and Franklin nodded.

Tee took the lantern, and after a moment of examining it, found the lever she needed to bring it to life. Its blue glow was similar to that of the study and lab.

As Christina returned, resettling her full backpack, she took the lantern from Tee. "Let's go."

They descended the mountain path in silence, until something caught Elly's attention and she stopped to look back.

"The house is on fire!" screamed Elly, spinning to Tee. To her astonishment, Tee was staring at the ground, her face hidden by her yellow hood. "Tee, your Grandpapa's house is on fire! Doesn't that mean something to you?" Elly grabbed Tee by the shoulders angrily, trying to shake her back to normal.

Tee reluctantly met Elly's gaze. She knew what this was doing to Elly, but her instructions from her parents had been clear. "What do you want me to say? If we stay here, we're going to get killed. There's no point crying over things we can't control," she said, her voice devoid of emotion. She couldn't bear to watch the flames destroy the home of her favorite childhood memories.

CHAPTER THREE

ALL THE KING'S-MEN

"Abominator was an excellent term to label our kind with, really. It's astounding to think that a hundred years ago, with one word and one night of horrific actions, King Falson turned every inventor, scientist, and engineer, every simply gifted person, into the target of everything that illed his realm. Imagine what it was like in those first days: friend turning on friend, neighbor turning on neighbor.

"I wonder if he'll ever be recognized for how brilliant that was. I still find it hard to imagine what it was like to be in his presence in that first hour of him being on the throne. The new king surprising everyone with a vengeful royal edict, and then going with his closest guards room by room, executing King's-Men, including my grandfather. It showed a savage level of conviction," said Marcus Pieman, staring out the window of his carriage as the beautiful Frelish landscape raced by.

He turned to Nikolas Klaus. "I've read the accounts,

over the years," continued Marcus. "How they broke down the doors of my grandfather's royal suite and beheaded him in front of his family. They killed all of the King's-Men that night. Loyalty, years of service, strategic advantage for the kingdom didn't mean a thing. Falson wanted to ensure that everyone understood he had supreme authority over all matters. And thus, a dark age was born—all out of one man's adolescent anger."

"None shall shine brighter than the king," said Nikolas, quoting a famous line from the long-dead king.

Marcus rubbed his thumb and fingers together. "Do you know what is so beautifully sinister about that phrase? It reaffirms not only the supremacy of the royals, but that everything is justifiable in order to preserve it. It was the spark to a dry age ready for a brush fire. Like all such fires, it destroyed in an instant that which took ages to rebuild."

Nikolas rubbed his bald head, thinking back to how he'd lost his family in just such an attack. Marcus was the closest person he had to a brother. Yet, in all the years he'd known him, Marcus had never mentioned his tie to the dawning of the Era of the Abominator. "Your father survived by the kindness of a soldier, yes?" said Nikolas.

"No, actually," said Marcus, staring out the window again. "There was so much blood in the room that my sleeping baby father was thought dead. The soldiers were so excited, with the king right there with them, that they went on to the next execution. My father simply slept through it. The next morning, a maid was sent to clean the room and found him."

Nikolas closed his eyes, fighting to recall. "Maven, yes?"

"You remember the name?" replied Marcus, chuckling a bit, rubbing his short white hair. "Your memory never ceases to impress me. Maven Senior, yes. She ran off with my father, and delivered him to a wealthy family. Her daughter, Maven Junior, was my nanny."

"Hmm," said Nikolas, "I did not realize there was a junior and a senior Maven."

Marcus nodded.

For a while, they sat in silence. Marcus resisted the urge to get to work. He was enjoying spending some time with Nikolas. Though occasionally throughout his life he'd found someone with whom he could have a truly intelligent conversation, it was never the same as with Nikolas.

Nikolas studied the interior of the carriage once again. It was a remarkable piece of engineering. Twice the length of a regular carriage, yet the ride was smoother than anything he'd experienced before. They were sitting in the back half of the carriage, the two sections separated by a wall. The back compartment allowed them to sit beside each other; a table with food was in front of them and a wall of caged books was behind them.

The front compartment was Marcus' mobile office. It

was lined with books and slots for managing letters from the field and orders to go out, and had a map and instruments on mechanical arms dangling from the ceiling.

Marcus reached forward and sliced the remaining piece of cake in half. He offered the final piece to Nikolas, who smiled in polite refusal.

Nikolas unbuckled the secured teapot, and refilled both of their cups. He paused, examining the iron ring in the center of the table that the teapot sat on, keeping it hot.

Marcus noticed Nikolas, teapot in one hand and a cup in the other, frozen in midair.

"The heating ring?" he asked, smiling.

Nikolas nodded.

"Have you improved it yet?" joked Marcus, thinking back to the old days.

Nikolas shook his head gently. "No. I'm just contemplating the ways in which you have done this. Was it you or was it Simon?"

"Oh, it's mine. I wouldn't allow Simon to touch much of this," Marcus said, gesturing to the carriage. "As always, I took my vision and had select inventors help me achieve it. Richelle did some pieces as well."

Nikolas nodded, barely hearing Marcus. Suddenly, his face lit up and he laughed. "Friction. Conducted from the shock-absorbing system, yes?"

Marcus laughed. "Yes! Now, before you accidentally burn us, please put the pot back."

Nodding happily, Nikolas complied. After securing the teapot, they sat drinking their tea, lost in thought once again.

As the landscape changed from forest to grassy plains at the outskirts of a town, Marcus turned to Nikolas. "Do you know why Falson did it? The real reason behind it all? I only learned it a couple of years ago."

Nikolas shook his head. "No. This, I don't know," he said in his classical, awkward fashion. He smiled to himself. It was rare that he stumbled on his words with Marcus, for some reason. Maybe it had to do with them switching in and out of languages, using whatever words came to mind, rather than sticking to one language throughout.

"It wasn't actually the Fare's grand failing," said Marcus. "That was a convenient excuse for Falson, having happened only a month before and killing hundreds of people in a neighboring kingdom. No, Falson had a very simple reason—a deeply personal one.

"When he was fifteen, he applied to the Institute for Unconventional Minds without the knowledge of his father or anyone else."

Nikolas' eyes went wide as he remembered the tales of that special school. "That was the highest of the age, of many things."

Marcus nodded. "Falson used a cousin's name to

create a sense of distance from the royal family, and to give his application more legitimacy.

"He fancied himself an inventor, though what he had was a good mind for planning and execution. Genuine creation? No. As well as being gifted, the institution required you to demonstrate that you were humble, thoughtful, and interested in the greater good." Marcus paused for a moment. "What fantastic, old-world ideals those were.

"When Falson was declined for the third time, he burst into the chancellor's office surrounded by his personal guards and demanded to be accepted. The chancellor died on the spot of a heart attack. When the king learned of all of this, he banned his son from the school, preserving the sanctity of that venerable institution. The prince unleashed a tantrum that was only quelled by his father giving him the designation of First Conventioneer. It was a made-up title; just something to make his son quiet down. Even before being crowned, Falson burned the institute to the ground."

Nikolas absorbed the story and stroked his salt-and-pepper beard. "Your father and grandfather suffered similar fates, then?" he said, trying to remember the details.

Marcus tapped the window absentmindedly. "I think of it almost like history was re-staging a moment, and each time the actor had their chance. My grandfather died as a King's-Men because he missed the signs that things were changing. My father was a better King's-Men, aware of the changes needed, but he was horrible at politics and seizing the opportunities before him."

"But you—you didn't die a King's-Men," said Nikolas.

"No, no, I didn't," said Marcus, turning to his old friend. "I'm changing history entirely."

CHAPTER FOUR

MAKING CRACKS

Five hooded figures quickly entered a small, octagonal room below the grand theater of the capital city of Relna. Each one identified the symbol on the edge of the round table that told them where to stand.

Taking their places, they put their lanterns on the table and pulled down their beige hoods. Once they were all ready, a red-hooded figure entered and stood opposite the door.

"Do you all understand what is expected of you?" asked the Red Hood. He turned to the man immediately to his left, and looked from man to man as they each nodded.

The Red Hood waited until music from upstairs could be heard. He knocked on the table, and the thick, wooden door was sealed from the outside. He pulled out a pocket watch and notebook, and marked down the time. "We have ten minutes. Report on the proxy war," he said in a gravelly voice.

The old man to his left glanced about nervously. Unbeknownst to him, none of the others had been to any such meetings before either. Like him, they'd only been recruited several weeks ago to serve as cryptic messengers.

He scratched his very short, blond-gray hair and straightened up. His voice had a deep rural Frelish accent. "I was told to say: the armies are marching on Palais in six days. They have left ruin in every city so far, and have been sending as many citizens as they can to the Kaban coast for the slave trade." He glanced around. "Does this have anything to do with—" The man stopped as he noted the panicked expression spreading among the others, and then he remembered the rules. To get paid the handsome sum they'd been promised, they were all to report and ask no questions. Asking a single question could forfeit their reward.

"Next," said the Red Hood. "Are we certain they will be defeated by our new forces before they march on Palais?"

"Yes," replied the next man over. He was young and short, with long, shaggy hair. "I'm told the royal family and the King's-Men will seize power back from the parliament once attacked, and then our forces will arrive from the northern coast to provide them assistance. We have the numbers and the equipment needed."

"Excellent." The Red Hood thought for a moment. "What of the south?"

The third man, sounding much like a professor, continued the report. "The southern kingdoms are squabbling as expected, and allowed us to make deeper inroads thanks to their insecurity. We've solidified our hold in almost all of them."

"Almost?" said the Red Hood, tensing.

The professor swallowed hard, glancing at his unnamed colleagues. "There are some issues in Karupto. We are addressing them. There are two King's-Men who protect Queen Sarah from our influence."

"So kill them," quipped the Red Hood. "I mean, I do not see the problem." He rolled his eyes, realizing there was no point in giving such an order to the messenger, as his role was to communicate one way.

"I'm told we've tried. These two were apparently part of something called the Pieman's Trust." Despite his years of experience working for other nefarious people, his hands shook as he stood, waiting for the Red Hood's reaction.

"I'll need to report this," the Red Hood said ominously. He jotted down a couple of encrypted words in his well-worn notebook.

There was a knock at the door.

"We're almost out of time," he said, confirming with his pocket watch. "Where are we with the Skyfallers?"

"Why don't you take your hood off?" asked the man due to report. He was a thuggish, bald man with several small scars on his face and hands. "And why are we all new? I can see it in all of them. What's going on?"

All of the others dropped their gazes, trying to hide from the Red Hood's attention.

The sinister expression that spread across the Red Hood's face immediately chilled the room. "What is your name?"

The thug glanced at the others. "Randy."

"I'll answer your questions in a moment, but first I ask that we close out this last piece of business. We must strictly adhere to process at meetings like this."

Randy quickly moved his gaze to everyone and then back to the host. No one else was willing to say a thing. Straightening up, he nodded in acceptance. "They're preparing a demonstration for the stubborn royals of Myke and some place called Bodear. I was told that the Pieman has a secret thing in Bodear."

"My mistress will be pleased to hear that."

The door opened and a man stared squarely at the Red Hood. He wore a red jacket with two black leather straps crisscrossing over it, and two pistols attached to it on the front and on the back. He had a long moustache and shoulder-length, dark hair that gave him a dashing, enforcer look. "Are we done? The music will end in two minutes," he said insistently.

"Yes, Mister Jenny," said the hooded figure, putting his notebook away under his cloak, "we have concluded."

Randy was annoyed. "I thought you said—"

In a blinding flash, the enforcer gunned down all the men except the Red Hood. He made sure that each of the messengers were no longer among the living before putting his pistols away and asking, "Lord Silskin?"

"I'm fine, as always, Mister Jenny," said the old man as he took off his blood-splattered hood and cloak, and dropped it on the floor. "No matter how many times we do this, my nerves always get rattled by the noise."

As Mister Jenny's men entered the room to start cleaning up, one handed him a neatly folded red-hooded cloak with gold embroidery on it. Then Mister Jenny, with head bowed, presented it to Silskin.

"Thank you," Silskin said, putting it on. "That feels better. I hate those common things, but there's no point in ruining the real thing."

"So what now?" asked Mister Jenny, concerned that he might be about to face the fate he'd dished out.

Lord Silskin smiled and put a hand on Mister Jenny's shoulder. "This meeting was the last one of its kind, and you need not worry. Your assistance has been instrumental in the past few years, helping the Fare move in the Pieman's shadow while we've started to strike at him. Now, that phase will conclude and the aftermath will come. We'll need to root out pockets of resistance, the remnants of the Pieman's forces, and whatever factions of the Tub dare to raise a hand to us. You will be key then, Mister Jenny, once again. You can trust the Fare. We know who our enemies are."

CHAPTER FIVE

A GREAT FALL

The frigid night air roused Abeland with a coughing fit. He blinked, rubbing his eyes with the back of his manacled, dirty hands. He tried to get comfortable. His thoughts drifted to how different things had been a year and a half ago.

On the walk up to the towering gates of the Great Palace of Karupto, Abeland took his time, enjoying the wildflower-covered rolling hills. He always made a point of trying to find some element of nature to clear his mind and settle his soul before taking on a regime.

As the gates opened, revealing soldiers lining both sides of the street, he accepted that it was time to get down to business. The soldiers formed a corridor all the way to the throne room, where Abeland and his party would be officially received.

Abeland studied the body language of the mix of soldiers as he walked past them. It was clear they'd been told to take the slightest excuse as a sign of hostility and attack. Several times, he stopped and observed the crowd peeking out from behind the soldiers. The soldiers in his line of sight would start getting anxious, and each time, just before things boiled over, Abeland moved his gaze and started walking again. At no point did he or his entourage seem to be the least bit concerned.

He'd had similar treatment recently in the neighboring kingdoms of Genouia, Perguntia, and Beleza. His arrival had become almost mythical, like a great demon descending upon a regime and asking a hefty ransom or else the land would face its own apocalypse.

The glowing ring of Abeland's monocle was usually the first sign of things to come. He'd often stand outside a city's gates in the wee hours of the morning and activate his monocle's glow. He'd stand there for hours, allowing for rumors and panic to spread throughout the capital city, as he waited for them to finally open the gates and allow him entrance.

He was flanked by five members of his personal guard, the Order of the Pieman's Trust. They were well-trained, ruthless, and permanently at the ready. Each was armed with an array of weapons, from firearms to blades.

When Abeland and his entourage stepped into the castle, the soldiers had weapons drawn. "That's more like it," he said, bringing about some snickers from his men. "I thought they just had fake ones like in… where was it that most of their soldiers had fake weapons?"

"Beleza," replied Francisco. "That's the one on the coast, west of Roja, right?"

Abeland smiled and nodded. "Odd little place," he mused, bringing about chuckles from the two that had been there with him.

Without another remark, they continued until they were in the heart of the extravagant throne room.

Two towering statues of the King were central to the room, his large stone palms holding up the high ceiling. Flags decorated the walls, with the official colors of blue and gold on plaques representing each of Karupto's five regions.

The corridor of soldiers came to an end on a red carpet, with two soldiers blocking the path with crossed pikes. The King sat on an enormous throne with a court of twenty people surrounding him. They were on a black marble platform two steps up, a few yards behind the pike-wielding soldiers.

King Hamed had a thin, old face and greedy eyes. His robes were bright blue and gold. His bald head caught some shine from the morning light that poured in from the windows extending three stories up the sides of the throne room.

Abeland quickly noted that there was no queen present. He couldn't remember if she had died or been banished, as the kings of Karupto were famous for disposing of their wives quickly after they bore children.

He smiled at the court like a fox greeting the chickens. "Good morning, everyone," he said, passing a quick gaze up to see a dozen crossbowmen and riflemen on the second floor balconies behind and to the sides of the King. "I hope that the thieves in the capital are honest ones, because it seems there isn't a guard or soldier tending to any other matter than the arrival of me and my friends."

There was some muttering among the court; clearly not everyone was in alignment with the will of the King. Abeland caught one particular glance and nodded. Slowly that person slunk further into the background.

Abeland raised his left, black-gloved hand, and touched a switch on his monocle. As the soft green glow changed to a piercing gold, Abeland adjusted to his new view of the world.

"Get out!" yelled King Hamed, standing. He took out a battle-axe hidden beside the throne and leaned on it.

Abeland tilted his head and smiled. *How long have you been itching to say that?* he wondered. "What—right now, Your Majesty?" he asked sarcastically, peering around. "We just got here."

"Do not pretend to be one of us, speaking our language with that fake local accent," said King Hamed angrily.

Abeland frowned. "You do know that if we leave, everyone will be so disappointed. It would be anticlimactic. Where's the fun in that? Where's the drama? I mean, just imagine what your master Exchequer would say about all this expense. You could have just left a note on the gates saying, 'Abeland, please go away.'

And by the way, my accent is genuine."

"We call it the Director of the Kingdom's Wealth," said a voice from behind the King.

"Thank you," said Abeland quickly.

The King banged his axe and gave the man a glare that promised retribution later. He straightened up as much as his aged, bent body would allow, and pulled out an ornate, jewel-encrusted pistol from under his robes. "I will shoot you myself, demon! I will put an end to your menace if you don't leave my kingdom. You won't carve up my lands and feed them to your lap dog, the Caixian."

Abeland had rewarded the kingdom of Caixa for their quick compliance by giving them pieces of the lands he conquered later. Already a progressive kingdom, they had often been pounded on by their neighbors, and for the first time wanted to be the one delivering the blows and claiming the reward.

Smiling at the balconies, Abeland twiddled his fingers at the soldiers up there. While it seemed like a greeting, he actually did it to show he had nothing in his hands and thus to reduce the chances of anyone firing unexpectedly. As he lowered his hands, he glanced at the row of silver buckles on the inside of his elbow-length gloves.

King Hamed, hearing the muttering echo throughout the throne room, turned to glare at his court members behind the throne, and accidentally dropped his axe.

As it clanged loudly on the floor and slid down the

steps, suppressed chuckling and outright laughter broke out. The King, enraged, pointed his pistol at the members of his court.

"I hear treason in this room!" he yelled at everyone. He turned back to Abeland. "Get out of my kingdom."

Abeland rubbed the edge of his mouth with his thumb before stepping up to the crossed pikes in front of him. "To be clear, this posturing is entertaining, but I'm on a strict timeline. You've received my terms, and I hereby ask for your agreement."

A dandily-dressed prince came to his father's side. "We can't do that, father. He doesn't even have an army."

"I know that!" replied the King in frustration. "Let me deal with this."

Abeland faced the two soldiers, whose pikes were now pointed right in his face. His monocle caught the light, blinding them. "Gentlemen, if you'd be so kind, I would like to look directly at the King. Also, if he's going to shoot at me, I'd prefer you weren't in the line of fire. I promise not to take another step forward. The carpet ends here anyway." There was something so politely commanding in Abeland's voice that, to the surprise of many, the soldiers moved aside like double doors opening.

The King stared at his own men, befuddled. He shook his pistol threateningly at them, but only ended up making it clear to everyone that he'd never used one before.

Abeland's entourage took the opportunity to fan out. Putting his arms at his side, Abeland said, "I've put my arms away, Your Majesty. I suggest you do the same. Then we can talk."

As some of the crowd chuckled, Abeland jerked his arms out behind him abruptly, as if knocking an enemy off his back. Hiding a satisfying series of clicks, he said to the King, "I felt the chilly blast of your displeasure!" He shook a bit more, feeding the crowd. "All posturing aside, can we talk?"

King Hamed shook his head. "No," he said, walking down the steps, his ornate pistol pointed squarely at Abeland's chest.

Abeland put his left leg back to brace himself and pointed his arms at the King. A quick squeeze of the small metal triggers in his palms released a series of shots from his sleeves. King Hamed flew backward just as explosives went off in the balconies, bringing them crashing down. Abeland covered his face as stone and dust flew everywhere.

Abeland's entourage dispatched the stunned soldiers surrounding them, then quickly closed ranks around Abeland.

"Look at that," said Abeland, pulling his coat sleeves back and inspecting the custom firearm attached to the inside of his gloves, "one of the buckles ripped. I'll need to get that fixed."

"I'll make a note of that," said Francisco, smiling.

"Thank you, as always, Francisco." Abeland glared at the cowering members of the court glancing about in shock and horror. He smiled, then yelled in a commanding voice, "Who's next in line? I am not here to destroy your kingdom, just to usher in a new age that is better for the people."

The whimpering sounds grew louder as people tried to shove each other forward.

Abeland pointed an arm at one of the grand windows and fired, shattering it in dramatic fashion. "Who is next in line? Who will bring about this new chapter in your country's history, or is this to be another kingdom that I must have governed?"

"I abdicate or yield or whatever! I don't want to be king!" yelled a male voice.

"Me, too!" yelled another.

"Wait! What are you doing?" screamed a young, dark-haired woman as she was shoved to the floor beside the dead King.

"It's her!" said two adult men trying to back away.

"Are you next in line?" asked Abeland, gazing down at the terrified figure.

The woman glanced around, tears in her eyes, and nodded as she stood back up.

"I have a couple of questions for you—do you mind? What is your name?" asked Abeland, as if they were in a tea room rather than a destroyed throne room.

"Sarah," said the young woman, straightening her dress. Her hands were shaking.

"Are you yet sixteen?"

"Yes," she replied, nodding repeatedly.

"Excellent," said Abeland. He bowed gently. "Queen Sarah, may I offer you some advice?"

She followed his gaze over to her two brothers, who were trying to slink away.

"Gentlemen," said Abeland to his men, two of whom quickly apprehended the princes.

"I recommend that you execute these two. Anyone so willing to sacrifice you in a moment like this won't think twice about trying to reclaim the throne from you afterward."

"But…" Sarah turned to her siblings as they pleaded to be let go. "They're my brothers."

"It is just my recommendation, Your Majesty," said Abeland. He remained quiet, allowing the new queen to think. He could see the wheels turning in her head, thinking through all the possibilities that lay before her.

She smiled back at Abeland. "I appreciate your counsel, but I will have them imprisoned. What shall I call you?"

Abeland showed no signs of having any issue with the decision of the queen. "Lord Pieman is my father. Some call me the Baron Pieman, but I'd prefer if you simply called me Abeland. If I may ask: can you read,

Queen Sarah?"

She stopped, realizing for the first time that she was truly the queen now. Sarah took in the broken remains of her father's legacy. The entourage that she'd been a part of, standing at first so confidently around the King and then cowering behind the throne, had mostly deserted in recent minutes.

With her head held high, she replied, "No. My father didn't feel it was important to educate women. As his daughter, I was to be married off for the purposes of an alliance." She paused. "I've heard rumors that you're of a different view."

"I am indeed, Your Highness. I have a niece, Richelle, who I taught to read long ago." Abeland turned to one of his men. "Can you send word we will need Anciano Cervantes? We can't have a leader who cannot read."

Abeland descended to one knee and bowed his head, a move quickly mirrored by his entourage. "Your Majesty, we will help fix this oversight. You and all women of your nation will need to read if they are to help shape its new laws and ways."

The queen smiled, for the first time feeling respected for who she was, rather than what she was. Slowly, she turned to face her brothers. She thought of Abeland's earlier words. "Execute them," she commanded, "by order of the queen."

With his eyes focused on the ground, Abeland smiled.

Sometimes, the patriarchs made it all too easy.

————————

Things had turned for Abeland several months later, near the end of July. Karupto was taking longer to get its act together in terms of reforms and transferring power to a parliament, but that wasn't the sole concern. There had been signs throughout the southern kingdoms, from Augusto to Caixa, from Zouak to Ganounia, that something was going on. He just couldn't put his finger on it.

In another week, he was going to need to leave the beautiful southern coast of Jannia and head back to his home just outside Belnia's capital of Relna. He was running low on his breathing medicine, and he looked forward to surprising his love by coming home early from his travels.

Until then, he'd focus on business and appreciating the last of Jannia's great weather and views. Abeland handed over the reins of his horse to a servant before closing the elegant wooden gate to the inner courtyard of his home behind him. He tugged the sleeves of his black, gentleman's long coat as he walked through the garden until something caught his attention.

He noticed that the courtyard garden was unusually silent, empty of birds and servants. The longer he listened, the more it bothered him that he couldn't hear anything.

Abeland pulled his repeating flintlock pistol out of his

thigh holster and clicked a gear on the monocle, making everything appear extremely sharp.

"Maria? Eduardo?" Abeland called out to his head servants. He slowly turned around until he saw the main gate being closed, and five of his top men from the Order of the Pieman's Trust coming up the path.

Abeland studied the men carefully. Their hands were resting on their weapons. Francisco's dual-pistols were sitting in their holsters on the front of his belt. Roberto had his six knives and a pistol showing on his belt, with his hands on his hips, holding his coat back. Guillermo had his rifle in hand, leaning against his shoulder. Enrico and Baltano had their hands behind their backs, ever the wildcards of the bunch.

Nodding to himself as he took in the situation, Abeland asked, "Francisco, you do realize what you're doing—right, amigo? We've been through a lot together."

Francisco rubbed his long, leathery face. He smiled at his boys, and nodded as he returned his gaze to Abeland. "We do."

Abeland twiddled his fingers as his mind ran quickly through the dozens of scenarios he saw before him. "Roberto, are all of you in agreement?"

Roberto looked a little uneasy. "It seems, Anciano Pieman, that your time in the sun is done."

"Okay," said Abeland, nodding and thinking. He'd personally found and trained each one of these men. Francisco had been with him the longest—nearly ten years—while Baltano was coming on two years.

Abeland slowly raised his arms. "Before you do whatever you need to do, I just want to understand why."

Francisco scoffed. "We agreed to stay true to the code of the Pieman's Trust—a code you created, amigo. But I am afraid it has been proven that you betrayed it. This, we cannot let stand." Francisco scratched his stubbly chin. "Respectfully, I must ask that you stay quiet. We all know that your words can bend steel and mind. We've all seen it, heard it. Please don't make this more difficult."

"Please," urged Enrico. It surprised Abeland to see the same conviction in his eyes as in the others.

Abeland lowered his gaze. He raised his arms up another couple of inches.

Roberto and Enrico approached carefully, pistols drawn.

"Huh, those are new repeating pistols. Very new," said Abeland, peeking up at the weapons.

"Please, Anciano Pieman, no talking," said Enrico respectfully. "We are only to take you to prison to await trial."

"Don't worry, this won't be difficult," said Abeland, thrusting his arms down quickly. With a click beneath his coat, Abeland punched Roberto, hitting him in the chest with a springing steel baton from under his sleeve, winding him. He then rolled into Enrico and used him as a shield as the other three shot at him. He dropped Enrico to the ground, dead.

The gate opened, drawing everyone's attention.

"They should have waited," said a familiar voice.

Abeland stared in confusion. "Simon?"

Simon St. Malo smiled and strode in confidently. "Gentlemen, you may leave."

Grudgingly, they picked up Roberto and left Enrico.

Abeland wasn't sure how to read the situation. "Are you really going to take me on by yourself?"

Simon nodded. "It's been a while, Abeland. How far we've come, from kids playing together to now. Even since Lennart's death, you just never found the opportunity for some one-on-one time, so here we are." He was savoring the moment.

Abeland's face wrinkled. "You've never been the talkative type."

"No, I haven't. I've been the thinking type, and the learning-things-about-people type." Simon smiled at the open gate as a small amount of white fluff started blowing in. He gestured to it, very pleased with himself. "I love learning all kinds of things about certain people."

"Your weapon of choice is puffballs? You're even dumber than I thought," said Abeland, knowing that anger and ego were Simon's two greatest weaknesses.

Simon smiled sinisterly. "If I'd wanted to kill you, you'd never have seen it coming. You would've been getting off your horse and then BOOM, nothing but bits of mess. No, I was given a challenge and I decided to see just how subtly I could do it."

"Subtle isn't usually your style," Abeland started coughing profusely.

"Ah," said Simon, pointing at Abeland with an eyebrow cocked. "See, by my calculations, right now your lungs have lost more than half of their capacity. In another minute or two, it'll be nearly nothing."

Abeland felt his legs turn to jelly as his chest hardened. He knew the feeling all too well. It had been his single greatest secret over the past couple of years.

Simon grinned as Abeland fell on all fours. "Pollen. Not guns, not spears, not even machines of serious imagination. It's poetic, really. They are the seeds of your destruction.

"I had to have one of the servants steal a couple vials of your homemade medicine in order to figure out just how much pollen, and what types I needed to completely overwhelm you. It seems I owe him a bonus."

Abeland blacked out.

CHAPTER SIX

THE POINTY STICK INN

Nikolas yawned as the carriage door opened. It was nearly midnight. One of Marcus' soldiers stood with a lantern, holding the door. The light cut a path in the night between the carriage and the inn. Nikolas was hungry and looking forward to a warm meal and a decent bed. It had been a whirlwind day.

Marcus stepped out the door of the double-length carriage's front section. He'd been working for the past several hours. They'd stopped twice in seemingly strange places. Nikolas had made a point of not paying attention. He knew what was going on, but the less he was seen witnessing, the better for him, he figured.

Despite the late hour, and the remote location, the Pointy Stick Inn was bustling with well-armed men and women inside and out. Nikolas didn't recognize their colors.

A few of Marcus' soldiers remained to guard the carriage and horses, while the rest huddled around

Marcus.

As he gave them instructions, Nikolas wandered off, taking in the sweet spring air. It was different here; more humid and warmer than back in Minette. It reminded him of home.

"Where are you going?" asked a gruff voice.

Nikolas slowly turned, his hands clasped together behind his back. "I am appreciating the night and the opportunity to stretch my legs. It is good to move about. It allows the mind to move in concert with the body once again, yes?"

The soldier was one of Marcus' scouts and clearly didn't like what he'd heard. He was wearing gray leather armor, and had a crossbow on his back. His belt held a dagger and a shiny pistol.

Nikolas hunched over, exaggerating his old man status. The moonlight bounced off his bald head. "Why do you have that?" he asked, pointing to the interesting firearm.

The soldier tried to grab Nikolas by the arm, but Nikolas nimbly sidestepped him, nearly making the younger man tumble to the ground.

Nikolas leaned in to examine the pistol. "That's not a flintlock. That's new... very new. Why would you have one like that?" he wondered aloud, reaching for it.

The soldier cursed and went to grab Nikolas more forcefully. Nikolas turned, leaving his foot strategically placed, and watched as the soldier fell on his face.

Some of the patrons started laughing and clapping. "Nice one, old man!" yelled someone.

"What's the problem?" asked Marcus in a sharp and stern voice, walking up to them.

Nikolas showed Marcus the pistol he'd taken from the soldier as he'd fallen. "Why does he have such a pistol? Its newness is... unexpected, yes?"

Marcus squinted at the pistol in the moon-and-torch light. He glared at the soldier as he scrambled to his feet, face red with anger and embarrassment.

"Tell me where you got this," demanded Marcus.

The soldier shifted his angry gaze between Marcus and Nikolas. He'd only been working for Marcus for a couple of weeks, and had been pretty much invisible to Marcus up until then. "It's mine. I bought it. What's it to you?" said the soldier. He started to reach for it, but the glare in Marcus' eyes stopped him.

Nikolas shook his head, holding the pistol up to the light. "No, you couldn't have bought this. Unless you're rich and you're doing this job for... for no reason I can imagine."

"Indeed," said Marcus, narrowing his eyes as he studied the soldier trying to inch away from him. "I asked you a question. Where did you get this?"

The soldier started to sweat, his eyes dancing around at the numerous people now paying attention.

Marcus took the pistol from Nikolas and held it up to the moonlight, studying it some more. He muttered to himself as he noted key things about its design. He brought it down and held it in his hand. "The weight is very good, the grip quite nice. You have a good piece here," Marcus said to the soldier in a friendly tone. He then extended his arm and pointed the pistol, point blank, at the soldier's face. "It hides the repeat loader well, but given the size of the pistol and the siding that accompanies the barrel, I surmise that it contains three shots. Now answer my question."

"Lord Pieman, your table is ready," said Marcus' captain from behind.

"Do you recognize this?" Marcus asked his captain, raising the pistol over his shoulder, but keeping his eyes locked on the soldier.

The captain hesitated for a moment. "St. Malo gave them to some of us. He wanted to make sure that we had a superior weapon with which to protect you. He didn't want us telling anyone."

Marcus dropped the pistol to his side. "Even me?" he said in disbelief, staring his captain squarely in the eyes.

The captain glanced at the problem soldier before answering. "I guess St. Malo may have been too emphatic in his instructions of telling no one."

Nikolas furrowed his brow. He didn't like the answer.

Marcus gently tossed the pistol in the air and grabbed it by the barrel. He then held it out for the soldier to take.

The soldier looked at it, then at the captain, and then at Marcus. He stretched out his hand to take it. When he gripped it, Marcus held on to it firmly.

"Never forget who you work for," said Marcus, his tone and eyes burning into the man. The soldier nodded nervously in reply.

Marcus turned to Nikolas. "Let's not keep our table waiting. It's been a long day."

Just as they were about to walk into the inn, Marcus noticed a man loading a cart with barrels, and stopped. Marcus bowed his head, tired. "Nikolas, forgive me. There's apparently something I need to attend to."

Nikolas noticed the man was loading the barrels at an unusually even pace, indicating to him both that they were empty and that he had no sense of urgency about getting home.

"Captain, if you'd please see Nikolas to our table," Marcus said as the captain caught up to them, the scout in tow.

"Of course, Lord Pieman," said the captain with a definitive nod.

Nikolas eyed the captain and the scout. The light from the inside of the inn defined them better. As he stood there, holding the door open, he could see they were very rough, tired-looking characters. They hadn't shaved in days, and had scars on their hands, faces, and necks.

"Get in there, tubby," said the captain, stopping himself before laying a hand on Nikolas, afraid of what the old man might do.

Nikolas cocked his head to the side and studied the captain's expression. "You think this joke is funny, yes? You've heard of the Tub and think yes, it is clever, but no. I am not fat and I am not very involved in the Tub, so therefore your joke is either extremely ignorant or you are attempting to conceal something which you are afraid I will notice."

The captain scowled at Nikolas and shoved him forward. "Get in there before we smack that grin off your face."

Nikolas steadied himself and stepped through the doorway. "What grin? Am I grinning?" he said to another one of Marcus' entourage who was motioning for him to come to a particular table. He couldn't help but smile. These men were professionals, but they were sloppy, tired, and might just give him the opportunity he needed.

The inn seemed bigger on the inside. Nikolas loved that sense of disparity between how something appeared on the surface, and how it truly was. The inn was essentially a two-story rectangle, with chairs and tables swarmed by patrons. There was some smashed furniture piled up in a far, dark corner. Despite oil lamps hanging every six or so feet, the inn seemed intimate; it was just dark enough to feel you had some privacy while being light enough to give you confidence that the food you received was likely what you'd ordered.

Laughter regularly erupted from various parts of the

inn. Servers swam through the sea of people, trying to keep up with the impossible demand, and flipping from exhaustion to elation as drunk patrons showered them with coins, paying many times over what was owed.

Nikolas felt a shove from behind and started making his way towards the table. As he walked, he noticed the stone wall and hearth at the opposite end. Decorating the giant fireplace were many small shields, each about the size of a hand. They were all perfectly lined up, except for one near the bottom that caught Nikolas' eye. Its paint was faded, but he could still make out two lines with a spring around it. He knew the symbol well.

Just as Nikolas arrived at the table, he pretended to trip, knocking over a woman who'd been balancing flagons on her head to the delight of her comrades. The flagons came crashing down.

"You made me lose a week's wages!" yelled a large, shaggy man, drawing a dagger from his belt.

Nikolas gave them an innocent look, and then pointed at the captain.

"Oh, he did it?" said the flagon-woman angrily, grabbing the captain.

As a tussle started, Nikolas carefully made his way to the fireplace. He double-checked that there was only one shield out of alignment, and then overcorrected it, taking it from leaning too much to the left to leaning too much to the right.

He turned around, scanning everyone. To his

surprise, it was a young barmaid who locked eyes with him.

"Ever the perfectionist, but clearly missing your specs," said Marcus, correcting the shield to be perfectly straight. He handed Nikolas his spectacles, which had been left in the carriage. "That would have driven you mad all meal, wouldn't it?"

Nikolas nodded. He quickly thought out how to reinforce the idea. "It's only gotten worse with age," he said.

"Now, let's sit and eat," said Marcus, putting his arm around Nikolas.

He glanced up at Marcus, who was a couple of inches taller than him. Marcus had always made him feel like the welcome little brother, even though there were fifteen years between them.

"These soldiers, you don't know them, yes?" asked Nikolas as they sat.

Marcus turned his studious gaze to Nikolas. He relaxed, and rubbed his short, white hair as if shaking off the vestiges of responsibility for a moment. "No, I don't. I should know them, however. Though my memory isn't what it used to be, I should be able to recognize the party they are pretending to represent."

Nikolas examined the soldiers' uniforms.

Marcus pointed to one. "Take the loud man there, with the long sideburns and no beard. The line that separates the red and the gray on his uniform—it's slightly curved on him, but not on the woman next to him. That's not a design detail; it's a manufacturing flaw. I've had those problems before. They were made in different batches, at different facilities. I count at least five different batches."

Nikolas nodded in agreement. "But by skilled hands. They are still well-made."

"Yes," said Marcus, leaning in. "I'd guess they would have had to produce a lot to not notice.

"That all said," Marcus rolled his shoulders back, straightening himself up, "I heard that they are marching out in the morning. We're safe regardless."

Nikolas turned back to Marcus, wondering. His old friend sounded certain about that last part, as if he knew that even if all of the soldiers in the inn turned on them at once, he would win.

Leaning forward, bowing his head a bit and putting his hands between his knees, Nikolas yawned and then looked up. "I know you are not wanting to discuss business any more, but—"

Marcus could see what was on Nikolas' mind. "You're worried about your granddaughter."

Nikolas nodded.

Marcus took out a folded piece of paper from the breast pocket of his black vest. "Here, this was with Richelle's letter, which I received from the man at the cart."

Nikolas tried to act surprised.

"Don't do that," said Marcus, waving off Nikolas' feigned expression, offended. "I know you too well, even when I'm exhausted and we haven't seen each other in years. I know that you noticed him. You noticed the pistols, and just so you know, I haven't stopped thinking about that either." He removed his monocle and rubbed both eyes. "There are a lot of things to keep in mind when you're playing a hundred games of chess at the same time."

"Such as giving me the piece of paper from Richelle?" asked Nikolas, pointing to the paper still in Marcus' possession.

Marcus laughed and handed it over.

Nikolas was surprised to find the letter was addressed to him directly. Richelle wrote about how she'd tried to reason with Tee, but Tee'd been too upset to listen. Ultimately, she hadn't captured Tee and could confirm that she'd left the battlefield with only minor bruises.

Closing his eyes, Nikolas smiled. He imagined Tee in the trap that he'd been too trusting to help her avoid, a fireball against the impending darkness. She'd grown up so much in the past several months. The LeLoup incident had changed her, but the core of who she was had made it through unharmed. He felt a mix of guilt and pride in having seeded her upbringing with the tools she'd recently needed. A thought then occurred to him.

Nikolas sat back and stared at Marcus curiously.

Marcus lowered the letter he was reading. "Now that look, Nikolas, I *don't* recognize."

"The Tub's rule about not passing knowledge or training on to successive generations," said Nikolas, pausing.

"Yes?" asked Marcus, putting the letter away. He slipped the strap of his geared monocle back on and fit it into place.

Nikolas' eyes danced around the room as several things that had bothered him for years finally fell into place. "It was you, wasn't it?"

Marcus tried to hide his smile. He leaned back and folded his arms, his eyebrows going up. "What would make you think that?"

Nikolas' eyes narrowed. "It bothered me when I first heard of this rule. It is one thing not to share your prejudices and misshapen beliefs with another generation, but to pass nothing on? To believe that the victory over the Fare was permanent? I always found the reasons given to be excuses, but every question I asked led in a circle, and in the end, the Tub wasn't mine to fix. It is clear now."

"That I had already started dismantling the Tub before we met? Yes," replied Marcus, a bit uncomfortable. "As I've mentioned before, it didn't bother me that you were still peripherally involved with the Tub after you left. You had to be, given your son-in-law. You did as you promised: you didn't tip the balance, not that they would have allowed you to…"

There was much about his ambitions and strategies that Marcus had never spoken to Nikolas about. Nikolas had always been caught in a moral conundrum when it came to him and his plans, as he could see both sides of the equation. Ultimately, it had always come down to his faith in the man.

Nikolas closed his eyes and rubbed his bald head as he thought. He muttered to himself as he tried to determine how Marcus could have done such a thing. Finally, he opened his eyes, his hand over his mouth in surprise. "The old candlemaker, Alan Waxman. I remember noticing that the bylaws had been changed when he fell ill. That was you, yes?"

Marcus' steely eyes told Nikolas that it had gone much deeper than that.

"But how did you do this so early?" asked Nikolas, leaning forward.

Marcus waved at a barmaid as she rushed by before turning back to Nikolas, unsure how he wanted to answer.

"Back in a second!" she yelled over her shoulder.

Leaning forward on his elbows, Marcus glanced around to see who was listening, as if anyone could hear over the ruckus. "After I took control of the remains of the Fare by… means that were less than savory, I moved quickly to undermine the Tub. They were already highly dysfunctional. Their leadership was old, worn, and about to change hands. Successors were not obvious yet, so I acted quickly.

"As candidates came and went, I had new laws put on the books. I had the ethos changed. When you got involved, I knew it would be relatively harmless. Yes, there were some skirmishes here and there between the Tub and the Fare, but that was more often than not with remnants of the Fare that wouldn't follow my lead, rather than with anything I was doing.

"I couldn't have the Tub undermining what needed to be done. They were supporting the status quo—a status quo that still allowed our kind to be killed or jailed without question."

Nikolas scratched his beard as he tried to remember his Tub history. "So this was all before Eleanor DeBoeuf took her role. How did you convince her? She—"

"Everyone has a price, a weakness, or a blind spot. Except maybe Samuel Baker, you'll be happy to know. He's a different matter altogether. I have high respect for the man."

Nikolas rubbed his chin, thinking of Tee's other grandfather.

Marcus smiled. "Those that you can't attack directly…"

"You render unable to harm you," said Nikolas, quoting a popular saying in military history.

Marcus nodded.

Nikolas was impressed. "Very well-executed," he said, in genuine appreciation of the complexities involved. "Anna was a dangerous wildcard, yes?"

"To be honest, I never intended for her to take the role she did. I made a mistake; rare, I know. For a long time she was simply disruptive to DeBoeuf and Baker, and then when I took DeBoeuf out of the equation, it surprised me to find Anna Maucher taking the leadership reins of the Tub. It wasn't long before I heard of the peace deal she wanted. My spies told me, however, that she had no real support from the factions that made up the Tub."

"What may I offer you gentlemen this evening?" asked the barmaid.

Nikolas recognized her from earlier, when he'd been by the fireplace.

"Alright, everyone!" boomed a decorated military man at the entrance. "Time to haul out. We leave at dawn and we've got a long march to camp. Let's go!"

Nikolas understood the words, but couldn't place the language at first. "Karuptaf?" whispered Nikolas to Marcus.

Marcus thought about it for a moment, then nodded. He leaned over the side of his chair and watched the soldiers drop their coins, collect their things, and start to head out. "I wouldn't have thought them from Karupto," said Marcus, thinking.

"Does Abeland still write you letters every month?"

asked Nikolas.

Marcus eyed Nikolas suspiciously.

"You always wear that expression when you're worried about Abeland."

Marcus sighed, letting out a half-laugh. He'd been around geniuses and master inventors all his life, but there was no one like Nikolas.

He paused for a moment before smiling at the barmaid, who had been standing there patiently. "I'm sorry, my dear."

"No worries," she said. "I appreciated having a moment to myself. It's been quite the hectic day, and a very long night."

"Is it always this busy?" asked Nikolas.

The barmaid's eyebrows went up. "Oh, it's been a madhouse lately, but it's usually pretty quiet. The other night, though, we had another rowdy bunch like these ones, dressed similarly, too. They headed out west, I think." She put the tray she'd been absentmindedly holding in front of herself under her arm. "What would you like to eat? We still have a couple of items off the... oh, I didn't bring you menus."

"It's okay," said Marcus, sporting a charming smile. "Do you have that meat pie? I had it when I was here before."

"Yes..." she said, glancing over her shoulder at the innkeeper, who was starting to collect the coins left everywhere. "Em, do we have meat pies in the ov'?"

"A couple."

Marcus continued. "That, and a cup of hot water."

The barmaid was staring at Marcus intently, and then snapped her fingers. "Oh, you're Lord Pieman." She did a sloppy curtsey. "I've never met a lord before."

Marcus stiffened, his jaw tensed. "Pardon?"

The barmaid went flush. "Oh, sorry, was I not supposed to say anything? It's just that the reservation for all the rooms was under that name. When you said—"

"That's fine. I was just… surprised," said Marcus, his smile shifting to a plastic grimace. He found it hard to believe that for the first time in decades of traveling, one of his aids had made such a reservation in his actual name. This felt deliberate.

Turning to Nikolas, the barmaid asked, "And for you, sir?"

"Does the pie have a baked crust?" asked Nikolas.

"Yes, it does," said the barmaid cheerfully.

"Do you have anything else that is baked?" he asked hopefully. "I have a craving for this, yes?"

The barmaid looked back at the innkeeper for a moment. "We might have some pastries left. Would you like me to check? I think they might be two days old."

Marcus shook his head as he watched the last of the soldiers leave. "Dessert discussion before the meal? How absurd. Never mind discussing stale pastries."

Nikolas gave the barmaid a serious stare, and said in a soft tone, "I'd really appreciate it, even if they are two days old. Some things are important to me."

"Emery, do we still have any of those pastries?" she yelled over her shoulder, maintaining eye contact with Nikolas.

"Go look for yourself! Who works for who?" he yelled back.

"Whom," muttered the barmaid.

That got Marcus' attention. He reached for her hand as she started to leave.

"Pardon my rudeness," said Marcus, "but what did you say?"

The barmaid was startled. "What?" she said, frowning at Marcus blankly.

He glanced at Nikolas, who was equally surprised. "Never mind. My apologies. Rash actions of a tired mind," he said, leaning back in his chair.

CHAPTER SEVEN
AN EG UNSCRAMBLED

Richy and Egelina-Marie approached one of the eastern entrances of Mineau very carefully, staying well- hidden in the brush at the edge of the Red Forest.

The strange glow against the midnight sky had turned out to be towering flames. The closer they'd gotten, the less real it had seemed. Somehow a war had taken place in a matter of hours, with buildings set ablaze and wreckage strewn about. The snapping and popping of the flames were occasionally interrupted by rifle, pistol, and cannon fire. Every now and then they could hear people screaming.

Advancing on their hands and knees, Richy asked anxiously, "What the yig happened here?"

"Richy!" said Egelina-Marie, surprised to hear him curse.

A smile broke on his tense face. "What? You're not my mom," he replied cheekily.

Egelina-Marie laughed at herself. Of all the things in

that moment to be concerned about, she'd jumped on him for a silly word choice. The youthful side of her didn't want to apologize, so she smiled and said, "I claim big sister privilege, so watch it, buster."

"Buster? I'm a buster now. Okay, got it," said Richy. "What's a buster?"

"Someone who is about to get busted up for asking lots of stupid questions," she answered, nudging him with her shoulder and chuckling.

Their banter was silenced by the appearance of a dozen soldiers coming towards the entranceway from inside the walled city. Four of them marched behind a cannon that was being pulled by a horse, and all of them had rifles slung over their backs and torches in hand.

Richy strained his eyes. "Are those Mineau soldiers or foreign ones like we fought earlier? I can't tell." It felt like forever ago that they'd been in the battle with Richelle Pieman and the Red Hoods, never mind the foreign soldiers they'd dealt with afterward.

Egelina-Marie shook her head. "I can't tell. If they are from Mineau, then that means the magistrate and maybe others were in on this. We'll need to get a closer look," she said, scanning about.

Richy nodded. "Do you think our friends are in trouble?" he asked, worried.

Eg's face fell as she thought of them, in particular Bore and Squeals, who she and Richy had dropped off in Mineau only a few hours ago. "Trouble? Nah. I'm sure if something happened, they had fun with it. That's what you Yellow Hoods do, right?"

"Yeah," said Richy, trying to convince himself.

She pressed herself flat to the ground. "Something's coming up behind the soldiers. They've got a convoy of some kind."

Lying flat as well, he noticed something. "Why aren't they using lanterns?" he asked. "It's not like they're a new invention or anything. And if they were Mineau guards, wouldn't they be using standard issue ones? So why use torches?"

"Ah, I don't know," said Egelina-Marie, thinking. "Too expensive, maybe?"

"Maybe," replied Richy.

They sat quietly, hidden in the brush as the soldiers marched past only ten yards away, followed by a procession of horses pulling wooden cages.

"They're mercenaries," said Egelina-Marie, pointing.

"Huh?" said Richy.

"These guys are wearing Mineau colors, but their march isn't right. No kingdom's army is going to wear another kingdom's colors, or another city's. It's a macho-ego thing. That means these guys are paying for their own supplies, and if they have torches, it means they're a bunch of cheap pargos."

Richy nudged her with his shoulder jokingly. "Woo, watch the mouth there, Mademoiselle Manners."

"Pargos! Pargos! Pargos!" she whispered, making him chuckle.

The laughter stopped as the cages came close enough for them to see people inside.

"Are they alive?" squeaked Richy, horrified.

Egelina-Marie clamped her hand over his mouth as two soldiers walked right up to their position. The soldiers were standing only a few feet away, torches in hand, scanning about.

Slowly, Egelina-Marie and Richy started to back up.

"Hey, there's something shiny in the bushes," said one of the soldiers, pointing.

Egelina-Marie glanced around and saw the light bouncing off Richy's Yellow Hood cloak. They scrambled backward to the path, and took off as fast as they could into the Red Forest.

A shot fired.

"They're chasing us!" yelled Egelina-Marie, grabbing Richy's hand and running blindly down the dark path.

Richy felt his hood snap against his face as a rifle shot bounced off of it.

A minute later, Egelina-Marie skidded to a stop at a fork in the path. She moved back and forth, hoping for something to help her decide which route they should take.

"What is it?" asked Richy, glancing around, breathing hard.

"I can't figure out which way our stuff is," she said, a mix of emotions in her voice.

When they'd left her horse and his sail-cart, they'd marked the path carefully so that they'd be able to find their way back with only the moonlight and Egelina-Marie's small mirror from her backpack.. She didn't have time to rifle through her backpack to find the mirror, and couldn't find any of the markings.

"Over there!" yelled a voice in the darkness.

Egelina-Marie's heart sank. She'd failed herself and someone she cared about for the second time today. She could hear the voice of inner doubt attacking her about every decision she'd made so far. Fear started creeping in, trying to paralyze her limbs and root her to the spot.

She glanced back and saw the little dancing balls of torch flame getting closer. For the first time in a long time, she felt the younger side of her nineteen years of age, and wished her father was there.

The shine of the moonlight in Richy's blue eyes reminded her that he was only thirteen. His face was filled with fear and hope that she would get them out of this. She didn't know what to do.

"Should we fight?" asked Richy nervously.

Egelina-Marie glanced at his hands. His shock-sticks were still in his yellow cloak's hidden pockets. His actions and words didn't line up.

"Eg, we need to do something," he repeated, worried

she was locking herself up in her head again.

She squeezed his hand and chose the path with better moonlight. "I've got an idea," she said as they skipped over tree roots and ducked low branches. "It's a stupid one. It's really stupid, but it might work."

"I'm all for stupid right now," said Richy eagerly.

Eg smiled at the sense of relief in his voice. "Do you think these guys are tired?" she asked, halting at a tall tree stump.

Richy nodded emphatically as he bent over to breathe.

"Good. Charge up your shock-sticks," she ordered, diving into her backpack to get Tee's slingshot. She'd almost left it when they were taking Pierre's body from the battlefield, but something had nudged her to take it. Now it was going to be vital.

Minutes later, four soldiers arrived, pistols drawn.

"Hey!" said one of the soldiers, seeing the light bouncing off of Richy's cloak a few steps into the forest.

"Turn around!" said the lead soldier in a booming voice. "Let me see your face, or we'll kill you where you stand." He stepped forward towards Richy's hooded form, glancing around suspiciously. "I thought there were two of them."

"I don't see anyone," said another soldier.

"Hey, he's a Yellow Hood! We'll get a reward!" said a third soldier. All four of them grinned excitedly.

"I'll give you one chance to surrender," said Richy, trying to sound as confident as Eg had told him to be. "Be warned, for I have magical powers. So drop your weapons!"

The soldiers laughed.

"Nice try, kid," said the lead soldier, reaching out to grab Richy's hood.

Just then, one soldier dropped to the ground, unconscious.

"Get up, you lazy—" said another soldier, just before he dropped to the ground as well.

"Surrender!" boomed Richy.

As the leader turned around to see what had happened to his friends, Richy reached out from behind a bush and struck him in the foot with an armed shock-stick. The soldier lit up with blue lightening and flailed madly before falling to the ground.

The remaining soldier dropped his rifle and put his hands up. "I'm just here for—"

Egelina-Marie clonked him from behind with a log.

"Oh," whined Richy, standing up and brushing himself off. "I wanted to hear what he was going to say."

"Yeah, that's a heartbreaking cliffhanger," she replied, picking up two torches and handing one to Richy to put out. She was thankful that the ground was moist. The last thing they needed was to try and outrun a forest fire.

"Give me their pistols," said Egelina-Marie, putting

one in her backpack. She slung a repeating rifle over her shoulder and found the belt pouch of refills for it.

Richy took his yellow cloak off the tall tree stump and handed the pistols over to her. "I didn't know you knew how to use a slingshot."

Egelina-Marie paused, her eyebrows rising in thought. "I… ah… I never tried before."

"Impressive! Can you teach me?"

"Sure. In fact, you take it," she said, handing him Tee's slingshot. "Just in case."

After putting it away, Richy looked at Egelina-Marie, confused. "What are you doing to that soldier?"

"Searching for money. I'm going to listen to my gut, and that means,"—she glanced around, trying to find where Mineau was, and then just pointed randomly— "we're trusting that our friends can take care of themselves over there, and you and I are going after Bakon. We've got weapons now, and I know where we can buy some supplies, so the only thing missing is money. We can sell a couple of the pistols, but nothing beats actual currency." She pulled out some coins from one of the soldier's pockets before moving on to the next one.

"You're robbing them?" exclaimed Richy. "Isn't that wrong? I mean, aren't we the good guys?"

Eg searched about. "We are, and these," she said, pointing, "are the bad guys. These bad guys took stuff from good people, so we,"—she removed another small bag of coins—"are going to allow them to make it up to the world by funding us. Anything extra we have," she said, standing, "we'll give to some orphans or something."

Richy wasn't convinced. "Are you sure about this?"

"What, that these are bad guys? Yeah, pretty sure," she replied. "We don't have time for a philosophical debate. It's pretty straightforward in my book." She caught sight of approaching torches. "Looks like these guys have friends. We better get going." She put a hand on Richy's shoulder. "Can you live with this?"

Richy thought about it for a moment, then nodded.

"Good. Let's get out of here." Eg grabbed his hand, and they took off at a careful run.

"Where are we going?" he asked.

Egelina-Marie glanced over her shoulder. "Away from those guys. In the morning, we'll find our stuff and head out."

"To where? Bakon's trail will be gone," said Richy.

She refused to let her heart sink again. "Let's not over-think this, okay? He's trying to find a Pieman. That red-hooded woman you told me about—she said her name was Richelle Pieman, right?"

"Yeah," said Richy, dodging a high root that seemed like it wanted to grab his foot.

"They must be important people, so that means that someone in a capital city's got to know of them. So either we go to our capital city of Palais, or over to Belnia's capital city of Relna. We ask around, and see where it takes us."

"We're going to Relna," said Richy with conviction.

She smiled and scanned about, trying to find where the little balls of torchlight had gone. "Why?" she asked, wiping sweat off her brow.

"You said you were going to follow your gut, right? Mine says Relna."

"Okay. Relna it is."

They walked in silence, checking periodically to make sure that there were no torches following them. Half an hour later, they arrived at a grassy area and plunked down, exhausted.

Egelina-Marie doused the torch in the dewy grass and leaned up against a tree. She was about to drift off when she chuckled. She reached for her backpack and pulled out a small blanket. Then she pulled out the sandwich her father had packed for her that morning, as he did every morning, regardless of whether or not she was working. In all the years, she'd never appreciated his religious devotion to making sure she had a small pack more than now.

"Are you hungry?" she asked Richy, who was all curled up in his yellow cloak.

"Starved," he replied, unmoving.

"Here," she said, handing him half the sandwich.

Richy had forgotten how hungry he was and took the sandwich as if it was holy. "You had this all along?"

She laughed. "Yeah. It's a long story. I'll tell you tomorrow on our ride east."

After several ravenous bites, he asked, "How are we going to find Bakon?"

With the back of her hand, Eg wiped the side of her mouth where the scrumptious tomato and butter had left their mark. "We're going to find the biggest mess we can. I'm positive that's where Bakon will be."

Richy came to the disappointing conclusion of the sandwich. "What makes you think he'll be there?"

She let a touch of the emotional storm raging inside her seep into her expression. "Because if he's not in life-threatening danger, he's going to be when I find him."

Richy took note never to anger a woman like Egelina-Marie, ever.

CHAPTER EIGHT

HOMECOMING

"We're almost there," whispered Elly, scanning the moonlit forest road.

Christina hadn't been happy at Elly's insistence on going to check out her home to see if her parents were okay. Though Tee had repeated Christina's point that her parents were fine, Elly'd been relieved when Tee had supported her request and everyone had decided to come along.

They'd managed to avoid two patrols of troops by sticking to the forest edge and hooding their lantern just in time, making them invisible in the night.

They'd also managed to determine that some of the soldiers were wearing Minette uniforms, while others were wearing the foreign ones they'd seen earlier. It confirmed for Christina that something larger was at play.

Christina scanned around, her pistol in hand. Its design was unlike anything the rest of them had seen, and only served as another point of irritation for Franklin. He'd managed to stop himself twice from asking about it, as he knew he wouldn't be able to manage a civil tone.

Tee put a hand across Elly's chest as she was just about to step out into the clearing surrounding her house.

"Someone's in there," warned Tee, pointing.

Elly locked on to the flicker of light moving through the house. "We've passed a bunch of other houses, but there was no sign that anyone had gone into them. Why are they in my house?"

Tee passed a knowing glance to Christina, who gave a confirming nod.

Christina turned to the team. "Franklin, Mounira, I want you to stay here. If anything happens and we don't come out, get out of here."

Mounira frowned. "Where would we go?"

"We'll be fine. We'll go to Herve. It's a nice city," said Franklin, nonchalantly.

Christina felt the tug of Mounira's hand on hers. "I guess I better come back," she said, feeling better as a small smile eked out on Mounira's face. She then handed the lantern to Franklin, and her backpack to Mounira. "Keep this safe, even from him, okay?"

"Got it," Mounira replied, eyeing Franklin. "Don't go making your shins hurt, okay?"

Franklin scoffed.

Quickly and quietly, Christina led Elly and Tee to the west side of the white, two-story house. With her pistol at the ready, she peeked through a window. "I saw three of them. Probably a few more are in there."

Elly reached into her cloak's hidden pockets and panicked. "I don't have any shock-sticks!"

Tee checked hers as well, and then shook her head. "We lost them at the fight with the Red Hoods."

Christina thought for a moment, then pulled out her one shock-stick. "This isn't like your regular ones. It's a prototype. It's already charged; just push the button here, and then throw it. You don't want to be holding on to this one, or you'll get shocked too."

Elly accepted the familiar weapon and studied its weight and balance for a moment. Other than what Christina had noted, it was identical to the ones she was used to. She quickly tucked it away.

Checking the siding of the house, Christina asked, "Can you guys scale the wall?"

"No problem," said Elly, starting to climb up to her bedroom window.

"You don't happen to have another shock-stick, do you?" asked Tee sheepishly.

Christina gave Tee a half-smile. "I don't, but I've seen how you handle yourself. I don't think you need one. Just keep a cool head. Anyway, I don't want you guys looking for a fight. Stay out of my way, stay hidden, but if you need to, defend yourselves. Got it?"

Elly slid the window open and carefully climbed inside, and a minute later Tee joined her.

Glancing over to Mounira and Franklin to make sure they were okay, Christina started making her way to the back door.

She flipped up the dark wood barrel-cover of her pistol, revealing a tightly wound coil. She picked some pebbles off the ground and dropped them into a chamber in the barrel-cover, and then closed it. She cocked it sharply, and listened for the awakening hum of the coil. "Three minutes," she said, reminding herself how long she had before the coil would lose its charge.

Tee followed Elly to her parents' bedroom, and watched the confusion play out on Elly's face as she found no signs that anyone had been home since she'd left. She tried to catch Tee's eyes, to glean anything she could, but Tee hid behind her hood.

As Christina opened the back door, it creaked, and a lantern shone in her direction.

"Someone's there!" yelled a man's commanding voice.

Immediately, shots were fired in her direction.

Christina dropped to the ground and squinted. Finally catching sight of someone, she pulled the trigger. A high-pitched whistle from her pistol was followed by a scream as the target dropped to the floor, struck by the stream of pebbles.

Elly and Tee peered down the stairs and saw one soldier fall, with two others surrounding someone in a red-hooded cloak.

Without thinking, Tee leapt down the stairs. Her mind was flooded with images of Pierre's death at the hands of a Red Hood. She knocked the Hood to the ground, surprising everyone.

Elly hopped onto the banister, and timed throwing the shock-stick at one of the soldiers perfectly. The soldier screamed as he lit up with purple lightening, and as he flailed, he hit the soldier beside him, who also yelled and then fell to the ground.

"Woo, that has some punch," said Elly.

Christina rushed in and smacked the wounded soldiers with the butt of her pistol. She glared at the girls. "I told you both to be careful. Elly, you almost hit Tee, and Tee, what was that about? I told you—"

Tee was trembling as she got herself off of the unconscious Red Hood. "I'm sorry, I just... I lost control."

"You could have gotten us all killed," scolded Christina. "That was really sloppy. Clear your heads or sit out next time."

Elly and Tee nodded.

"You know, my mom's going to be pretty upset with this mess," said Elly, gazing at the four bodies. "Especially the blood from that guy. Man, I bet that's not going to come off the wall easily."

Tee tried to laugh, but failed. "Your mom has a special skill at cleaning things."

"True," said Elly, examining the two lanterns. "These

are almost out."

Christina flipped the Red Hood over. Her face hardened as she noted the gold embroidery on the edges of the cloak.

Tee noticed Christina's expression. "He's not from the battle, is he?"

"No," she replied, slowly standing.

"And he's not like the Red Hoods we fought, is he?" asked Tee.

Christina sighed. "No. It's the same red, though. I figure that's intentional. But the writing in this stitching—my father showed me old books with this stuff in it. We have to go."

"What does it say?" asked Elly, watching Tee out of the corner of her eye in case she showed any signs of knowing.

"We've got bigger trouble than I thought," replied Christina. "We have to get going."

"Wait," said Elly, chasing after Christina out the back door. "Who? What do you mean by bigger trouble?"

Christina scanned about, confirming Mounira and Franklin were fine, before returning her gaze to Elly. "You've got to trust me when I say we need to get going - now."

"Where are my parents?" asked Elly.

Tee shifted her gaze from the back door's frame to Elly. "They're safe. That's all I know." There was a new certainty to Tee's voice that both relieved and bothered Elly. She felt like she was one of the kids left out when she and Tee would speak in code. She hated the feeling.

"What about your parents?" she asked, following Tee's gaze as it returned to the doorframe. Elly wasn't sure what was of interest to Tee. "Do you want to check your house?"

Christina interrupted. "We need to go. They'll be fine."

Elly put her hand on Tee's shoulder. "Don't you care —"

"My parents were in Mineau, remember?" replied Tee sharply. "They left me that note yesterday morning. They wouldn't have returned with everything that's happened."

"Okay," said Elly, leaving to join Mounira and Franklin.

Tee sighed deeply, letting out a bit of the emotional pressure inside. She rubbed the subtle marks on the back-doorframe. "I love you too, mom. I'll take care of her. I won't let you guys down."

Wiping her tears, she took out a piece of white chalk from her backpack and marked a few symbols on the other side of the doorway.

"Tee, let's go!" commanded Christina.

With a big breath to steady herself, Tee rejoined the group.

CHAPTER NINE

FLAKY ROADS AHEAD

As the sun started peeking over the hills and breaking over the horizon, the barmaid put her broom away in the closet of the inn's main room. She smiled at Emery, the innkeeper, asleep at a table. His hand was still clutching a wet rag.

Everyone else had left an hour ago, but she'd dutifully stayed as always to make sure that everything was properly tended to.

She leaned against the open doorway, gazing out at the orange sky. It was going to be a nice day for a ride. She turned and walked the main room, double-checking that everything was spotless for when Lord Pieman and his entourage came for breakfast.

Emery stirred as she walked by. "Alice?"

"Just doing my final check, Em," she replied softly.

"Oh, I must have nodded off there for a bit," he said, rubbing his stubbly, gray face. He yawned and gazed out the front door at the morning sky. "What a crazy week it's been."

"It has," replied Alice from somewhere behind him. He heard her get the dousing pole and start to put out the hanging oil lamps.

"I couldn't have handled these rushes without you, Alice. You know that, right?" he said, leaning on the chair and watching her expertly dousing oil lamp flame after oil lamp flame.

Alice stopped and smiled sweetly at him. "You've been good to me since I asked for a job a year ago, Em."

He nodded and chuckled. "I know! You haven't missed a day of work since. I don't know what I would have done without you. It's like you came out of nowhere and helped me turn this place into... into a place that people are making a point of coming to! It's like we're on the map."

Alice shrugged happily. "I just helped straighten up a bit, that's all."

"Ha!" laughed Emery, not buying it for a second.

Alice put the dousing pole away and picked up her bag of coins from the bar.

"Quite the haul last night, eh?" he said. "I think Marlene walked out of here lopsided."

Alice nodded, then turned to face him. "I'm going to be gone for a couple of days."

Emery's face went white, then he laughed, wagging a finger at her. "Oh, you had me there for a moment." He put his hand on his chest. "Oh my, you gave me a scare."

Alice's sweet smile turned up at one edge. "Sorry, Em. I really do mean it."

The innkeeper stood. "Wait—what—why?" he asked, worried. "Did... did something happen?" He wiped his hands on his apron and smoothed his stained, brown shirt.

Alice's expression turned regretful. "I'm sorry, Em." She pouted. "I forgot to tell you, and I just realized as I saw the sun coming up and thought oh no, I haven't told him. I should have told him last week."

"Oh, don't blame yourself," he said, gesturing with his chubby hands that everything was okay. "It has been so crazy here, I'm sure even I could forget that it's already Tuesday, given half the chance."

"It's Thursday," corrected Alice.

"Really?" Emery stared at Alice in disbelief. "What am I going to do without you?"

Alice lowered her head, keeping her eyes locked on Emery.

Two shots rang out, startling them both.

He waved for her to calm down. "It's likely just some straggler soldiers. Grunts who've just had the scare of their lives from their captain or lieutenant firing a pistol right by their heads to wake them from their drunken stupors. It happened last week as well, only a little later in the morning," he said, peering at the doorway and hoping he was right.

Alice smiled. "Right, that makes sense," she said, a bit rattled.

"It's okay, Alice. You go and I'll... ah... I'll manage," he said. "As... ah... as long as there isn't another night like last night, we'll be fine."

She leaned over and gave the old man a kiss on the cheek, immediately perking him up. "You will do fabulously. You'll hardly notice I'm gone."

Blushing and staring at the floor, Emery replied, "Well, I doubt that on both counts, but... I'll be fine." He nodded convincingly.

Alice walked to the open doorway and held on to it for a moment. She turned back to Emery. "I'll need to borrow a horse."

He was a bit surprised, but shrugged. "Sure, why not? No problem, Alice." He rarely lent his horses to anyone. "Um, Alice?"

"Yes, Em?" she said, giving him her adoring attention once again.

"Where are you going?" he asked, folding his arms nervously. There was something about Alice that always made him nervous to ask her anything about her life.

"Oh," she thought for a moment. She could read the concern on his face, and couldn't have him stop her from borrowing the horse. She really didn't want things to get messy. She'd been sent to serve as eyes and ears, and now needed to report back quickly. "I'm off... to find a Baker," she said. "It's about some special pastries." She waved and left.

The innkeeper stood there, dumbfounded, staring at the empty doorway. "Um, Alice? Alice?" He tapped his chin, shaking his head. "But, the baker's just down the road. And... and he's not open yet."

As Alice walked towards the stables, she froze as she saw Marcus in his distinctive black long coat and monocle, walking to the entrance of the guest rooms, a pistol smoking in his hand.

When she heard the door close behind him, she let out her breath and continued on her way.

CHAPTER TEN

MERCY OF THE RED HOODS

Snapping twigs and boots scuffing along the ground stirred the Hound from his agonizing slumber. Layered over the top of the horrific pain was the early morning chill that drilled into his bones.

He struggled to open one eye. Trembling from the pain, he caught a glimpse of three shadowy figures in the bright and blurry world around him. Mustering up his first words since having been hit with the rocket-cart the day before, he whispered, "Help me."

The Red Hoods observed the scene. The entire area was a mess. Pieces of the rocket-cart were scattered all about, as were pieces of the Hound's shock-gloves and the tank he'd worn on his back. Three trees had fallen, and black grass marked a trail that led to the crumpled Hound. He lay almost naked against a golden oak.

Hans bent down and examined the shredded metal tank. There was a green liquid pooled in parts of the beaten-up battery pack. Hans gave it a sniff. "It smells horrible. Worse than Mother's tomato soup," he said, chuckling.

Saul picked up a twig and stuck it in the liquid. It hissed as the end blackened. "Nasty stuff."

Hans turned to the Hound. "I guess that's what did this to him."

Most of the Hound's head and face were bare and burned. Only matted tufts of his red-brown hair and big beard remained, some of it fused to his skin. His legs, arms, and chest were covered in tatters, mostly exposed to the elements, with parts severely burned. A broken shock-glove lay at the end of one hand, the last remnant of how he'd looked the day before.

"It's acid," said Gretel.

Hans glanced up at her. "How would you know that?"

She rubbed a scar on her left hand. "Mother showed me." Gretel shrugged off the memory and turned her gaze to the shivering man at their feet.

Hans put his nose right up beside the Hound's head. "It smells like... like bacon, really."

"Disgusting," said Saul.

"No, seriously, come and have a sniff," said Hans, trying to grab Saul. He enjoyed the discomfort on Saul's face. Smiling at the Hound, he leaned in and whispered, "You should be dead, you horrific beast. But you smell good enough to eat." Hans went to give him a slap on the back and Gretel grabbed his arm.

"What are you doing?" said Hans angrily, shaking his arm free. "Don't touch me. How dare you do that!"

Gretel gazed upon the broken man. She could see parts of his arms where he must have tried to protect his face as the acid splashed while he'd tumbled. For the first time, she could see the handsome face that had been buried underneath all the hair.

Hans shoved Gretel back. "This thing is disgusting. It's unlucky to still be alive. It'll be dead by dinner though, one way or the other. The least we could do is put it out of its misery."

Saul wanted to say something, to argue Hans' point, but he just couldn't find the words. His brother had been oddly twitchy since Mother's death, and he didn't want to provoke him immediately after Gretel had.

Hans caught the look in Saul's eye and shook his head at his siblings. "Disgusting," he said, nudging the Hound with his worn boot. "This thing was supposed to bring us to a new life, to give us purpose, to make us matter. Now look at it. It can't even stand up! Let's just have some fun with it, put it out of its misery, and find the woman in the red cloak on our own."

"We do have the red cloaks," said Saul, trying to get Hans' approval. "We'll just try to find others like us and we'll find her. Maybe she'll want to help us."

"See!" said Hans, slapping his brother on the shoulder. "Now there's some reasonable thinking. Come on Gretel, let's—"

Saul felt ashamed when Gretel met his eyes. He'd allowed a moment of weakness and fear to overwhelm him. "No," said Gretel softly, bending down. She observed the tensed muscles in the Hound's face, how his eyes were shut so tightly that it seemed like a thousand layers of armor were trying to block the world from the fragile soul inside. She shielded the sun from his eyes with her hand and watched the muscles relax slightly.

As Hans and Saul started bickering about what to do, she waited. After a minute, the Hound's eyes fluttered open.

She gazed at him, curious. She'd never seen a man so helpless or injured before. The nightmares that had started since Mother had died, that had mostly featured a yellow-hooded fury, seemed to relinquish their hold on her while she looked at him.

The Hound had never seen such a tender smile. He tried to whisper to her, but couldn't.

Gretel felt his pain as he closed his eyes again.

"It's okay," she said, thinking. "I'm..." She paused, squinting, her face tense. "I'm... going to help you." She was surprised by the words that came out of her mouth. She'd been thinking strange thoughts since Mother's death, experiencing emotions she couldn't remember ever having before.

"No, you won't," said Hans, pulling out his rapier.

Gretel turned to see Saul picking himself up off the

ground.

Hans shoved his sister aside. "We are not wasting what little we have on this hideous beast!" He took a step forward, and found his sword-hand stopped by Saul's staff. Hans' eyes burned with fury at Saul.

Saul pleaded, "Hans, we need to think about this. I know you're still upset about Mother—"

"You don't get to talk about her!" yelled Hans, lunging for him.

Gretel caught a flash of steel out of the corner of her eye. Kicking off a tree, Gretel pulled a short staff from under her red cloak, and smacked Hans across the face. He dropped to the ground immediately.

Gretel helped Saul as he picked himself up again. He'd been grazed on both arms and a leg by Hans' blade, but was otherwise all right.

Hans was on one knee, rubbing his jaw. "I always forget that you can do that. Master Kutsuu never taught me that type of thing. I hate that sissy stick of yours," he said, standing up.

Gretel smiled, relieved that the fire was gone from his eyes. "You've been calling it my sissy stick for too long. I told you one day you'd think differently about it," she said, joking.

"Yeah," said Hans smugly. "But I'm still going to kill him. That's how it's going to be."

Gretel felt a wave of disappointment. She frowned as

she tried to find some way to stop Hans. "The red-cloaked lady doesn't know us. We could have stolen these cloaks. We need him," she said, trying to make sure there was no weakness in her voice.

Hans glanced at Gretel. "We'll just tell her that Thomas gave the cloaks to us, that's all." He was annoyed. He stepped past her and leaned over the Hound. "Bye-bye, doggy."

"Hans," said Gretel in a sharp, disapproving tone.

He paused, the tone going right through him. He glared over his shoulder at his twin sister. There was something she didn't recognize in his eyes, and it curdled her soul.

"If you're wrong, this is our new life you're destroying. Is this what you want?" asked Gretel. "Do you want to show Saul and me that you get your way, no matter the cost to all of us?"

Hans positioned his rapier above the Hound's heart. He could see Gretel's grip on her emotions wavering.

Fighting any signs of tears, Gretel said in a lower, controlled tone, "We don't know anything about Thomas. What's his last name? Where is he from? We know nothing."

Saul piped up from behind. "That red-hooded woman had the Hound in her carriage. She stood right beside him. Don't you think she'd want him alive?"

Hans thought, pointing his rapier at Saul. "Don't say

a word to me—not a word. Understand?"

Saul froze.

Hans sheathed his rapier and started to walk off, then stopped. His head tilted towards the ground, his light-blond hair falling over his eyes. Peeking through it menacingly, he said, "I will find a cart that we can use to load this... thing into. You two stay here. If you follow me or intervene in the slightest, so help me, you'll wish to be in as good condition as that *thing* is," he said, pointing angrily at the Hound.

Gretel and Saul didn't move until Hans was out of sight.

Finally, letting out a breath, Gretel sat down beside the Hound's head.

"Thank you," he whispered.

CHAPTER ELEVEN
SAFE HOUSE

The sunbeams gently nudged Christina, Elly, and Franklin towards wakefulness. Christina's eyes snapped open as a floorboard creaked. She quickly glanced around the room without moving a muscle. To her surprise, Tee was sneaking back into the one-room cabin and heading off to bed.

Christina had led the team to the safe house in the middle of the night. They'd all agreed that Tee should take the bed, given the injuries she'd sustained in the battle with the Red Hoods.

Tee carefully slinked through the room, stepping over Elly, who was sleeping protectively at the foot of the bed.

Franklin sat up and rubbed his face. He noticed Christina's open eyes. "Morning," he said, stretching and yawning. "Though I wouldn't say good, really. This floor is a touch less comfortable than I had imagined, and I'd imagined it to be rather uncomfortable." He smiled inside as Christina's nose flared and she shook her head. He figured he might as well enjoy himself, even if he had to admit it was petty.

Christina sat up and started checking her belt pouches. She'd made it a ritual decades ago to check everything she had on her, and not to assume anything. Finishing with the small hidden pouches at the tops of her boots, she felt settled.

Christina signaled for Franklin to give her a hand, and they moved the heavy, thick oak table a couple of feet over. Christina reached under the table and pulled out a foot-long stick. She carefully put it into a series of holes in the floor that had been covered by the table legs. With the last poke into the floor, there was a satisfying click and a two-foot-by-two-foot section of the floor raised slightly. Christina grabbed it and revealed darkness below.

"What's down there?" asked Tee.

"That shiner's looking quite sporting," said Franklin to Tee.

Elly roused and stared at him, confused.

Franklin tried to clarify, "It means—"

"I figured it out," said Tee, waving him off.

Christina waited to see if they were done, and then answered Tee's original question. "It's a cellar. It should have dried fruits and meats we can eat."

"What is this place?" asked Franklin, studying the simple cabin again. "I thought we were just stopping at random."

"What's what?" asked Mounira, uncurling herself and coming out from under the bed.

Christina was about to answer, and then hesitated. She stared at Elly and Tee, and thought some more. She smiled as she saw Mounira rub her face with her one arm, her hair a complete mess. The young girl's ferocity and innocence were wonderfully mixed together.

"Well?" asked Franklin, a bit offended at her pause.

Christina shifted her gaze to him and held out for another beat before answering. "It's a hideout I use every now and then," she said quickly, leaving everyone feeling there was more to the story.

Elly surveyed the small cabin. Other than the bed, dresser, table and chairs, it was barren. "I don't see a lantern or anything we could use for light. It's a shame our one from last night smashed to pieces just before we got here."

"I'm surprised it survived using the sliders down the mountain," said Mounira.

"To be honest, I'm surprised you survived that," said Franklin.

"I've had practice," said Mounira, winking at Elly and sharing a smile.

"It's nice to have a name for the pulleys and weights. 'Sliders' works," said Tee. While Christina had mentioned in passing being responsible for them, she hadn't said why they'd been built.

Christina lay on the floor and reached into the dark cellar as far as she could. After a couple of grunts, she managed to snag something and pulled out an old, simple oil lantern. "Elly, there should be a flint and steel in the middle drawer of the dresser there," she said, pointing.

A moment later, the lantern was lit and Christina lowered herself into the cellar. She crouched down and got some preserves. She was debating grabbing some other supplies when she saw Franklin's head pop in through the ceiling and ask, "Are you done? I'm starving. Hey, what is that stuff? Do you need a hand?"

"No!" said Christina. "I'm coming."

"Someone needs a cup of chamomile," said Franklin, going back up. "Or maybe a clonk on the head."

With their stomachs full and the floor restored to its original state, Christina asked everyone to exit the cabin, allowing her to do a final check to make sure they hadn't forgotten anything.

As the door closed, Franklin turned to the others. "Christina's a ripe weird one, right?" he asked, hoping to get some camaraderie going against her.

Elly glared at Franklin. "Weird? Weird how?"

Mounira folded her arm across her chest in disapproval.

Franklin scratched his neck and looked around the misty morning forest. "I don't know, she's like… paranoid or something. Like we're going to go off and tell her enemies all her secrets. Do we even know who she is? I mean, think about it. We've never seen her with anyone we know, and yet we're following her to the ends of

Eorthe." He ran his fingers through his hair. "I don't know, she looks like a bit of a weirdo too, don't you think?"

Mounira stepped forward, piercing Franklin with her deep brown eyes. Her darker skin stood out in sharp contrast to his. "You're talking about the brilliant woman who saved your life and everyone else's? That one, right?" she asked, defending her hero.

"I don't find her weird at all," said Elly with a big smile. She glanced over at Tee to see if she was going to get an elbow to the ribs. Tee hadn't noticed there was a conversation going on.

Christina exited the cabin, closing the door firmly behind her. "Okay, now we need to get moving. We have a bit of a hike to get to the horses."

Elly, Tee, and Christina started walking. Mounira ran up and took Christina's hand.

Franklin stood there. He detested not being in the know. "Hey, guys, did you notice that?" he said, pointing to the smoke in the air south of them.

"That's..." Tee searched for the sun in the cloudy sky to orient herself. "That's Mineau." She saw Mounira's hand start to tremble and Christina grab it a bit tighter.

"What do you think happened?" asked Elly, worried.

Christina fixed her eyes forward. "The world's falling to pieces, so it can't be by accident. Keep your eyes peeled for trouble." She could sense there was a grand plan being executed, but she had no sense of by whom.

Tee watched the smoke for a minute, and as nonsensical as it was to her, she asked the wind to make sure her parents were safe. Of all the crazy things she'd learned about her Aunt Gwen, putting a wish on the wind had seemed to top everything, until now.

CHAPTER TWELVE

LIKE A BROTHER

The ten-year-old Abeland peeked through the crack in the door. He loved spying on his father in his secret meetings. Marcus had such presence and command in his voice that his boys would often pretend to be him, ordering their wooden toys to do one thing or another, and then dying of laughter.

Abeland loved how everyone who came to the house was dressed, and how they spoke to his father. One day, he wanted to be just like him.

"What are you doing?" asked his five-year-old brother, Lennart.

Abeland turned to see the little guy, standing there in his shorts and shirt, smeared with tomato jam. Lennart peered through long bangs. Abeland thought he needed a haircut, but Mother loved his curly locks.

Lennart had a teddy bear under his arm, one that father had bought for him on one of his many trips away. The face was well worn from cuddling.

"I'm listening to Father," whispered Abeland.

Lennart frowned and wagged his finger at his big

brother. "You're not supposed to be doing that, Mother said. Father doesn't like to be dis-tur-bined."

Abeland rolled his eyes. "Disturbed. We're not going to disturb him, anyway. Come, listen. He's talking about moving horses and cannons around."

Lennart dispelled his frown and cuddled up beside his brother, putting his ear to the door. "He always tells us we shouldn't do this."

Abeland tapped his brother on the head. "Shh!"

"But I'm not doing anything!" yelled Lennart.

Abeland grabbed Lennart and clamped his hand over his brother's mouth. "Shh, don't make us get caught."

"Boys?" came a weary female voice.

"Mother!" whispered the boys with wide eyes.

"Okay, Lenny, let's go! Come on!" said Abeland. He grabbed his little brother by the hand and tore off in the opposite direction of the approaching footsteps.

They ran through the kitchen, where a dozen servants were working diligently. "Excuse us!" the boys whispered as they wound their way through and out the back door. Then, to their surprise, they found a boy who appeared to be the same age as Abeland standing there in the backyard.

The boy had a black eye and filthy clothes. His hands trembled at having been discovered. Abeland quickly followed the boy's eyes to a pie and a loaf of bread that were cooling on one of the kitchen window ledges.

Lennart pointed to the stone wall that surrounded their inner-city backyard. "Did you climb the rock wall? It's very high."

The dark-haired boy stared at Lennart and then at Abeland, unsure of what to say.

"Did you climb it?" asked Abeland.

The boy nodded.

"Huh. You must be a pretty good climber," said Abeland, impressed.

"Really good!" said Lennart excitedly. "Will you show me how you did it? I can't get up very far."

The boy eked out a smile.

Abeland turned back to the food on the ledge. "I'm guessing you smelled this fare here. Are you hungry?"

"Yes," said the boy nervously.

"What's shiny?" asked Lennart, pointing to something tucked into the boy's frayed rope belt.

Abeland stopped himself from walking over and having a peek. He understood that if he got any closer to the boy at this point, he'd make him feel anxious and threatened. Abeland smiled as he remembered his father teaching him that about injured animals recently.

The boy slowly and carefully pulled out a geared bird. He turned a tiny metal rod and it flapped its wings. Abeland and his brother were impressed.

"Did you make this out of broken watch pieces?" asked Abeland.

The boy nodded and smiled.

"This is really good," said Lennart.

The boy let out a big sigh. "I sell them for money, but this is my last one. I made this one from my dad's watch."

"Where's your daddy?" asked Lennart, glancing around.

The boy's face fell. "He's dead."

Abeland studied the boy. They were the same height, and likely no more than a couple of months apart in age. "What's your name?"

"Simon," said the boy. He straightened up, showing that he was clearly from a better background than it had first appeared. "Simon Stimple."

Abeland put his arm around the boy. "Simon, I want you to meet my father. I'm sure he'll let you stay with us and you can have all the fare you can handle!" he said, pointing to the food. "But..." Abeland removed his arm and gave it a sniff. "We better get you bathed first. Otherwise Mother will kill us."

Simon gave the sleeping Abeland a nudge with his boot again, rousing him. "I thought I'd say goodbye before I left. I don't suppose I'll see you again. I need to get back to the store before anyone notices it's unmanned, so to speak."

Abeland blinked hard at the morning light assaulting him from the open doorway. The weight of his manacles quickly reminded him of where he was.

Simon tapped him on the chest. "Your breathing sounds terrible. Haven't they been giving you the medicine I've been sending? Oh, wait, I haven't been sending any," said Simon, smiling to himself. "Mind you, you look terrible from head to foot, so why not inside and out? I never really appreciated just how well-groomed you've always been until now.

"You know, I'm sure Lennart would have found a way to still look good. It's a shame you killed him."

Abeland sat up, leaning against the cold stone wall. "What are you talking about?" he whispered, coughing. His throat was dry, his lips chapped. His lungs felt like they barely moved when he breathed. He focused on Simon, surprised to find him crouching down beside him, instead of keeping his distance as usual.

"Oh," said Simon, tilting his head from side to side, "little secrets that I've been let in on. I'm not mad, even though he was my best friend. I always idolized you, but you never seemed to have time for me like Lennart did. I suppose it's like my friend Charles says: it's survival of the fittest. Though, I have to admit, I would have preferred if the tables had been turned."

"You aren't making any sense," said Abeland. "I didn't kill my brother. I loved my brother."

"Well, that part I know isn't true," said Simon. "But I don't care. Anyway, what was it I was talking about? Ah, medicine. I hate to see you in this state, so I brought you a little something. See, after I leave here, only one more person is ever going to come. You'll get a final meal and that's it. But don't worry, you shouldn't starve. The plants around here," he said, pointing at the walls, "they'll be in full bloom in the next couple of days, maybe the next week. That wonderful breeze you have from that barred window will make sure it's over soon."

Simon took out a two-inch vial of green/blue liquid from his vest pocket. "What if I offer you some breathing medicine in exchange for some truth? I want to know when you got this lung disease. You didn't have it until recently."

Abeland glared at Simon with his brown-and-gray eyes. "Give me the vial first."

Simon toyed with it for a moment before popping the cap off. "I don't see a way I can lose, so why not?" He poured the contents into Abeland's mouth, and smiled as the chained man nearly spat it out.

"Did I mention I made some changes to your formula? I made it extra bitter and gave that hallucination side effect an extra kick. Just my little way of ensuring that you enjoy your final days."

Abeland forced himself to swallow all of it.

Simon took out a small red cloth and wiped Abeland's mouth. "There, some decorum. Now, I have to admit, I was really surprised to learn that you had such an accessible weakness. When did it happen?"

A twinge in Abeland's chest told him the medicine

had contained a potentially dangerous amount of nightshade. "It was the battle of Tangears, before I came to the southern kingdoms. They had a weapon that set fire to the air. I inhaled some of it as I yelled for my troops to take cover."

"Hmm," said Simon. "That'd be about four years ago. I've seen you several times over that period, and yet I didn't know."

"I keep my secrets well-hidden," said Abeland, taking a slightly larger breath than he had in months.

Simon leaned back against the wall. "I've also heard you built quite the apparatus to process the deadly nightshade into something helpful and harmless. Why not share that with the world?" he asked mockingly. Abeland always seemed to wrap whatever he was doing in explanations about how it was better for the world in the end.

"Because we don't have a world that shares well," said Abeland, coughing.

Simon started to stand, then crouched back down. "In all these months together, you've never asked me once why you were here, or who asked me to do this to you."

Abeland glared at Simon.

"You know, don't you?" said Simon.

Abeland just silently stared, his breathing calm and steady.

Simon put on a fake smile. "Dear old dad's plans not

so subtle then?" As he went to stand, Abeland grabbed his legs and pulled them out from under him. As he sat up, Abeland hit him in the nose with his forehead.

Abeland quickly put a chain across Simon's windpipe and whispered into his ear. "Unlike my lungs, your weakness of supreme overconfidence and love of picking at other's pain has no remedy."

Simon struggled to no avail. Abeland was still stronger than him, even in his reduced state.

Abeland yanked the chain, making Simon squeal in pain and flail his arms in desperation. "I know you wouldn't have come sit beside me unless you had the key to my freedom on you, you sick pargo." He tightened the chains around Simon's neck. "So where is it?"

"You broke my nose," screamed Simon.

Abeland held the chains as tightly as he could, cutting off Simon's air. Abeland himself was starting to see stars as he strained his lungs so much. "Words are expensive, so you shouldn't be wasting them like you've wasted the opportunity I gave you all those years ago. All you've done from day one is act entitled and been a pain. My father should have listened to me years ago and tossed you out."

Simon tapped Abeland, yielding like he had when they had fought as teenagers. He relaxed the chains slightly, and Simon slowly moved his hands to his left boot heel. A moment later, he produced a key and handed it over.

With his hands free, Abeland smacked Simon's head against the stone and shackled him in the chains. He paused at the doorway, debating whether or not he should just kill Simon and be done with it. His tactical mind didn't really believe that it was Marcus who had orchestrated his downfall. Abeland figured the most likely path to the truth was through the mistakes a desperate and panicky Simon would make.

Abeland stumbled out of the small underground building and found himself standing in the middle of a field surrounded by a forest in the distance.

"What the...?" he said, turning around and around in confusion. "Where am I?" He'd been pretty certain he was on the grounds of a castle.

A wave of dizziness hit him, making him stumble to one knee. He put his hands down to brace himself as the feeling slowly passed. He wobbled back to his feet. "Simon wasn't kidding when he said he'd been messing around with the side-effects. This is going to be bad, I can just tell," he muttered to himself.

"Better be careful," said a deep voice.

Abeland glanced around. There was only a horse, stocked with saddlebags. Otherwise the green-and-brown grassy field was empty.

He walked around the horse, searching for someone, before turning to look it in the eyes. "You didn't just talk, did you?" asked Abeland.

"Me? No," said the horse, shaking its head. "You

must be hallucinating."

"Wonderful," said Abeland, rubbing the horse between the eyes.

"Have you ever had hallucinations before?" asked the horse.

Abeland nodded as he stared at the horizon. "Back when I first started experimenting with nightshade. After the battle of Ganounia where my lungs got burned, I did a lot of research to find something that would work. But I never had a talking horse hallucination."

The horse raised its head. "I thought you told Simon that it happened in Tangears."

Abeland laughed. "Are all horses so trusting? I lied," he answered, opening up the first of the saddlebags to check it.

"If there's an apple in there, I'd appreciate it," said the horse, nodding.

"Um, okay." A moment later, he handed the horse a green apple and then prepared himself to get on. "Do you mind if I... um, mount?"

"No, go ahead," said the horse, gazing about. "I think we're safe. Just be careful. You're seeming... a little off."

"I'm a bit woozy, but I'm okay," said Abeland. He finally got up on the horse and then slowly slid down the other side.

"Maybe you should have a rest first?" said the horse, staring at Abeland lying on the ground.

"I'm fine. Just… another sign that this medicine wasn't made right. Its muscle relaxation properties are too strong."

Focusing hard, Abeland mounted successfully. He took hold of the reins and they trotted a couple of yards in one direction, then turned around, and then turned around again.

The horse raised its head and said, "How about we take the trodden path over there?"

"Okay, listen," said Abeland, leaning over and patting the horse on the side, nearly falling off. He noticed his hands and forehead were sweaty. "Um, thanks for the advice, but from here on out, don't talk, okay? I can already feel my mind going squirrelly as it is."

The horse's head moved from side to side. "Squirrels? Please tell me you don't see talking squirrels. Those little beasts are pure evil, especially the purple ones."

Abeland rubbed his face. "Now I have a paranoid hallucination." He tapped the horse's side. "No talking unless you absolutely have to, okay?"

"Got it," said the horse, bobbing its head up and down.

Finding the main road, Abeland took it eastward. Every now and then, he rubbed the palm of his hand on his bearded face, using it to judge how much sensation he had left. After an hour, he couldn't feel anything and nearly tilted himself off the horse when he raised his arm.

His mind was now a mess as well. Several times, he

asked the horse if it saw the imaginary creatures in the shadows, but true to its word, the horse said nothing.

A while later, as Abeland was leaning heavily on the horse, drooling and almost asleep, he heard a woman scream. He rocketed himself upright, nearly flying off the back of the horse. He clutched the reins like a man dangling off a cliff. He was soaked to the bone in sweat.

Abeland searched about. "Richelle? What's that little girl gotten herself into this time?" he said to himself, slurring his words. He blinked awkwardly as he noticed he couldn't feel his tongue properly or see clearly. When the scream came again, he zeroed in on a woman with a food cart up ahead.

He shook his head, surprised at how much it weighed. "Richelle, Richelle, Richelle. What have you gone and done this time? It's nearly time for your dance lessons."

The horse moved from side to side. "You're in no shape to go and help."

"Shh," said Abeland, waving his hand, his gesture wildly exaggerated. He patted the horse's neck and smiled. "Lennart, you really should be taking charge here. She's your daughter. I don't understand why you didn't want her. Well, I mean, I know why, but still.

"It was clever of you to change her name to Mother's right when she died. So sneaky to have kept her full name from Father the whole time. He didn't even notice you manipulated him into taking her away!" Abeland tapped his nose. "I think it was the only time you got the best of him. Don't worry though, your secret's safe with me."

An old man fell to the ground and the woman screamed again.

"You missed out though; she's really a good kid. By the way, brother to brother, Lennart, you really need a shave." Abeland struggled to focus on the road ahead. "Okay, here I go. I'm coming, Richelle!" he yelled, sliding off the horse. His legs immediately buckled and he fell to the ground, hitting his head. He was out cold.

CHAPTER THIRTEEN

PASCAL'S DILEMMA

LeLoup smiled at the devilishly handsome, green-eyed man in the full-length mirror. It felt good to be back.

Convincing a soldier to steal a horse and bring him to Palais, the capital city of Freland, was child's play. The soldier had been a bit skeptical at first, but a few words and timely tapping of the brass tube containing Nikolas Klaus' plans for a horseless cart, and the soldier was his.

The soldier had waited for his payment outside the brownstone townhouse, as instructed. LeLoup had escaped out the back, having given him a fake name. He wondered if the soldier would be hunting down Maxwell Watt for the year's salary he'd been promised. LeLoup chuckled at how clever he was as he checked out his backside in the mirror.

He wondered for a minute about the wisdom of selling the plans to that woman, instead of taking them to Simon. He'd intentionally never dealt with her before, having heard she had ties to unscrupulous people, even by his standards. But he needed money, and if he was ever going to see Simon again, he wanted to make sure he was in a position of strength.

"I have to say, Pascal, you have such wonderful new clothes," said LeLoup, brushing his neck as he lifted his chin and inspected the new style of shirt. He'd stopped for a hot shave and haircut on the way, and was already feeling like a new man. He loved the look of the high-collared white shirt, especially with the gray tailed coat and pants. It was incredible to him that people seemed to have abandoned pantaloons and britches so quickly. The world seemed so eager for change these days.

The well-dressed, bald tailor at his feet took the pins out of his mouth. "Thank you, Andr— I mean, Monsieur LeLoup." The chubby old man tried to hide his nervousness, but he was dripping sweat. His round face was tense and his mouth puckered.

When LeLoup had walked in the door, Pascal had greeted him warmly and all was good, until Pascal had addressed him as Andre. LeLoup's green eyes had come alive with disdain, drilling fear into the old man's heart.

"Pascal, just LeLoup. There's no need to be formal; we've known each other too long for that." LeLoup gazed about the small shop, at the rolls of cloth lined up against the wall on wooden poles, at the wooden mannequins with their dashing new and classic suits. Pascal's two assistants, who normally did all the pinning work, were huddled against the back wall.

LeLoup had yelled at them earlier, wanting only Pascal to do the work. They had stayed rooted to that spot ever since. LeLoup could smell their fear; he found it calming.

"Yes... sir... LeLoup," replied Pascal, putting the pins back in his mouth and finishing his work on the pant legs. "There we go." He brushed off his hands and then, putting his hands on his bent knee, stood with a huff. "I can have them ready—"

LeLoup put his hands on either side of Pascal's cheeks. "In about an hour. An hour sounds reasonable to me. What about you?" he asked, his words laced with threats and malice. He knew it was impossible.

The old man's eyes dashed around the shop, landing on his two assistants. "All four suits? But..."

LeLoup took another peek at himself in the mirror. "Well, it's not like you had to make them. They were already made. They just need adjustments."

Pascal stopped himself from saying that, as LeLoup already knew, they had been intended for other customers. LeLoup had threatened him and offered a lot of money to Pascal to make them his.

The tailor clasped his hands together gently. "Could you give us until the end of the day? What with the jackets and... we want to do a good job for you. You deserve that much, LeLoup."

A genuine smile crept across LeLoup's lips and he released the fat man. "Pascal, I trust you. If you say you need until the end of the day, then you shall have it. I have some other errands to run that will keep me busy.

How's Manny doing? I'm a couple of months late picking up something special from him."

"He's good," said Pascal, wiping his brow again. "He's… he's good."

"I'm so glad," said LeLoup, smiling. "You know what? I'm rather...what's the word for it?"

"Peckish?" blurted one of the assistants.

"Yes!" he said, snapping his fingers and making the assistant jump. "Peckish! Goodness, how I've missed civilization and real words. Is Blaise's Conundrum still around? I love that pastry shop, with its two small pastries for one price. Which one to devour first? Should I keep one for later? So clever."

"It's still in the same place it has always been," said the other assistant.

"Still wonderful, best in town," said the first, wiping his forehead with his sleeve.

LeLoup gave them all a sinister, toothy grin. "Excellent. I do so love devouring things."

CHAPTER FOURTEEN
KING'S-HORSES

Christina stopped and put her heavy backpack down. The forest clearing was about twenty feet in diameter, big enough to camp in if they needed to. She gazed up at the high forest canopy and got a rough sense of the time. The sunlight was partially diffused, giving the forest a warm, golden light.

With a nod, Christina confirmed to everyone that they could rest for a bit. Tee took off her backpack and plunked herself down on the cool, moist earth.

Elly grimaced at the backpack, and then glared at Christina. She'd offered to carry it, but Christina had insisted that Tee do it. Elly had thrown up her hands and walked away from it.

Christina smiled at Tee. She'd heard about her over the years, starting with when Jennifer had first been pregnant. Nikolas was so proud of his granddaughter, and had remarked on every little achievement or precious moment. She'd felt Nikolas' angst when he'd shared William and Jennifer's plans. They'd been cramming as many of the secrets, and special skills, into Tee that they could in a few short months, rather than over years. Ultimately, Nikolas come around to their point of view, realizing that the world was more dangerous than he'd wanted to admit.

Christina had been no stranger to secrets growing up, but she and her father had never stayed in any place long enough for her to make a friend like Elly. It had been clear from the moment they'd left the battlefield and made their way back to Minette that there was an incredible bond being tested. She envied the relationship, but not the conflict that clearly was going on inside Tee.

Tee saw the seriousness of Christina's expression. "My legs hurt, my back hurts, my ribs and arms are bruised, but I'm hanging in there."

"Good," said Christina, smiling.

Elly bristled at Tee's words. Too much of her didn't want to feel sympathy for Tee, but she couldn't help it.

"Do you feel like the oil is leaking out of your lamp?" asked Mounira. "Does that make sense in Frelish? It's an expression from home."

Tee nodded as she thought it through. "I think I know what you mean. No, I don't."

"Phew!" said Mounira. "I felt that way after I lost my arm. It took a long time to feel better."

Christina pointed at her sidekick and scooped up her backpack. "You're with me; the rest of you stay here. If there's any trouble, make as much noise as you can."

Mounira gave Tee a pat on the back and skipped off after Christina.

Franklin kicked the ground as they left. "I really hoped she'd leave that backpack. She slept with it like it had the blooming crown jewels in it. I wonder what's in it?"

"Your soul!" said Elly, getting a laugh out of Tee and a grimace from Franklin.

He sat down on a log, and soaked up the forest view. He'd never hiked so much in his life, but he was keeping up better than he'd thought he would.

Intellectually, the task was trivial: walk through miles of forest, avoid hitting trees, and keep going until he was at the destination. In reality, uneven terrain was exhausting at times, and the temperature could vary greatly from one area to another. As a scientist, he found it fascinating.

"Have you ever had a black eye before?" Franklin asked Tee, realizing he was staring at her. She was pretty, even with her shiner. Franklin quickly dropped his gaze, having learned that if he allowed himself to think of Tee as a pretty girl for long, his words and thoughts would get jumbled up.

Tee shook her head. "No. I've had plenty of bruises, but no black eyes or broken bones."

"What about that time we were six and we fell off my

house?" asked Elly.

Tee paused for a moment, recalling the memory. She chuckled at how much trouble they'd gotten into for having a tea party on the roof. "I think I sprained my arm. I can't remember."

Elly nodded. "That sounds right. You had a sling for a while."

Franklin threw a stone, swimming through the mess of his thoughts and emotions. Every time he tried to do what seemed right, it came out twisted and he was rebuked for it. It felt like home. "My sister gave me a black eye once. Took about a week to heal. I tried to take her teddy bear, and she let me have it. Probably the best right jab an eight-year-old ever threw in the history of pugilism." He noticed their expressions and got annoyed. "Boxing. Punching. Pugilism means—"

"I know what pugilism is. You have a sister?" said Elly, surprised. "You never mentioned her."

Franklin sat down and crossed his legs. "Oh… yeah. Mean little thing. Well, I shouldn't say that, but she's a lot like my mother and, well… my mother and I aren't an award-winning pair at the county picnic."

Tee and Elly glanced at each other and shrugged.

"Have either of you ever been this far outside of Mineau before? The trees are a brilliant yellow and green. I'd guess we aren't in the Red Forest anymore," said Franklin.

"No," said Elly. "Before yesterday, I'd never been

further than Mineau."

Tee stared at Elly and Franklin. There was an uncomfortable pause before she replied. "I've been to visit my Aunt Gwen. She–"

Franklin cut Tee off excitedly. "Hey, I have a question. When do you go to school? I just realized I've been gone for months now. I'm actually starting to miss it. I figure you must be on a break."

Tee and Elly shrugged at each other.

"What's 'school'?" asked Elly, turning back to Franklin.

He laughed. "Nice! No, seriously. Were you on break when I showed up?"

Tee scrunched up her face. "Are you asking if the school thing is broken?"

Franklin stood up and rubbed his hair in frustration. "Are you playing word games with me again?" he asked, annoyed. He felt like every time he spoke to Tee, something caused his darker, defensive side to flare up.

"No," said Tee, motioning for him to settle down. "We don't know what you mean by 'school'."

Franklin was a bit taken aback. "School is... um, a place you go to learn lessons about history, language, maths, and whatnot. You know, school."

Elly bounced her hand off her forehead. "Oh, lessons. You mean lessons! Why can't he just say lessons?" she asked Tee.

Tee shrugged and shook her head. "He's a boy."

Elly nodded in emphatic agreement, then stopped, tilting her head. "Richy's a boy, though."

Tee smiled at her, eyebrows raised.

"Too much hanging around with us, you think?" asked Elly.

Tee shook her head. "No, just the right amount. I'm sure he'll make some woman very happy one day. We'll have boiled enough of this—" she gestured at Franklin —"out of him that he might just be loveable."

Elly giggled and Tee smiled. For a moment, things felt almost normal between them.

Franklin folded his arms. "Are you quite done? I have *some* dignity left, I'm sure."

Tee waved for him to calm down. "We have lessons every day. Different lessons for different things at different times of year. We go to the person's house or meet somewhere, like a blacksmith's forge or a baker's kitchen. Wherever the lesson needs to take place," said Tee.

"Oh," said Franklin. "That's... that's actually rather interesting."

Elly stood up and pointed. "Wait, what are those?" she said, her mouth agape. Tee and Franklin followed Elly's astonished gaze.

Christina was leading what at first seemed to be a convoy of three horses, with Mounira on the first one and tan blankets on the backs of the others. However, as they got closer, Elly, Tee, and Franklin saw that these horses were not alive. They were entirely mechanical in nature.

"What are those?" asked Franklin.

"They're amazing!" said Mounira excitedly. "They were just hiding in the forest under a sneaky blanket that looked—" Christina frowned at her, reminding her that she wasn't supposed to say anything until Christina gave the all-clear.

Letting go of a trigger in the mouth of the first horse, Christina brought the three horses to a quick stop. She removed a cable that went from horse head to horse head, and pulled off the blankets. "These are the remaining King's-Horses. They were created more than forty years ago by Nikolas Klaus and my father, Christophe Creangle."

Franklin's eyebrows shot up. "They were made forty years ago?" he said, flabbergasted. "Them? These here? No way. They look almost new."

Christina gave a tight-lipped smile and nodded. "We know how to take care of our toys," she said.

Franklin moved about the King's-Horses in complete disbelief. He'd never witnessed such art and technology together before. The quality of the machining was something that he'd only recently started seeing at home. "There's nothing like these around today, at least not that I've heard of, and my father's told me about a lot." His arms were folded, his fingers drumming on his face in astonishment.

Each King's-Horse was covered in brilliantly sculpted wood and dark bronze panels, giving it the appearance of a real horse from a distance. There were numerous holes through which gears and belts could be seen. Where the joints of a horse would be, there were rotating plates. Its motion had been remarkably natural.

Tee moved her hand along the side of the third mechanical horse. "Wow. My Grandpapa helped build them that long ago?" She kept stuffing her emotions down deep inside herself as she thought about him. "I had no idea."

Elly shook her head as if to wake up from a crazy dream. "I thought the sail-carts were amazing. He must have taken no more effort than to yawn."

Christina's face said she wasn't entirely comfortable sharing the information about the horses, but she knew if she withheld everything about them, she would quickly have a little rebellion on her hands. "Nikolas and my father wanted to prove to the King of Teuton that the purging of inventors was wrong. They thought, as Conventioneers and nearly King's-Men themselves, that they had enough credibility to risk creating these and showing him what could be made outside of the restrictive boundaries of the Conventioneer Act. The High Conventioneer didn't even know what they were doing.

"The King came to a private showing of the four

King's-Horses. After having a terrified servant ride around on one in the inner courtyard, the King mounted one.

"He loved it so much, he took it out and rode it through the capital's streets and back. After several days, his ambitions came alive. He realized that Nikolas and my father had imaginations worth tapping, but he wanted weapons that the other Conventioneers said were impossible. Nikolas and my father refused to make them, and were arrested.

"The King gathered his best Conventioneers, and asked them to make him a hundred King's-Horses. He figured that, in making a hundred, they would learn everything about them and be able to build him whatever he wanted afterward.

"He initially offered them one of the four King's-Horses to disassemble, but they went through three trying to figure out how the machines worked, without success. When they came back to ask the King for the final one, he took a mace to it right in front of them, smashing it to pieces.

"He raged for a week, but finally, under the repeated suggestion of his High Conventioneer, he went down to the prison and freed my father and Nikolas on the condition that they make him some new King's-Horses.

"For two months, they worked under the watchful eye of the High Conventioneer. The new ones were simplistic copies, built to be of little value for weapons-making, and likely to fall apart within a year. While they worked on these, Nikolas and my father plotted with the High Conventioneer to escape.

"On the night my father and Nikolas escaped, Nikolas took one of the original King's-Horses and my father took the other three. You see, they'd actually secretly made eight rather than four in the first place, but they'd kept this from everyone, including the High Conventioneer."

"From what I heard, the High Conventioneer was caught trying to escape. I don't understand how he wasn't executed, but he eventually became the regent of Teuton. Some years later, its people ousted the monarch and it became a democratic republic. He serves as their president for life." Christina scratched her cheek, her eyes away from everyone.

Franklin, Mounira, Tee, and Elly were quiet as they absorbed the tale. Christina took the time to double-check that the saddles were properly secured. She then folded down some pedals and adjusted their height.

Detecting something in the way the story had been told, Elly asked, "Who was the High Conventioneer?"

Christina sighed. She liked Elly. The girl was sharp, funny at moments, and apparently held her own in a fight. Christina uncomfortably replied, "Marcus Pieman."

Franklin's jaw dropped as he realized that Nikolas and Marcus knew each other. Any lingering effects from Nikolas' speech two days ago were dispelled, and

Franklin's anger intensified. Who was Nikolas to tell him what to do and how to behave? He felt disgusted that he had thought that maybe one day he could be like Nikolas.

His hands shook as the rage built up inside him. He glared at Christina. "Pardon?! Did you just say the name of the man who tried to kill us? Are you telling us that saintly Nik is best buddies with the Pieman?" Franklin stormed about. "It was probably his blooming army that burned Mineau to the ground. Is that why he took Nikolas? Picked up his old chum before the scorching started?" He scowled at Tee. "What's going on here?" He wanted to believe she didn't know. He immediately wished he'd asked her and not accused her, but he'd missed the moment.

She held Franklin's gaze, saying nothing.

Elly fired on Tee too. "What do you know, Tee?" she said, shattering the fragile sense that things were back to normal between them.

Tee pulled her hood up. "Nothing. We should get going."

"Good idea," said Christina, chiming in.

"Why don't I believe you, Tee?" said Elly, her fists clenched.

When Tee answered, her voice was devoid of emotion. "That's your choice, Elly."

Elly stomped her foot and shook her fists at Tee. "Stop locking me out! Stop it!"

Franklin shook his head and caught a glimpse of a panel where the mechanical horse's heart would otherwise be. "What's that spot for? That... heart-panel," asked Franklin, pointing to the six-inch square door.

"Storage," snapped Christina.

"Storage?" repeated Franklin incredulously.

"Deaf?" asked Christina, annoyed.

Fuming, Franklin quieted. Deep down, he wasn't sure how much of the truth he could handle. His sense of superiority stemmed from his and his father's work, and was part of the foundation of who he was. Now, he was tormented by the idea that his father's invention wasn't even relevant, never mind that the very man his father had looked up to had been playing him for a fool.

As Christina finished her checks on the third King's-Horse, Franklin snuck up to the first one again. He peeked through the holes and muttered to himself as he thought through how it might work. There was something about the pedals that bothered him. For such a brilliant and elegant design, they seemed rather... crude, almost like they were an afterthought.

The more he thought through how the mechanical horse might work, the more the anger boiled inside him. He tried to open the panel that Christina had said was for storage, but it was locked.

"What are you doing?" yelled Christina, knocking Franklin to the ground.

Franklin pointed at the panel angrily. "That's got to be

for an engine. An engine, forty blooming years ago? That small?! What's going on?"

Christina stared at Franklin without blinking. "I don't know what you're talking about," she said in a firm, dismissive tone.

He scrambled to his feet. "You know exactly—"

Christina's hand instinctively went to her sidearm as she took a quick step forward, forcing Franklin to cower back. Her expression could have stopped a falling tree. In a fierce, eerily calm tone, she said, "The more you act like this, the more you become a liability. If you want to feel insecure about your daddy's work, go right ahead, but understand that I need to get us moving—with or without you."

Franklin scoffed at Christina's bravado, on the knife's edge between anger and tears. "Then good luck finding the steam engine plans without me," he said, folding his arms and trying to match her glare.

Elly, Tee, and Mounira watched the confrontation silently.

Franklin looked away, running his hands through his hair. "Why are we even going after the plans? I mean, given what I've seen in just a couple of days, it's all been a colossal waste of time. Better things already exist! My father's engine isn't of any value to anyone."

Christina took a second to breathe. It was loud enough to make everyone feel like she was trying to stop herself from just shooting him. She closed her eyes and opened them, more centered.

In a controlled tone, she said, "That steam engine is going to revolutionize the world. The world is ready for it and it can scale up, powering huge things."

A sinister grin swept across Franklin's face. Christina had stepped right into his trap. "How would you know? You haven't seen them. Or have you? Because my father hasn't sent anyone a copy of them. He's been extremely careful who he's told about it as well."

Christina couldn't believe she was having this argument, let alone with a fifteen-year-old in the middle of nowhere. "So the attack by the Fare—" she started to say.

Franklin threw his hands up. "Actually, I don't know if it was the Fare. My father thought they were behind everything, but he burned Mister Klaus' letter without reading the whole blooming thing. For all I know, it's the Tub who sent the troops, or maybe it's just blooming coincidence because world politics never make any sense!"

Christina pointed a finger sharply at him, her other hand still on her pistol. "Get on that middle King's-Horse, now. This conversation is over. If you're not ready in five seconds, I'm leaving you here."

"You can't do that," said Franklin, clearly rattled.

"Try me," she said, her voice scorching his soul. She mounted the first horse, positioning herself behind Mounira. "I'm done with having a liability. Contribute or die. I'm done with you."

Christina shot a glance at Tee and Elly, who were just standing there. "You're riding the last one together. Get moving."

Elly stiffened at the thought of riding with Tee, and immediately felt a sense of sadness and guilt for it.

CHAPTER FIFTEEN
THE LIAR

Every time the boutique's door opened, Manny twiddled his fingers nervously. Each customer who'd shown up in the past hour had made him jump, and for good reason.

It had been a regular morning until Pascal had run in, sweating like a pig and stammering like a fool. They'd had a complicated, uncomfortable friendship for decades. Manny felt that Pascal was pretentious and self-centered, but at the end of the day, he was the only person Manny trusted to make clothes that looked good on his large frame. Pascal didn't approve of the weaponsmith's line of work, but he appreciated the quality and artistry. Even though he was a pacifist, Pascal had purchased a custom blunderbuss rifle years ago and mounted it above his fireplace at home.

"Is that you, Manny?" asked LeLoup, peeking his head around the door. He was much later than Pascal had predicted. His green eyes shined eerily, making Manny stiffen. "You look like you've lost a couple of pounds. You look good." He stepped in and admired the store. It had been a while.

The boutique was a nice box, with its dark hardwood floor, creamy walls, and exposed wooden beams in the ceiling. Manny had decorated it such that it felt like a living room with a counter in the corner, where he often stood. Firearms and crossbows hung on the walls and in special glass cabinets. Sometimes clients would sit and read a book while they waited, enjoying the fire and a glass of wine.

"Um," said Manny, rubbing his fat-fingered hands together. "I'm planning to see my feet by next Solstice." He straightened up, trying to appear confident. He hadn't wanted to believe what Pascal had said about LeLoup, but he could already see it. The man before him moved differently, and though his voice was the same, there was a sting to it that was new.

LeLoup walked up to the counter and leaned on it, piercing Manny with his green eyes. "You didn't believe those rumors about me going into hiding or dying, did you?" He started to laugh. "I mean, dying at the hands of a yellow-hooded child, really?" He laughed harder.

Manny chuckled against his will. He hadn't felt intimidated like this since he was in elementary school. His size and a false-gruff personality had been his defense ever since. "No," he replied, nervously laughing.

LeLoup wiped a tear as he calmed down. "Good, I'm glad. I was worried that you'd have sold my *beauty*," he said, gravely serious.

Manny breathed a sigh of relief. "I have it right here,"

he said, reaching under the counter and putting out a two-foot-long, elegant wooden box on it.

LeLoup stared at the box, then gave Manny a questioning gaze. "How did you know I was coming?"

After a moment of internal debate, Manny decided to come clean. "Pascal let me know. He said you'd be dropping by."

"Oh," said LeLoup. "I didn't know the two of you were friends." He was intrigued that there was a relationship he was unaware of.

"We're not really friends," replied Manny, wiping his forehead with a kerchief from under the counter.

LeLoup moved his gaze back to the box and started tapping on it in thought. He stopped and asked, "Who else do you think he ran around and told?"

Manny shifted his stance uncomfortably. "Um... no one. He said he had a lot of work to do for you," he replied, shaking his head.

LeLoup frowned as he considered the picture Manny was painting. "He does have a lot of work to do for me," he said, tapping the box and staring at the front door. "Yet, his non-friendship with you was so important to him that he... ran, I presume... all the way here to tell you I was coming." His face twitched. "It must have been a funny sight, him running."

"He was all sweaty and everything," said Manny, trying to laugh, but LeLoup's gaze squashed the humor.

"So he told no one else then, Manny? Okay. I believe you. He knows that I'm not one to let people break promises, and he promised to have my work done. But how about you, Manny? Who did you tell? Because I don't like people spoiling my surprises."

Manny stared at him silently, unsure how to answer.

"Mind if I have a look at my pistol?" asked LeLoup, ignoring Manny's blank look. He carefully opened the hinged lid and peered inside.

"I call it the Liar," said Manny, relieved to talk about something he was comfortable with. "I had to modify the three-barrel design from the prototype, and I was able to improve the weight. Oh, and I improved the barrel rotation speed as well. They rotate in a fraction of a second now.

"This little lever here is why I call it the Liar. You see, every barrel is double-loaded, and so after you've shot your sixth bullet, you flip that switch, and it'll load one more bullet."

LeLoup picked up the long, three-barreled pistol. Its handle was a thick, beautiful, stained wood. He ran his hand along the smooth casing that hid the geared mechanism. "So when I've fired my six," said LeLoup, standing back and pointing the weapon at Manny.

Manny dug his fingers into the counter for all he was worth so he didn't flinch. He kept reminding himself that he knew the gun was empty. He'd made sure of that three times after Pascal had left, yet he feared that somehow the maniacal look in LeLoup's eyes could change reality.

"I'll then pull the trigger, an empty barrel will rotate up, and it'll be clear I'm out of bullets." LeLoup pulled the trigger at Manny repeatedly. "All the fun is gone."

Manny's left arm went numb. Despite a growing pain in his chest, he stayed silent, his fingernails scarring the counter.

LeLoup straightened up and put the pistol against his shoulder. "Then when that Yellow Hood thinks me harmless, I'll flip this switch." LeLoup slapped the switch. It got stuck halfway.

Manny was horrified. "It probably needs some extra oil, that's all."

LeLoup slapped it again, frowning at Manny. "It's fine." He pointed the pistol at Manny's head and pulled the trigger again. "Liar. I like it. Very... me."

Manny grimaced, ignoring the wash of pain in his chest.

"The dark mahogany and gold accents, and the detail work... well done," said LeLoup, putting the gun back in its case.

"Thank you," said Manny, sweating profusely.

LeLoup examined Manny for a moment before rifling through his wallet and putting a note on the counter. "I know you won't be telling anyone I was here, right? Of course not. Goodbye, Manny."

As the door closed, Manny fell to one knee, and then to the floor, clutching his chest.

CHAPTER SIXTEEN

ABOMINATORS AND FRIENDS

Christina slid off her King's-Horse, handing the reins to Mounira. She double-checked the deserted back road for prying eyes, then led the team deep into the woods.

The few people they'd passed hadn't had enough time to determine what it was about the horses that didn't seem quite right as they'd ridden past.

"This is a good spot. We'll cover them up and leave them here. Dismount and I'll bring them side by side," said Christina.

Mounira tumbled backward off the side of the horse, barely making a successful landing. "*La la* - right, Tee?" she said, glancing over at her big sister figure.

Tee dismounted and gave Mounira a nod. "Yeah, that was a good one," she said flatly, pulling her hood over her head.

Elly slid off and scowled at Mounira. "No. You don't get to use *La la*," she said, then turned to Tee. "If you're not going to use it anymore, then, like so many things, it's just gone. Just… gone."

Mounira shrugged. There was something going on that she wasn't following, nor cared to.

Christina pulled the camouflage blankets out of one of the saddlebags of each horse and covered them. She then stepped back several yards and examined them. "Yeah, they look okay there. Someone passing quickly by should miss them, and no one should be this close in the first place."

"How long did you have them at the bottom of the mountain?" asked Mounira.

Christina smiled at the embodiment of never-ending questions. "Months."

Franklin wondered what other inventions Christina had access to, and what other secrets of the world had been kept from him and his father.

"Wow, I guess that blanket works really well," replied Mounira, studying it with newfound interest.

"It does," replied Christina. She remembered her father telling her when she was six that if she'd stop asking questions for ten minutes, he'd give her a diamond. He'd never had to pay up.

"Okay, make sure we've got everything. Let's go, everyone. We've got a couple of miles to walk," said Christina.

After a minute of walking, Mounira asked, "Why can't we just put the King's-Horses in a stable? You know, like real horses? Why do we have to hide them?"

"We need to keep going," answered Christina, hiking on. She shifted her backpack, trying to find a more comfortable position for it.

Tee moved closer to Mounira as they walked. "We can't just bring them into town. Someone would notice them and we'd have a lot of trouble."

"Are they illegal?" asked Mounira, worried.

"No, but we are," said Tee, grudgingly sharing some of what she'd learned recently. "They have a special word for inventors, scientists, and engineers who don't work under a set of strict rules—"

"Abominators," said Franklin. "That's what your uncivilized part of the world calls people like us. We might just find ourselves getting our heads cut off, depending on what this kingdom's High Conventioneer recommends." Franklin ran his finger across his throat.

Mounira gestured wildly with her one arm. "For what? Horses?"

Tee put her hands on Mounira's shoulders and said in a very calm tone, "Remember the story Christina told us about how these were made? There was this king who decided he didn't want any people around who were smarter than him, or who made him look bad. Freland is better than most places, from what I hear, but it's still dangerous. Long ago, that thinking spread like fire through the kingdoms, and correcting it is a very slow process."

Elly said, panic leaching into her voice, "Wait, are you saying they still kill inventors? I'm not one though, right? I don't invent things." For the first time, Elly deeply regretted having left home.

Tee shot Elly a harsh glance. "You helped make that first sail-cart with me, didn't you? That's an engineer thing you did," said Tee. "Don't go pretending you're somehow not a part of this."

Elly started to get riled up.

Christina yelled over her shoulder. "It doesn't matter. If you look a certain way, build something that makes someone else jealous, speak a certain way, or—in some places—are just born a smart woman, they will label you an Abominator. If you're lucky, they'll let you become a Conventioneer.

"All of us are in danger no matter where we go, except for maybe the Republic of Teuton."

"Why are they called Conventioneers?" asked Mounira.

Tee avoided Elly's gaze as she answered, "Because they abide by the rules—conventions—set by the monarchy or whatever government. Nothing too imaginative, too weird, or potentially threatening."

Franklin piped up proudly. "Things are better in Inglea, though. We did away with the Order of the Conventioneers a few years ago and got those Abominator laws almost completely off the books. Now we have the Royal Society for Collective Progress. My father's even a member. It answers to Parliament and if you're doing anything big, you just need to go present to a committee. I'm not allowed to join until I'm sixteen, but I've already been pre-approved."

"Was the steam engine allowed? I can't see how there could be all this secrecy about it, if it was," said Elly, poking at Franklin's smugness.

Christina caught Franklin's scared expression, and couldn't help but smile. "We need to be careful. That's why we're not going directly into Palais."

Elly and Mounira were visibly disappointed.

Franklin glared at Christina. "What?" he said, feeling jilted. "Let me go at least. I'm older than the rest of them, and I survived on my own for months."

Christina considered Franklin's request. "The inn's about a couple miles southeast of here." She snapped her fingers. "Actually, Tee and Elly, put your yellow hoods into Tee's backpack. Mounira, give me yours. They're fine when we're walking through the forest, but not when we're close to town like this. I don't want anyone remembering us easily."

Franklin rolled his eyes. "Don't you think they'll notice an annoying, one-armed Southerner?"

Mounira kicked him in the shin.

"FOR THE LOVE OF—" yelled Franklin, hopping around. "How do you keep managing to do that?"

"I don't know what you're talking about," said

Mounira, walking away with a smile plastered on her face.

Franklin was fuming. "I didn't mean it that way. I meant simply—"

"Enough," said Christina, cutting him off. "After we're settled at the inn, you can go into town if you want, Franklin. But if you run into trouble, you're on your own."

Glaring at all of them, he curled his lip and nodded to himself. Clearly, his comments weren't welcome. "Thank you," he replied calmly, putting his leg down. He'd won a small victory, and hoped to turn it into a bigger one.

CHAPTER SEVENTEEN

TRUST ME

Bakon hardly noticed the hunger building up in him. The gravity of what he'd learned and the rashness of his actions still weighed on him, clouding everything.

One simple piece of paper in the Ginger Lady's house had made him betray so many people. He'd abandoned his father figure, Nikolas Klaus, by not rejoining Tee to help find him. He'd deceived his brothers, Richy, and the love of his life, Egelina-Marie, by running off without them. The ever lingering doubt that he wasn't good enough for Eg was having a field day. Why couldn't he just ignore that maybe once he'd had the name Beldon Pieman?

Bakon examined his fists, which he'd nearly broken punching a tree the night before. He'd swung at everything he could, except the horse, fighting through all of his mixed emotions until he'd finally collapsed on the ground at the side of the road and fallen asleep.

He'd decided to head for Relna, figuring if he'd never heard of the Piemans before, then they were likely not Frelish. His plan was simple: get there and keep asking about the Piemans until someone made him stop, one way or the other.

A woman's scream slapped him back to attention. Looking up ahead, he saw a riderless horse trotting up towards him around a bend in the forest road.

Bakon nudged his horse to speed up. "I hope that lady has some people I can mess with. I need a distraction."

As he came around the bend, he saw a bald man unconscious on the ground, and three thugs; one of whom was chasing a dark-haired woman around a toppled fruit cart.

"Hey, guys," yelled Bakon.

The Chaser froze and stared at Bakon. He was a wiry man, and Bakon knew the type well. Likely he was the kick-puppy of the Ringleader, and probably the one who did most of the work. He had noticeably bad teeth and bags under his eyes. His clothes were haphazard, not unlike Bakon's had been until very recently.

"Hey, yourself," snapped the Ringleader, taking a step forward. He looked scruffy and like he'd slept in his unwashed clothes for weeks. His long beard and wrinkled, boyish face made him look more comical than threatening.

Bakon scrutinized the third man, who reminded him of his brother, Bore. He was at least six-foot-six, with badly cut hair and stubble. He frowned at Bakon and kept glancing at the other two for direction.

"This should be fun," said Bakon to himself, smiling. Dismounting, he chewed his lip, trying to figure how he was going to play this out. Recently, Captain Archambault had been sharing some new ways he could deal with things if he found himself alone; ways that, honestly, he'd never have considered as they didn't involve punching someone.

Bakon walked over to the side of the road and picked up a good and sturdy stick. He smiled at the trio of thugs. He noticed they were all wet, but the ground and stick were dry. He looked up at the sky and saw dark clouds heading away from them.

"What are you doing?" asked the Chaser.

"I needed a stick," said Bakon as if there was nothing going on. "I found one. Do you need one?" he asked, offering his. "There are more."

"Um, no," said the Chaser, bewildered.

Bakon shrugged. "Suit yourself." He started walking towards the woman and the fruit cart.

"You don't want to do that, mate. You just want to leave," said the Ringleader, his hand on a flintlock pistol in his pants.

"Is that so?" said Bakon, acting a touch surprised. "I'm really hungry, and there's fruit right there. Now, I was planning on paying for it, but I don't have any coins." He patted himself down. "Hey, do you accept sticks as currency? It's a really good one." He waved his stick about for all to see.

The Chaser shifted his gaze between his buddies and then to the woman, who shrugged at him, having no idea what was really going on. "We're... ah, stealing this stuff," he said, pointing to the cart. "So we're not interested in selling nothing."

Bakon smiled to himself as he thought of what Isabella Klaus would have said if he'd used a double negative like that.

The Ringleader pulled out his pistol.

Bakon recognized the make. He had one at home.

"Get out of here," said the Ringleader. "This is none of your business. We're doing some stealing, and you don't need to be part of this. Just... just go away."

Bakon nodded in understanding, rubbing his chin. He rolled his shoulders and thought. He imagined Gabriel describing the situation, and asking him questions as to what he should do next. As much as part of him was itching for an out-and-out brawl, he was curious to see if leveraging his charisma could really work.

"Careful there, buddy," he said seriously. "I'm armed with a stick." The Chaser started to laugh, but Bakon's expression made him stop and look at the Ringleader, even more confused than before. Bakon noticed that the big guy was reacting about five seconds after everyone else. "This *is* my business. See, that lady's my sister." Bakon took a few slow steps towards the Ringleader.

"No, she's not," said the head thug. "Nice try."

"You're right, she's not," replied Bakon, smiling

sheepishly and taking two more steps. "She's my wife."

"She's not your wife," said the hyena-like Chaser.

Bakon winked at him. "Got me again." He took another step towards the Ringleader.

The Ringleader shook his old firearm at Bakon. "Just go away!"

"Hey," said Bakon calmly. "Tell you what. How about I drop this stick, and you point the gun at the ground?"

The Chaser caught wind of something and yelled, "Shoot him. I don't like him."

"He can't. It's wet," said Bakon, pointing at the flintlock pistol. "I can fix it though, for some fruit."

"What?" said the Ringleader. "It's not wet."

Bakon frowned at him. "Look, I'm hungry. I don't care what else you're doing, just give me some food, and I'm on my way. Everybody wins—"

"I don't," grumbled the woman.

"Fair point, but close enough," said Bakon. He pointed at the pistol again, now only three feet away. "See the shine on the top there? That means the chamber's wet. Even if it does fire, it'll blow up in your face."

The Ringleader stared at the firearm for a moment. "It's fine," he insisted.

Bakon shook his head, his expression annoyed. "Hey, guy, you're embarrassing yourself. I know you're a professional highwayman, and I'm just a country ruffian, but let's be honest with each other. That pistol's useless if you don't let me fix it."

The Ringleader frowned at his pistol. There was something about the way Bakon was talking that made the Ringleader feel that he genuinely had the thug's best interest at heart.

"I'll prove it to you," said Bakon. "Lady, come here." He stepped forward and snatched the pistol right out of the Ringleader's hands and handed it to the lady.

Everyone stared at Bakon in disbelief.

"Did he just do that?" asked the Chaser.

"Trust me," said Bakon, waving for them to calm down. He didn't know if they had another weapon, but he was certain that the pistol had at most one shot.

The woman stared at Bakon, confused. "Help me out, lady. Now, please try and shoot him."

"Um, where?" said the woman, waving the pistol around.

Bakon glanced at the man. "The foot's good."

"Are you sure about this?" asked the Ringleader.

"Positive," said Bakon, giving him an okay gesture. "Mademoiselle."

The gun fired. The Chaser, Ringleader, and woman all screamed.

"My foot!" yelled the Ringleader. "You flipping pargo! I told you it worked fine!"

Bakon snatched the pistol from the woman's hand, opened it up, took out the spent bullet, and closed it back up just in time to point it squarely at the face of the third big man, who was now just inches away.

The big man and Bakon stood there, gesturing at each other for a minute, until finally the big man nodded and went to collect his wounded friend.

"What were you doing?" asked the woman.

"He's deaf. My brother Bore has a friend just like him. The guy lives seconds behind everyone else. Bore taught me some of the simple gestures. Honestly, I'm surprised I remembered them - haven't used them in a while." Bakon paused, briefly wondering about how his brothers were doing. "These guys will be leaving now. The big guy knows I'll shoot them if they don't," whispered Bakon, keeping his pistol pointed at the trio of thugs.

"I can't believe you were able to reload it that quickly," said the woman, watching in disbelief as the men left.

A sheepish smiled appeared on Bakon's face. "Well, to be perfectly honest," he whispered, "I didn't. I don't have any bullets on me."

"So it's not loaded?" asked the woman.

"No."

She covered her eyes. "I can't believe I was just saved by an idiot."

"Some people are never happy," said Bakon, putting his gun arm down as the thugs started off. He peeked over his shoulder at the bald man, who was still unconscious on the ground. "He with you?"

The woman laughed. "Dad's fine. He fainted. Too much excitement and it's like someone doused his lamp —out he goes. Loud noises do it to him, too. He'll be up soon."

"If you don't mind sharing some of your fruit, we can hook your hand-cart up to my horse."

The woman nodded. "Sounds fair."

After attaching his horse and making sure that the old man was steady enough to walk, Bakon walked over to the fruit. Suddenly, the woman screamed and the old man passed out again.

Bakon rolled his eyes. "What now?" he asked, trying to find the imminent danger.

The woman pointed at an arm that was sticking straight up into the air from the side of the road some fifty yards away.

"I think it's a zombie," whispered the woman, crouching down as if the ground would somehow give her protection.

Bakon walked over to it, putting the spent pistol in his pants. "Can't you see that the fingers are moving? Why does everyone want to believe in magic?" he muttered to himself.

Arriving at the arm, Bakon turned back to the woman. "Hey, lady?" he asked. "Did you lose another guy? There's one here attached to the arm."

"That one's not mine," she replied.

"Huh," said Bakon, studying the rousing man. "Are you okay?" He helped the shaggy man carefully to his feet.

The man had a strange look in his eyes. "I was trying to help... someone. I heard a scream," he said, gazing about, confused. "How did I get here?"

"Did you happen to lose a horse?" asked Bakon. "One trotted past me earlier."

The man scratched his beard. "I don't think so. I seem to remember talking to my brother, though." He turned about, taking in where he was. "I'm guessing it was a hallucination."

Bakon sighed and shook his head. He'd run into this type before as well.

As they climbed out of the ditch and onto the road, Bakon got a good look at the man. He had a scruffy beard, sunken brown eyes, and clearly hadn't eaten well in a long time. He was Bakon's height, and dressed in tatters. Oddly, there was something familiar about him.

"What's your name?" asked Bakon as they walked towards the horse and cart.

"My name"—the man rubbed his head—"is Abeland." He stopped and studied Bakon's face. "You're... wait... you?... you're not, are you?"

"Pardon?" asked Bakon.

Abeland rubbed his head again and the strange look

drifted from behind his eyes. "Sorry. I was given some bad medicine and it's still messing with my mind. I thought you were my brother for a moment."

"Oh," replied Bakon. "Do you know where you are?"

Abeland studied the forest road. "I came from that direction. I was trying to go home," he said, finally orienting himself. "Do you know where this road leads?"

The woman, who had been slowly approaching, interjected, "To Evana, and then on to Relna."

"Relna? So I'm in Belnia... they moved me that far?" muttered Abeland to himself. He scanned the trees and landscape again to confirm. "Belnia..." He squinted at Bakon, thinking. "I need to get to Relna. I have a house outside of there. If you'll take me, I'll pay you handsomely for your help."

At first pass, the man appeared to be a crazed beggar, but there was something about his clear, crisp speech and the way he was standing that told Bakon he was far more than he seemed.

"Okay. My name is Bakon."

Abeland paused for a second. "Bakon?" There was something disturbingly familiar about that name.

CHAPTER EIGHTEEN
WHAT A SHARP
MIND YOU HAVE

LeLoup was enjoying his day in the Frelish capital city. He'd picked up a custom leather holster for the Liar, allowing it to rest comfortably on his right thigh. He'd also managed to squeeze a finished long coat and pants out of Pascal early.

He paused and appreciated his own reflection in a shop's window. "I really am ruggedly handsome, aren't I?" he smiled.

Seeing a crowd, LeLoup made his way over to find a street gambler at the heart of it. He had a makeshift table made with some crates and a piece of wood. On top of it were nine cards in a square, face down.

Small piles of notes and coins were on the table, and everyone was eager for the street gambler to flip two cards. After the first card, the crowd took an anxious breath, and with the second came the grand disappointment to most and celebration by a few. The street gambler smiled as he took his winnings and handed out what he owed.

LeLoup leaned against a brick wall, listening to the smooth pitch of the street gambler. It sounded so innocent, so inviting, so alluring, that people couldn't resist putting their money on the table and trying their hands at the game.

A blond-haired teenage boy came and stood beside LeLoup, watching the street gambler do his magic. "He's a good one," said the boy. "He isn't cheating. Most of them cheat, but this one is just very good at what he does. I've been watching him for a while."

LeLoup turned his gaze to the boy for a moment, before returning it to the crowd. "Now how would a boy such as yourself know anything about a game like that, unless you're a street gambler yourself?"

The boy pushed off of the wall and then rocked back. "I lost a bunch of money to one months ago. Even when I won, I lost. It didn't matter that I was smarter than everyone in that stupid town."

LeLoup nodded knowingly. "Some larger men helped you with the burden of your winnings, I take it?"

The boy nodded, scowling.

As the crowd erupted with yells and cheers, the boy nodded to himself.

"Predicted that one?" asked LeLoup.

The boy confirmed it with a quick glance.

LeLoup stroked the underpart of his chin. There was

something about this boy. He was confident, and clearly following every detail of what was going on. "Isn't it always the way? When the genius creates something, thuggery and ignorance try to bring it down?"

The boy turned to LeLoup, annoyed. "It shouldn't be that way. And even among the geniuses, there are liars and scoundrels."

"True," said LeLoup, scrutinizing the boy a bit more. His eyes were sharp, the wheels clearly turning inside.

LeLoup observed the crowd. No one seemed to be paying any attention to the boy. "Where are your parents?" he asked casually.

The boy shook his head. "I'm here with friends. We're traveling to Costello. They're back at the inn, though. I'm here alone."

Smiling to himself, LeLoup replied, "Costello is very nice this time of year."

Sounds of anticipation emanated from the crowd.

"Before he flips it over," said LeLoup, nudging the boy.

"Bottom left card and the middle top card," said the boy.

They watched as the street gambler flipped them over and held them high for everyone to see. The crowd once again exclaimed, mostly in disappointment, but with a few cheers.

LeLoup nodded. "Very well done."

The boy shrugged. "It's simple, really."

"There are many things in life that look simple," said LeLoup. "Why are you going to Costello?"

The boy moved his head away from LeLoup.

"Sorry. I'm being too nosey," said LeLoup apologetically.

"Speaking of Costello, I've met the Abbott once. Painful fellow, made me want to give him what for. Thick like a brick," said the boy, making them both chuckle.

LeLoup stared at the boy. "You know, it's one thing to see what should be done from the sidelines, but can you see things in the heat of the moment?"

The boy rolled his eyes, not dignifying LeLoup's question with an answer.

"I have some powerful friends—friends who would appreciate someone with your insight and abilities," said LeLoup, stroking the boy's ego. He could see the boy straighten up with a touch of pride. "But first, a test."

"Name it," said the boy.

"Let's see if we can win three times in a row." He walked over to the gambler and glanced back at the boy by the wall. "Are you going to change your life, or are you going to stand there in the shadows?" LeLoup grinned from ear to ear when he saw the spark in the boy's eyes as he approached.

"We're in," said LeLoup to the street gambler.

"Place your bet," said the street gambler, offering a

charming smile.

LeLoup reached into his wallet and took out a thousand coin note. His piercing green eyes caught the nervous movements of the gambler's gaze and the bead of sweat starting to form on his temples. "Is this too rich for you?" LeLoup asked coyly. The gambler followed LeLoup's glance to the Liar strapped to his thigh. "I'd hate to have to collect in other ways."

The street gambler smiled at the intimidating pistol, and then at LeLoup, and said, "We're good."

The crowd was gossiping about the amount and what would happen.

"Wonderful," LeLoup said to the street gambler. "Let's see if my young colleague is as brilliant as I suspect he might be."

A minute later, the crowd erupted, and the boy and LeLoup exchanged nods at having won. LeLoup glared at the street gambler and asked him, "You're good for the money, aren't you?"

The man sweated a little and glanced at the crowd. "Everything's good. We're all good here, sir. Everyone, place your bets."

"No, not everyone, just me," said LeLoup.

The street gambler smiled at him nervously. He knew if he backed out now, he'd never be able to work this part of town again. "Okay."

When the crowd erupted once more, both LeLoup

and the boy were excited and pressed their thumbs together in triumph. Members of the crowd immediately copied them.

"My young friend here has a talent, ladies and gentlemen!" yelled LeLoup, raising the noise level.

"You just wiped out a year of earnings, kid," whispered the street gambler angrily.

The boy gave him his own version of LeLoup's predator grin. "That's a shame. I thought we'd taken everything. Let's see if I can make this a bad decade for you, shall we?"

LeLoup gave the boy a slap on the back and grabbed him by the shoulder, pulling him in. "Win this one, boy, and the world is yours."

The boy nodded excitedly.

"What's your name?" asked LeLoup, releasing him.

"Franklin. Franklin Watt."

LeLoup couldn't believe the day he was having.

CHAPTER NINETEEN

A Neu Way

Marcus banged on the ceiling for the driver to stop the carriage. Moments later, the door opened.

"Everything okay, sir?" asked the new captain.

Climbing out, Marcus said, "We're going for a walk, no entourage."

"Sir, we—"

Marcus cut his new captain off. "You weren't going to say that you have orders from someone, were you? I'd hate to have to replace my captain twice in two days."

Nervously, the captain shook his head. "I was… I just… we are in the middle of nowhere."

"Actually," said Marcus, scanning the winding road carved through yet another forest, "we are very much somewhere. Remain here."

Nikolas was a bit surprised when the door opened; he'd been lost in a book. Marcus had been in the front office section of the carriage working since the early morning, leaving Nikolas in the back with books, paper, ink, and his thoughts.

Stepping out and having a good stretch, Nikolas took in the scenery. The sky was a deep blue, with a handful of gray clouds. The trees and other foliage gave Nikolas a good idea of where they were, but not why they'd stopped. He was about to ask Marcus about where they were headed when, for the first time, he saw the carriage in full daylight. It was quite something to behold.

The extended carriage had four sets of twin wheels, with a wheel-within-a-wheel design, connected with tightly coiled springs. The exterior was painted fairly simply, in black and gray. At the front was a bench seat for the driver with a flip-up armored panel for cover. Four crouched soldiers were stationed on top with rifles.

Nikolas bent down and studied the suspension and wheel system in detail. He muttered to himself as he pieced together how it worked and why certain engineering decisions had likely been made.

"Do you approve?" asked Marcus, curious, as Nikolas got himself fully under the carriage to scrutinize it up close.

Nikolas nodded. "It's a very practical design. The horses aren't the sole source of propulsion, though, yes? I noticed—"

Marcus laughed. "How long did it take you to realize that after you were under there—a minute?"

Nikolas pensively touched his fingers to his thumb, counting. "Approximately."

"It took Simon nearly twenty minutes," he replied. "I

wouldn't give him any of the details, however."

Nikolas took Marcus' hand and got back to his feet. "It's nothing obvious. You shouldn't worry," said Nikolas, brushing himself off.

"Indeed," said Marcus, smirking.

Nikolas added, "I was curious about it, as I had noticed a particular sound when we were traveling. There's a... a type of harmonic rubbing, metallic sounding. It occurred every two to four seconds when we were on an incline. I couldn't place it at first, but now it's clear to me.

"I realized that it must be related to this carriage being heavily armored, yes? So I calculated the weight it would have to be, and determined that it couldn't be pulled by four horses alone. Also, I assume it's meant to withstand a cannon blast from one hundred yards, yes?"

Marcus chuckled. "It's supposed to be eighty. I'll have to make a point of checking; I wouldn't want to make a horrible mistake. I've missed you, old friend." He gave Nikolas a friendly slap on the back. "So, tell me while we walk, what's the auxiliary propulsion system?"

Nikolas rubbed his forehead. "I assume that you have some form of pop-up armaments, yes?"

Marcus nodded, chuckling some more.

Taking off his spectacles and cleaning them on his shirt, Nikolas' eyes danced about as he studied the machine he'd constructed in his mind. "You are still after the steam engine, so that must be accounted for."

Marcus moved his head from side to side, not wanting to answer, but rather wanting only to acknowledge that it was an adept question.

"So given Simon's skills, and assuming no external factors, I'd say you used your expertise in alchemical materials to... no," said Nikolas, cutting himself off, "that would have been... too volatile. No, you'd need something more simple." He closed his eyes and scrutinized every detail of the carriage he'd imagined.

"When we went up that hill an hour ago," he said, putting a hand over his eyes, "the transition to the incline was smooth." Nikolas stood a few steps, eyes covered. "It couldn't be chemical, as there was no kick. It must be... springs. You've figured out an effective way of storing the kinetic energy when going downwards and using it when going uphill. The alchemical part is for something else." Nikolas took his hand away and squinted for a moment. "Did Laurent DeLau design this?"

Marcus stopped, flat-footed. He hadn't expected Nikolas to be able to make such a series of leaps. He straightened up and thought for a moment. He'd only ever underestimated Nikolas a handful of times.

He put his arm around Nikolas to get them moving again. "Just a little further. There's something I want to show you. And to answer your question: yes, Laurent was working for me. He passed away about two years ago. Lived like a king, and passed away one day rather suddenly."

A few minutes later, they arrived at an unassuming, small log cabin. It was only six-by-eight feet wide.

"Do you remember when we discussed what it would take to change the world?" asked Marcus, standing in front of the simple wooden front door.

Nikolas noticed that two trenches had been dug through the forest to the cabin from opposite directions.

Marcus cleared his throat, getting Nikolas' attention and a smile.

"We talked about a lot of things years ago," said Nikolas. "But do I remember that one? Yes."

Marcus nodded. "That discussion in particular provided me some much-needed clarity. It gave me a roadmap for what I needed to do, and what I soon will have accomplished.

"I believe I've solved all of the issues. Granted I've made enemies along the way, some of them more dangerous than others, but I'm very close to completing my plans. The solution to the biggest of the problems we imagined is right behind this door."

———

"You're still thinking about her," said thirty-three-year-old Marcus, smiling. It was rare that he got to tease Nikolas about something that had any effect on the young man. "I can see it in your eyes. You're completely distracted by her."

Eighteen-year-old Nikolas squirmed in his chair and

furrowed his brow. He pulled on his fledgling brown beard. "You don't know what you're talking about. Who is this 'her'?" he said, trying to wave off Marcus.

Marcus laughed and slammed the table. "I must get my wife in here to witness this. Nikolas Klaus, right hand of the High Conventioneer, is distracted by a woman! Richelle! Are you there? Richelle!"

Nikolas scanned about nervously.

"She's not home," said Marcus, laughing.

Nikolas tried glaring at Marcus, but the sheer joy in the man's face was too much for him to overcome. He got up and paced around the room a bit. "Do you think—" and then he stopped.

"What?" asked Marcus. "If she was interested in you? I don't know. She did ask you your name six times, as you stood there looking absolutely stunned at the beautiful, intelligent woman talking to you."

"I was... *thinking*... about big things! Important things," retorted Nikolas, gesturing at the ceiling. "Anyway, women are a mystery to me that no wisdom or advice seems to illuminate."

"Here's some that will. When spoken to, try to respond, preferably in a manner that somewhat resembles normal speech," said Marcus, chuckling.

"I was thinking! She confused me. This woman interfered with my thoughts, *that's* all. I always notice women as people, as entities that consume physical space. As entities with whom I can have intellectual conversations on any range of matters, yes? But this Isabella... she is different, she is... present."

Marcus held his sides as he laughed. "Try not to remark on that quality of hers. She may not take it as the compliment it is meant to be!"

Nikolas stared at the sheets of parchment covering the walls of Marcus' study, in hopes of buying himself some time to find a way out of Marcus' social trap.

They'd been writing ideas on the sheets all day, brainstorming about anything and everything, an exercise they'd started to do more and more often. Everything was written in the age-old secret scripting language of Crayo. What appeared so innocent on one level would surely have had him and Marcus arrested, if not beheaded, if anyone knew. Nikolas found the exercise very freeing.

"So what are these grand thoughts you were trying to wrestle with?" asked Marcus, leaning back in his chair, arms folded.

Nikolas stared at the floor to focus. "I was thinking about... what have been the core challenges and failings of every governing body, from kingdom to empire to nation state. More importantly, I was asking myself: can they be resolved? Is it a question of insight, innovation, or imagination?"

"Really?" asked Marcus sarcastically.

"Yes," said Nikolas, nodding.

"Indulge me," said Marcus, waving for Nikolas to

carry on. "Prove to me that you were not lost in the eyes of one Isabella von Delona."

Nikolas paced around the stone floor, looking at the bookcases and gas lamps hanging in the corners. "I'm ignoring problems such as agricultural yields, taxation, and such," he said, stalling.

Marcus shrugged. "I'm fine with that. They're solvable."

Nikolas continued, "Transportation is the first problem. One needs a superior transportation system to allow for a small military to cover a large area. Large armies have a high cost and are difficult to move, and therefore easy to outmaneuver. A superior transportation system needs to be developed that can make such a displacement quickly and effectively. A smaller military would have the peripheral benefits of less morale management and fewer recruitment issues."

"What about simply having horses for everyone?" asked Marcus, throwing in a question he already knew the answer to.

Nikolas scoffed. He couldn't believe what he was hearing. Marcus might as well have proposed riding pigeons. "Horses are too few. Never mind that it's too expensive to train them as well as the soldiers, plus there's feeding and caring for them. Also, there is—"

"Yes, yes, moving on," said Marcus, gnawing on the end of a wooden spoon. He took his feet off the table that divided the study in half and leaned forward. "Okay,

Conventioneer Klaus, I'm almost believing that you weren't thinking about... what's her name?"

"Isabella," said Nikolas, joy springing to his face.

Marcus smiled and shook his head. He loved Nikolas dearly, and hadn't imagined he'd ever see him like this. "What else?"

Nikolas was ready for him. "Then there's the art and science of communication. Every regime ultimately has failed because it doesn't have the ability to react quickly enough to crisis, particularly at its frontiers. Secrecy, security, speed, and efficiency are all vital. This is the greatest problem, yes?"

Marcus was impressed.

"So you believe me that I wasn't thinking about this... this woman?" said Nikolas, folding his arms and raising his chin.

Marcus stood up. "Oh, no, not in the slightest. You were thinking of Isabella, you can't fool me for an instant. However, you thought better on your feet than you ever have. That tells me you were seriously thinking about her. I promise I won't mention anything to Richelle, yet.

"But this line of thinking, it's very interesting. I think we should spend the rest of the day on this."

───────────

Marcus and Nikolas entered the log cabin. It was windowless and barren, save for a table with a large box on it, and two ceiling-hung oil lamps.

As Marcus lit the lamps, two shiny metal tubes

revealed themselves. They came out of the floor and through the bottom of the table. Most of the table was taken up by a secured wooden box.

"Any ideas yet?" asked Marcus, as he slid the puzzle locks on the box open and removed it. Underneath were the connected ends of the two tubes, and a lever.

Nikolas studied it, shaking his head.

"This is the key," said Marcus, opening a drawer and removing a small cylindrical canister from it. "I place whatever message I want into this, pull the lever to allow it to be inserted into the tube, then seal it back up and it speeds away to its destination. That destination could be one of several locations throughout the kingdoms. Which one is controlled by these rings on the side of the canister. Each location has a particular setting. I can have up to two hundred and forty-eight locations."

Marcus took out paper and ink from the drawer and wrote a note, and then put the paper in the tube. As he pulled the lever, there was a sudden 'thum' sound.

Nikolas gave Marcus a narrow-eyed gaze. "Tulu?"

Marcus was astonished. "Pardon?"

Nikolas tapped his chin in thought. "Tulu Neuma. You introduced me to him once, yes? Long ago. We were working with Christophe on the second set of King's-Horses and planning our escape. He was a Conventioneer... from the Angel Fingers islands? Short, bald man, with dark skin, yes? The mechanics of wind and air were something he understood like no one I'd ever met."

Marcus bowed his head slightly. "You have a memory like no one I've ever met. You really remember a five-minute long conversation in some hallway, decades ago?"

Nikolas stared at Marcus, confused, not sure what deception would have gained the other man. "You remember it."

"Yes, well, for a different reason. I took Neuma under my wing after my… failed escape. When I became regent, I gave him ten years to show me this idea of his could work. He called it the Tube von Neuma."

Nikolas smiled, remembering the rules for Conventioneers. Their inventions were required to be named with a simple noun, followed by their name, under the belief that over time, the name would be forgotten.

"I assume you changed that to the Neumatic Tube, yes?" said Nikolas, the rebel in him enjoying the moment.

"Of course," replied Marcus, smiling. "He was able to prove it in nine years, on a small scale. We were able to send messages from one end of a castle to another. Bit by bit, we took steps that led here."

"It must have cost—"

"A king's ransom?" interrupted Marcus. "And then some. I'm fortunate to have very deep pockets available to me. Anyway, in about thirty minutes we should have our response."

Nikolas examined the simple tube and wondered, "Where could the message go in thirty minutes?"

"I sent it to my home just outside the capital city of Teutork," said Marcus, with a catbird smile. "The outer ring determines its destination. There's a ring inside the tube here that would stop any messages intended for here from going past."

Nikolas calculated the distance, the speed the message would need to go, the amount of time for someone to hear and react to a bell or something indicating there was a message, the amount of time to respond, and then for the response to be received. "That's… incredible."

Marcus had a huge grin. "I haven't heard you give that level of commendation for an invention… ever. Mind you, Isabella was able to get those out of you every time she showed up. That is, provided she wasn't covered from head to toe in mud."

Nikolas let out his first genuine laugh since Solstice. "I'd forgotten about that time. Yes, the day of the heavy rains and that wagon that raced outside of your home."

Marcus grabbed the table as they laughed. "And Richelle tried to help her but then she tripped… knocking over the crates of flower petals."

"Oh! The flower petals!" Nikolas bent over, laughing hard. "They stuck to her. From head to toe, yes?"

"She… she looked like a chicken!" said Marcus, doubling over.

Nikolas roared with laughter, falling on his butt. "Oh, but she was a most beautiful and graceful chicken."

"Richelle kicked me so hard for laughing. I still have the scar," said Marcus, starting to calm down.

"I will never forget the image of everyone so horrified. Yet Isabella stood there, dignified, and then started to laugh and dance about, yes? She was an angel," said Nikolas, sighing. He'd forgotten how much he'd missed the good times, when Marcus had been an older brother figure to him.

Marcus sighed. "They were great women."

Nikolas nodded, a moment of sadness creeping over him as the memory of Isabella faded back into history.

Marcus patted Nikolas on the back. "We'll come back later, as I want to prove to you this works." He motioned for Nikolas to head out. "Let's have some lunch. I had one packed for us.

"While it is not perfect, does this solve the problem of communication?" asked Marcus, returning them to the points from earlier.

Nikolas had always assumed that Marcus' ambitions would hit a limit—whether the limit of his lifespan, or a limit of technology. Clearly, he'd been wrong.

CHAPTER TWENTY
BROTHERLY LOVE

Hans slammed Saul against the old wooden door of the cabin, his hand on the hilt of the rapier on his belt. Saul was stunned, his ears ringing. He'd barely caught sight of a flash of Hans' red hood before hitting the floor.

"Tell me!" yelled Hans, his eyes filled with fury. "Tell me why Gretel took half of the treasure? Was it all for medicines to heal her broken dog?"

"What? Where have you been? We thought you'd run off," said Saul, focusing on his brother. His eyes darted around, searching for his staff. The tip of it was peeking out of the grass several feet away.

Hans turned to see what Saul was focused on, then let him go. "Go on, pick it up. Let's see just how much of a coward you are."

Saul straightened his beige tunic and red hood.

"At least you bought yourself a new tunic. You didn't let her have all the money for that hideous beast," said Hans, feigning relief.

"Hans, she's—"

"Wrong!" barked Hans. He rubbed his hand through his dirty, light-blond hair. "This isn't how it's supposed to be," he muttered, taking out his rapier.

Saul kept his hands up and backed up. "Let's talk about this. You took off after you dumped us at this cabin. That was days ago. You're not well."

"I needed to think," said Hans. "I just needed to think. I'd never desert Gretel."

"Brother, look—"

Hans pinned Saul to the door again. "Don't ever call me that. You are no more my brother than that dog you're protecting."

"That's a bit harsh," said Saul, trying once again to shift the tone.

"Is it?" said Hans, leaning in so that they were only inches apart. "Let me share with you one of Mother's little secrets. Shall I?

"Why do you think you don't look like Gretel and I? Because she and I are the twins. You were just thrown away, left on Mother's doorstep the same week that she found us."

Saul didn't want to believe Hans, but he'd suspected it for a long time. He could see the delight in Hans' face at his pain and confusion.

Hans glared angrily at Saul. "My patience is running out with you and her over this dying dog. Leave, or I'll kill you."

Saul rammed his forehead into Hans' nose, and kicked him in the stomach. As Hans stumbled backward, Saul ran over and picked up his staff.

Before Hans knew it, Saul brought his staff down on top of him, knocking Hans to the ground. Saul then kicked the rapier away.

"That's a warning!" yelled Saul, wiping Hans' blood off his forehead.

Hans immediately pulled a knife out of his boot and scrambled forward, stabbing Saul in the foot. Saul screamed.

"You know the problem?" asked Hans, standing and wiping the blood from his nose. "You almost had me convinced that you weren't the worthless weakling I've always taken you for. Gretel at least has her bow, but you —you just have a big stick. A big, dull stick. It really is the perfect weapon for you." He grinned at Saul pinned to the ground, trying to pull the knife out of his boot. "Let me get that for you." He quickly removed it, and kicked Saul over. "Gretel's now got two wounded to worry about. I wonder who she'll focus on. The broken brother or the damaged dog. She won't be able to afford to save you both. I hope she was careful with her coins."

Saul rolled around in agony.

"See you in… shall we say a week? Let's see how you fare then, brother," said Hans, cheerily picking up his rapier. "I will have my sister back and to myself."

Hans started to walk off, and then turned back. "Oh,

you can keep the knife to remember me by." He tossed it at Saul, narrowly missing his head.

———————

Gretel was exhausted. It had been a long walk to the closest village. She'd almost gotten lost again, but thankfully had found the rocks she'd left for herself marking a trail home. She hadn't been able to find any of the canopy bridges in these parts, which surprised her.

She had been afraid to leave the Hound, but she trusted Saul and knew that he would do his best to care for him while she was away.

As the cabin came into view, Gretel saw a slumped, shirtless man leaning against the front door. She dropped her basket of food and medicine, and ran as fast as she could to him. "Saul!" she screamed.

Gretel fell to her knees and examined him quickly. He was sweating profusely, his right foot wrapped in his blood-soaked shirt.

"Hey," he said weakly, trying to sit up.

Gretel felt his forehead. He was feverish. "What happened?" she asked, panicked. "Is it that Yellow Hood girl?" She glanced around, fearing that the moment of reckoning had come.

"No," said Saul, shaking his head. "Hans was… a bit upset. He's taken the rest of the treasure. He'll be back in a few days."

Gretel had been relieved when Hans had left. Seeing him brought up inexplicable fear and anguish mixed with relief. Her stomach turned over and over as the emotions refused to reconcile.

She took off her red cloak and draped it over Saul, not sure what to do. "Let me have a look at your foot," said Gretel, gently unwrapping the shirt. "Saul, what really happened?" She couldn't understand why seeing the wound bothered her so deeply, especially given that she'd seen much worse, and had even done much worse to people in the past.

Gretel glanced back at the toppled basket and its contents. She hoped that none of the vials or jars had smashed when she'd dropped them. "I have vinegar; that will help. I hope."

"I managed to break his nose, I think," said Saul.

She smiled sadly. She knew that Hans had accomplished exactly what he'd wanted, like he always did. He was trying to force her to choose.

CHAPTER TWENTY-ONE
FORKED ROAD

Tee rolled her sore left shoulder as she walked the last yards to the inn. The sun was barely up, and she was dripping with sweat.

She quietly turned the doorknob of the inn, and opened the door.

Christina stepped in her way. "You're quite the early bird," she said, startling Tee.

Tee leapt back, pulled her hood down and had two wooden sticks at the ready in the blink of an eye.

"So what's your plan? Sneak back in, get up when Elly does, do your normal workout with her, and then do the full day's hike? You can't keep doing this every day. You'll wear yourself out. You'll get sloppy and make a mistake."

She studied the expression on Tee's face, recognizing the experience of having been unfairly given responsibilities and secrets. Tee was a younger version of her in so many ways. She hoped fate would be kinder to Tee than it had been to her.

She leaned against the doorframe, and finally

something came to her. "If you let things like guilt and duty infect you too much, Tee, they'll drive you to a dark place. Trust me. Sometimes you've got to make a tough call. Your life, or the life of someone you care about, might depend on it." Christina waited to see Tee's reaction.

Tee thought about it and nodded, her face showing doubt. She was not quite convinced that what had been said aligned with how she was feeling, but she could sense there was some wisdom in the message.

"Anyway," continued Christina, "I was hoping to catch you alone. I have to leave. You need to lead the others to Herve to search for the plans. I'm not expecting them to be there, honestly. From there, head to Costello. If something happens, go straight to Costello. I'll meet you there in a week or so."

Tee was surprised. "Wait, what? Why? And aren't you even going to ask me where I've been?"

"Did you kill anyone this morning?" asked Christina half-jokingly.

"What? No!" said Tee.

"Then I don't care," said Christina, smiling. "What you do, provided you don't get yourself or anyone else killed, isn't my business. My job is to get you to Costello, unless a bigger problem happens, which it just did." She was being a bit cavalier, but it fit the moment.

Tee sighed, staring at the ground, the extra burden weighing her down even further.

Christina gave her a light punch in the shoulder. "You'll figure it out," she said, taking her backpack off and crouching down to open it. She handed Tee a folded piece of paper. "I've written where you need to go. You can read Crayo, right?"

Tee had never heard anyone other than her grandfather mention Crayo until recently. He'd always joked it was their secret language and that's why it had such a silly name. They had a game where they sometimes left little messages for each other around town, in special places. As Tee had gotten older, the messages had required more skill to figure out. At one point they'd stopped being written only on paper and had shown up written in chalk at the foot of buildings, or on door frames. Her parents had told her the truth about it weeks ago, and how and when to use the code. She hoped she'd used it properly on Elly's doorframe.

Tee nodded, taking the paper and unfolding it. It was a map with instructions and marked locations, with code words all over it.

"You'll stay at this inn outside of Herve. It's safe," said Christina, moving around so she could point at the map easily. "This is the word you need to say to the wife of the innkeeper. Don't talk to the innkeeper before you do that, and don't say the word to him. They are very particular about protocol.

"If you need a second place on your way to Costello, stay here. Use this code with the innkeeper or her wife.

They are a very friendly couple."

Tee took a big breath. There was a lot of information to take in.

"Search Franklin's old room and then get yourself to Costello as fast as you can. I'm positive the Fare will have people looking for you and the plans." Christina reached into her backpack and then stopped herself. "You know how to tell the false arrows and notes on that map from the real ones, right?"

Tee nodded. "My Grandpapa drilled me on that regularly. He once—"

"I don't mean to be rude," said Christina, cutting Tee off, "and I'm sure it's a great story, but I really need to be heading out. Oh, and a piece of advice. Be very careful with Franklin. I don't trust him."

"He's okay," said Tee nonchalantly. "He just doesn't know how to handle being around smart girls all the time. He's outnumbered four to one."

Christina stopped herself from pressing the point. "Maybe." She pulled out four shiny new shock-sticks. "You might need these. Keep them charged and hidden. And try not to lose them."

Tee was confused as she took them. "You had these all along? Why didn't you give these to us earlier?" She eyed Christina suspiciously.

"They weren't finished," she answered. "They work properly now."

"Where are the handles?" asked Tee, letting the issue drop.

Christina buckled her backpack closed and slid it over her shoulders. "They don't have any. You just twist them along the centerline, back and forth. You'll know it's fully charged when it gets warm, and that'll happen pretty quickly. Don't let Franklin see them, okay?"

Tee nodded, sliding all four into the secret pockets of her yellow cloak. She couldn't figure out what Christina had against him, but maybe it was the real reason why she hadn't given them the shock-sticks earlier.

Christina was about to go back into the inn when she remembered something. "By the way, I'm taking Mounira with me."

"Oh?" said Tee, surprised. "You don't want her to slow us down?"

"Something like that," said Christina. She didn't want to admit it, but the youngest member of the team made her feel special in a way she didn't fully comprehend. Selfishly, she wanted to bring Mounira with her.

Tee stepped into the main room of the inn, and there on a chair, leaning against the closet door, was a sleeping Mounira. She looked like such a little kid asleep, even though she was only two years younger than Tee.

"Take care of her," said Tee as she took the stairs up to their rooms. "She's a good kid."

"I will," replied Christina, moving to wake Mounira.

Tee hadn't been lying down for more than two minutes before she heard Elly ask, "Tee, are you awake?"

"Of course she's awake," answered Franklin, sitting up. "She was downstairs chatting with Miss Mysterious Abominator."

Elly sat up and glanced around the small room that the three of them had shared. The three beds were in a tight u-shape, with just a bit of room in the middle for any of them to get in or out. Christina and Mounira had been in the adjacent room.

Tee grabbed her yellow cloak and backpack from under her bed. "Christina's taking Mounira with her. She has to go. There's some big emergency."

"What?" said Elly, shocked. "Christina's abandoning us?"

Franklin whistled and rolled his eyes. "Wow, I can't believe it. Oh, that's brilliant! Now that she's sacked Klaus' lab, she's off. Wow, were we suckers," he said angrily.

Tee put on her cloak, slid on her backpack, and walked to the door. She thought back to how Christina had been clutching the backpack. She wondered if there could be some truth to Franklin's paranoid suspicion. However, she knew as the leader that she had to stop that line of thinking. "It's not like that."

Elly threw off her blankets. "Then how is it, Tee?"

Tee looked at Elly, then Franklin, and back at Elly. She

didn't want to answer, and her face went steely.

"Stop doing that!" yelled Elly. "I hate that face!"

Franklin turned to Elly. "I think you and I are going to be on our own soon."

Elly pointed sharply at Franklin. "Stop doing that."

"Doing what?" said Franklin, with a hint of taunt in his voice.

"You keep trying to wedge in between people! Tee and me, and everyone and Christina. Just how insecure are you?" said Elly, bringing the room to an awkward silence. Elly flared her fingers in frustration. "I'm guessing we're still supposed to go to Herve, somehow?"

Tee pulled the map out of her backpack. "She gave me this map. We'll have breakfast, get on the King's-Horses, and head out."

"Let me see it," said Franklin, trying to snatch the map from Tee's hands.

Tee twisted around, avoiding him. Franklin grabbed Tee around the waist. Tee immediately threw her arms up, slipping out of Franklin's grip, and then punched the back of his knees. He fell to the ground with a thud.

"Don't you *ever* do that again," said Tee, standing over him.

Franklin looked up at the spinning faces of Tee and Elly. His head was only mildly sore, but at the back of his mind, he imagined his schoolmates laughing at him for being dropped by a girl—never mind a girl a year and a half younger than him.

"Show me the map," demanded Elly, as Franklin slowly got up.

Tee hesitated.

Elly's confidence started to shake. "Tee?" she asked.

With a heavy sigh, Tee laid the map on the floor.

Franklin wrinkled his face. "You call that a map? It's got arrows all over the place. What language is that even scribbled on it? That's not Frelish, that's for sure," he said, gathering up his clothes and heading for the shared washroom.

"What is this, Tee?" asked Elly. "Can you even read this stuff?"

Tee lowered her eyes as she thought, before raising them to meet Elly's gaze. "My grandfather taught me when I was little. I didn't know it was a real language."

Elly could sense Tee was holding something back. Her face fell as she realized that with every passing day, there seemed to be more and more that she wasn't a part of. There weren't supposed to be any secrets between them; they'd promised each other that a million times over. Elly remembered when she'd revealed her greatest secret to Tee, and how freeing it was to know that Tee accepted her for who she was. Now there seemed to be more of them piling up by the hour.

———————

Mounira quietly walked alongside Christina, eating the muffin she'd been given and taking in the early morning sounds and sights of the forest.

She caught a couple glimpses of Christina checking on her. There was something in those moments that reminded Mounira of when her aunts would look in on her and her cousins.

"Why am I coming with you?" asked Mounira, unable to hold in the question any longer.

Christina smiled. "I have my reasons. That's all you need to know."

"No, it isn't," said Mounira cheerfully.

A laugh spilled out of Christina. Only Mounira could be defiant and jolly about it, she thought. "A really bad thing happened near my home, and I'm afraid it's a sign of things to come. I want you close so that... I can protect you." Christina gave Mounira a tender smile.

"Oh," said Mounira. "Why?"

Christina's face shifted, revealing some of her discomfort in answering. She pushed herself to answer. "Do you trust me?"

Mounira took Christina's hand. "I do. We did save my friends the other day. I'm sure you're doing the right thing. We will come back and see them again, right?"

With her emotions just below the surface, Christina nodded. "Definitely. There's a storm coming and we're going to get umbrellas and coats."

"Then let's go," said Mounira, pulling Christina forward.

When they arrived at the King's-Horses, Christina's face fell. The horses were toppled over, some parts and belts were strewn about, and branches were jammed into the open areas.

Mounira watched quietly as Christina assessed the damage and opened all the panels. "I can repair one of them, I think, but the others will be useless."

"Who could have done this?" asked Mounira.

Christina gave Mounira a look.

"You don't think—"

"I do. Who else knew they were here?" asked Christina. "Give me that belt and that gear, please." She opened one of the pouches and got out some small tools.

Half an hour later, Christina put the key into the heart-panel of the operational King's-Horse and opened it. "We're lucky this one wasn't really damaged."

"The pedals are broken. Aren't you going to replace them? I mean, how can we... oh, what's that?"

Christina removed a copper cube from her backpack. "You didn't think that Nikolas and my father made big toy horses to go about the countryside only at the speed of a person running, did you?"

"Um," said Mounira, wondering. "Wait, this is the engine! Franklin was right?"

Christina attached some cable, closed the heart-panel, and locked the engine door. "It's called a mercury-copper-magnetic engine, or MCM. It is extremely rare to find them."

"Why?" asked Mounira.

"Because no one can make them anymore. Or so we thought," said Christina.

Reaching into the mouth of the King's-Horse, Christina flipped a switch and brought it to life. It started vibrating and humming. "I can't believe I still remember how to do this," said Christina to herself, thinking back to her father teaching her.

Mounira was in awe.

"Turn around. I need to put these on you," said Christina, taking a pair of goggles out of her backpack. "These used to be mine from when I was a kid. I never go anywhere without them. I've been dreaming of this day."

"Why?" asked Mounira, turning around and letting Christina tighten the goggles properly into place.

"I was six the last time I was on one of these with an MCM, and that one wasn't in anywhere near as good of a condition as this one," said Christina, smiling.

"What are these for?" asked Mounira, tapping the goggles as Christina tightened them.

"The wind," replied Christina.

"The wind?"

"You'll see, Little Miss Questions," replied Christina, helping Mounira up onto the King's-Horse.

"What about Tee and Elly?" asked Mounira, surveying the smashed and disassembled King's-Horses.

"Tee'll figure it out," said Christina hopefully. "Ready for a wild ride?" She put her feet in position and gripped the reins. "You better hold on tightly."

Mounira grabbed on to the reins with her hand. "We flew the rocket-cart. How bad could this be?"

Christina laughed as she moved her feet, and the King's-Horse bolted.

CHAPTER TWENTY-TWO
LADY IN RED

Simon walked quietly into his library. He'd started going through some papers he'd brought with him, when Cleeves discovered him.

"Oh, I didn't realize you'd entered, sir," said Cleeves. It was rare that Simon ever came into the library with anything but a booming demand for Cleeves to fetch him something. He'd suspected Simon had returned in the early hours of the morning, as he'd seen the driver Simon had used walking by earlier in the courtyard.

Simon's return was a relief, and meant that Cleeves could stop pretending that his master was simply unavailable or in another part of the manor or city. Simon had given strict instructions that no one was to know he'd left, including the regent. He'd ordered Cleeves to send any important messages to him by the fastest couriers or by the newly installed Neumatic Tube. It had been a harrowing task for the old man to keep track of where Simon was; fortunately, everything had gone flawlessly.

Simon glanced at Cleeves before returning to his

papers.

"Sir, it's good to see you. You have—" said Cleeves, interrupted by Simon's glare. He noticed that Simon had a purple-pink bruise on his forehead and a red, swollen nose. A quick inspection of Simon's high-collared shirt revealed it was hiding some bruising around his neck. Although it was rare for Simon to have any signs of physical conflict, the years had made it clear to Cleeves that it was best for all if he simply ignored it.

"What is it?" grumbled Simon. "Stop being a muttering idiot."

Cleeves pointed to the walled office inside the library where Simon often met with Marcus when he visited. "You have a guest, sir."

Simon had hoped to be undisturbed for a few more days to allow his injuries to heal, and to think how he was going to deal with Abeland being on the loose. It was only a matter of time before Marcus found out, and that would unleash an entire other set of problems.

Glaring at the old bald man, Simon rubbed his throat again. "I don't care who it is, send them away."

"Sir, it's—"

"Is it the Regent?" snapped Simon. "Because I don't have time for—"

"The Regent is dead. Things are about to change," said a woman's gravelly voice from the office.

Simon shot a sharp glare at Cleeves. He gestured,

asking who it was.

Cleeves leaned forward, and using a hand to shield the words, whispered, "She's wearing a red hood and cloak. Her face was hidden but she knew things about you and me."

"Richelle?" asked Simon, confused.

Cleeves shook his head.

Simon scowled at Cleeves. "You don't know who it is?" His nostrils flared as he raised his voice. "Why did you let her in?"

"Because I didn't give him any choice," said the woman, turning the corner. Her red-hooded cloak was embroidered with gold trim. Though her face remained covered, Simon could see a brown-and-blue dress underneath.

Simon straightened up quickly, his eyes going wide as he realized her rank in the Fare. They'd never met in person, always dealing through intermediaries.

"Um," said Simon, at a loss for words.

"It seems you've had a rather rough time recently," she said, her hands hidden in the folds of her cloak.

Cleeves started to sweat as he saw Simon's reaction. He couldn't remember the last time he'd seen Simon so visibly unsettled.

"Tea?" offered Cleeves.

"Yes, Cleeves, thank you," said Simon hastily.

Cleeves stood there, confused for a second by the

thank-you, before ushering himself off.

Simon rubbed his hands together, his shoulders rolling forward. "I don't mean to be rude, but... why are you here?" he asked nervously.

"Do you mind if we sit?" asked the woman, as if Simon had a choice.

He smiled and gestured back towards the office.

"No, that room simply isn't what I had in mind," she said, her voice laced with malice. "There's been too much treachery and failure in that room."

Simon couldn't see her eyes, but he could feel the heat of her gaze.

Simon pointed in the opposite direction. "I have a sitting area over here, by a fireplace. It's... not lit, but I could—"

"It will do," said the woman, settling the matter.

He led the way through the maze of tall bookcases to a pair of maroon velvet chairs. He stiffened as he realized that only one of them had a side-table.

She gracefully maneuvered around Simon and sat in the chair with the side-table. "Sit," she said, gesturing with a red nail-polished hand. "I know how much you enjoy that seat."

Simon stared at the empty seat uncomfortably. He was repulsed by the idea of sitting where he'd planted others and tormented them. He kicked himself for having chosen the wrong sitting area.

"Simon?" asked the woman. There was a familiarity in her tone that surprised him.

He scratched the back of his head as he tried to think of a different solution. Finding none, he sat.

The woman leaned forward. "Isn't that better? Now we can discuss the Abeland problem. You know how critical it was to our plans that you handle this properly, and yet, you made a mess of things. This needs to be addressed anew, doesn't it?" she asked venomously.

Simon's face went white, and he bowed his head.

"Please, Simon. Don't you expect us to know such things? We have ears everywhere. We have news run on the wind back to us," she said, gesturing about with red-nailed fingers. She watched the discomfort play out on Simon's face. "I can see that I'm going to need to resolve the Abeland situation. You just aren't filling me with confidence. It'll be fun seeing him again; it's been a long time."

Simon nodded as he shifted in his seat.

Out of the corner of his eye, Simon saw Cleeves coming with the tea tray. He gestured with his head for Cleeves to hurry up, and as Cleeves tried, he tripped and fell. The china dishes smashed, the metal tray clanged as it skidded on the marble floor, and tea and cream went everywhere.

Simon's face went red with rage, but he stayed anchored to the spot, glancing at the red-hooded woman.

The woman jumped up instinctively, her hood

slipping back for a split-second, revealing a scarred, heart-shaped face. Her hair was black with streaks of gray. Her skin was blotchy, signs of an illness not long past.

Simon stared at the floor, hoping she hadn't noticed. His blood froze as he realized who the woman was, as impossible as it seemed. He couldn't believe that he'd been coordinating his treachery with *her*. His mind was reeling at the implications. He, like everyone else, had thought her dead.

The woman hastily pulled her hood back up, glaring at Cleeves, who had been staring at her. She turned to face Simon, her eyes biting into his soul, her voice harsh and angry. "It's that type of impatience, that type of incessant need to manipulate things, that will cost you greatly. Trust me when I say that the Fare has never allowed anyone to jeopardize its goals, not for hundreds of years."

Simon didn't move a muscle. He'd seen over the years what they did to anyone they were displeased with, and it chilled him to the bone.

The red-hooded woman watched Cleeves trying to pick up the pieces, settling herself. After a minute or two, she said, "This will cost you, Simon. You will get instructions shortly." She turned and left.

Simon listened to the subtle sound of her soft boots gliding along the floor towards the main doors. His mind was like a clogged machine. He couldn't get past the realization of who she was.

"Oh," said the woman sweetly. She had paused by the door. "I have a present for you. A little thank-you for helping convince Richelle to create her Order of the Red Hoods, which allowed us to walk out in the open." There was the familiar sound of a brass tube being dropped on a worktable somewhere in the study. "It seems that someone got their hands on some interesting plans in Palais. Plans from one Nikolas Klaus. We expect you'll be able to give us a written report on them in a few weeks. If you can't have it done by then, well, you'll have answered the question of whether or not there is a role for you in the next phase of our plans."

Simon, his hands in his lap, stared at the floor. "Thank you," he said grudgingly. "I will not fail you."

"No, you won't, and it was no trouble," said the woman. "We'll be in touch."

As the library door closed, Simon let out a huge sigh and put his head in his hands. How had his reckless desire to become the master of the grand game turned him into a pawn? The last of the petty victories, like tormenting Abeland, were now meaningless. He couldn't shake the feeling that no matter who won in the end, he was going to lose.

CHAPTER TWENTY-THREE

Not a Moment to Breathe

"That was a nice horse you gave them," said Abeland, turning to Bakon.

They'd parted ways with the woman and her father twenty minutes before, as Abeland and Bakon turned on to a dirt road that bent away from the Belnian capital of Relna. Bakon shrugged. "They needed it more than I did."

Abeland nodded. "Are you typically a good man?"

Bakon shrugged again. "I don't know. Sometimes."

"Ah, there's my abode," said Abeland, pointing to a white manor as it came into view.

"Not exactly a humble one," said Bakon, realizing it was enormous.

"Nor my most immodest one, either," replied Abeland, smiling. He found himself regularly glancing at Bakon, trying to figure out where he knew his face from.

"You should have gone with them. The woman

seemed interested in you," said Abeland.

"I've got a—" Bakon stopped his answer and mumbled. "I don't want to talk about it. So this is your place? Is anyone even home?"

As Bakon got closer, he realized that the manor was smaller than he'd first thought; but still, it was a stately home with a sense of grandeur. The gardens in front of the house were overgrown, with some weeds more than four feet tall.

"Well, the gardener isn't, that's for certain," said Abeland, grinning.

"How's your breathing doing?" asked Bakon, stopping and scanning around for anything to be concerned about.

"I'm doing okay. Some of the tightness in my chest is slowly returning," said Abeland, stopping for a moment. "It seems Simon's lack of chemistry skill is helping me, for once. He simply doubled the concentration, which was very much what I needed. He could have created something truly nasty. I'll have to repay him for that one day."

Bakon wondered who Simon was, but figured it best not to ask. He was certain that Abeland hadn't fully recovered yet from the drug. He couldn't imagine a man like him letting a name slip by accident, and wasn't sure what he'd do if he realized his mistake. During the walk with the woman and old man, Abeland had demonstrated his charm and ability to answer questions with as little actual information about himself as possible. Every now and then he'd slipped, often having a momentarily confused look on his face.

"I should warn you," said Abeland, stepping in front of Bakon. "There might be a very angry—"

"Abeland? Is that you?" screamed a woman's voice from a second-floor window.

"—woman," finished Abeland, turning around. "Never mind. By the way, thanks for saving my life. You might need to do it again in a moment," he said half-jokingly.

A woman in a light-blue dress with curly, light-brown hair came racing out of the house. "Abeland! How dare you—what happened to you?"

Abeland smiled uncomfortably. He had originally planned to be away for six months, instead of the year and a half he'd been gone. He was honestly surprised to find her home, given the remarks she'd made when he left. She'd waited for Abeland to drop the secrecy around their relationship and marry her, and he hadn't been ready. That, however, now seemed like thoughts of a different man altogether.

Scratching his beard, Abeland said, "Hello, Lana. I would have been home earlier, but Simon and some old friends asked me to hang around for a bit... in prison. I just decided I'd had enough and needed to come home. I guess I lost track of time."

Lana curled her lip and glanced at Bakon quizzically.

Bakon took the cue and extended his hand. "My name is Bakon Cochon."

"Ha!" snapped Lana. "You couldn't have made up a more fake name?"

Bakon clenched his jaw. "It's my name."

"Oh," replied Lana, embarrassed.

Abeland nodded towards Bakon. "This man saved my life, so if you're done making him regret it, I'd love to go inside. I need a shower, a shave, and a good meal." Abeland gestured forwards.

"Well, we only have one cook left," said Lana, turning to go.

"Is it Margaret?" asked Abeland hopefully.

"No, it's Alfonso," retorted Lana.

"Hmm, maybe leaving the prison before lunch was a bad idea," sighed Abeland.

———————

Bakon was about to wipe his mouth with his hand when he caught a glimpse of Abeland using a napkin. Remembering his manners, he found a napkin and wiped his face properly.

He sat across the rugged kitchen table from Abeland. The kitchen was bigger than Bakon's house, with white cabinets that went up to the twelve-foot-high ceiling. The blue walls gave the room a sense of warmth.

The shower had been an interesting experience and taken a few minutes to get right. He knew none of the servants would complain about the mess he'd made, but wondered what they'd say to each other. The guest room was so grand that Bakon found it hard to imagine why someone would build something so big.

The shirt Abeland had loaned Bakon fit remarkably well, which surprised Abeland. He hadn't noticed how similar their height and build were. He examined Bakon's eerily familiar face, now clean-shaven, and wondered.

Abeland folded his napkin and placed it on his empty plate. "Something's on your mind, and I'm guessing it's not having a third one of Alfonso's tasty sandwiches."

Bakon smiled and gazed at his crumb-filled plate. "No, that was amazing. I was worried when you made those comments outside."

Abeland smiled. "Well, if I'd said it was going to be excellent, you might have expected something greater than you got. There's a lot to the psychology of things that one should consider."

There was something in the way Abeland said that last sentence that reminded him of the way that Nikolas usually spoke. Bakon looked up from his plate. "I'm trying to find someone," he said uncomfortably.

Abeland snapped his fingers, getting Alfonso's attention. He waved him away.

Bakon glanced over his shoulder at the departing servant. "I didn't mean—"

"Now that I'm cleaned up and have had a reasonably good meal, I have some of my better habits coming back to me. Making sure there are no unintended ears is one of them. Now, before we start talking, I need a dose of my breathing medicine. Care to accompany me to my den?"

They walked through the grand, echoing corridors of the manor, arriving at the oak double doors of the den. Opening them revealed a room with bookcases lining the walls, two chairs, and a fireplace.

In the middle of the room was a huge wooden chair, reinforced with steel. It had two bronze arms that held a huge metallic-and-glass helmet, with ribbed tubes coming out of it. The tubes connected to a desk-sized apparatus with levers and buttons that sat behind the huge chair.

"Before you ask—no, it is not some type of torture device," said Abeland, smiling. "This is my breathing machine. It infuses the medicine I make directly into my lungs and exercises them." He stared disappointedly at three pegs on the wall where his custom-designed monocles would normally be. He wondered what Lana had done with them.

"How often do you need to use this?" asked Bakon, trying to make heads or tails of the machine.

Abeland thought back. It had been a while. "I was using it about twice a month previously. I had a version of this I brought with me to Jannia. I'm not sure what happened to it. I have another one at my father's main house outside of Teutork. I'll need to use it every couple of days to stretch my lungs and force the medicine into them. After about a month, I should be able to reduce the frequency."

"Does it hurt?" asked Bakon, curious.

"It's uncomfortable but—"

Suddenly, there was a loud rumble.

Bakon and Abeland looked at each other.

"That sounded like—" said Abeland.

"A cannon," finished Bakon, his eyes wide.

Abeland ran over to one of the bookcases and flipped down a fake shelf of books. He quickly moved his finger along a dozen fluid-filled vials.

"Maybe this one," he said to himself, taking one and holding it up to the gas light. "No, too old." He rifled through the other vials. "They're all too old." He flipped the shelf back up and shook his head.

"Are you going to be okay?" asked Bakon, wishing he'd kept the pistol from the thugs.

"Only one way to find out," said Abeland, hurrying out of the den, a hand on his chest as it started to constrict.

Abeland and Bakon ran through the corridors to the main hall, where they found soldiers and a smoking cannon. The front entrance had been blown to pieces.

Lana was standing with the soldiers. "There he is!" she yelled. "I want him dead!"

Skidding on the black marble floor, Abeland grabbed Bakon by the shoulder and pulled him back into the corridor. "I guess she's a bit more mad than I'd thought.

Head for the den!"

They ducked bullets as they rounded the first corner. Bakon could see Abeland leaning into his run; it was obvious he was starting to have real trouble breathing.

Arriving in the study, Abeland closed and locked the door. Without a word, he swiftly moved around the breathing machine to the bookcase behind it and pulled down another fake shelf of books, revealing a heavy lever.

Abeland huffed as he pulled on the lever. "The mechanism's a bit stiff. Help me push this open. Push the bookcase in on the right."

Both men put their backs into it as the sounds of footsteps echoed down the hallway.

Finally with enough room to squeeze through, they entered a dark, dank corridor and pushed the bookcase closed, sealing themselves in.

Abeland's hands hunted around in the darkness until he found a lantern. After a few quick cranks, a white glow filled their stone-walled surroundings.

Bakon studied the lantern. It was remarkably similar to some that Nikolas had.

"This way," said Abeland, taking a step and feeling his legs wobble.

"Who are you?" asked Bakon, putting his arm around Abeland's shoulder to stabilize him.

Abeland studied Bakon's face. He was thankful he'd

trusted his gut and not poisoned Bakon's food. He'd been tempted to, fearing that Bakon was somehow connected to one of his enemies.

"Head left," said Abeland as they got to a fork in the tunnel. "This way leads to the edge of the back garden, right by the forest. We can make our way to Relna from there."

At the end of the stone corridor was a wooden door, daylight showing between the slats and around its perimeter.

Abeland turned off the lantern and put it down. They took a moment to listen for anything on the other side.

"Okay. Let's make a break for it," said Abeland, pushing the door open.

They stepped out into the early-evening garden and found a dozen soldiers waiting for them with rifles drawn.

"Well," said Abeland, disappointed. He raised his arms. "I'm starting to feel that Lana might actually be upset with me. Also, she's had so much time on her hands, it seems she's found all my secrets." He bit his lip as he scanned about.

"You know," said Bakon, raising his arms as well. "I'm worried what Egelina-Marie will do to me the next time I see her."

"Who's that?" asked Abeland, turning to Bakon. The ignored soldiers weren't sure what to make of their casual conversation.

Bakon struggled with emotion. "My girlfriend, who I abandoned to try to find the Piemans."

Abeland looked away, hiding his surprise for a second. He turned back and studied Bakon's face.

"Excuse me," said one of the soldiers, waving his rifle that was trained on them. "Could you... ah, stop talking?"

Abeland straightened up and glared at the man so strongly that the man recoiled a step. "Excuse me. Do you mind? We're not going anywhere, so allow us to finish this." Something shiny in the forest caught Abeland's attention.

The soldiers exchanged looks, not sure what to do.

Abeland dropped his arms. "That's it. I've had it with you lot," he boomed. "Do you know who I am?"

"Abeland Pieman," stuttered one of the soldiers.

Bakon stared at Abeland, surprised.

Abeland smirked at Bakon. "Yeah, well, you don't have to keep looking."

"Put your hands up... please?" asked the lead soldier.

Scowling at the soldier for interrupting, Abeland said, "I'll consider it—" He then caught sight of something else in the forest behind the soldiers. "No. Thanks for the polite request though." He made a pistol with his fingers and pointed it at the soldiers. "You've forced me to use my last, most secret weapon." The soldiers started to laugh. "Bang," said Abeland.

A shot rang out, then another. Before the soldiers could figure out what was happening, they were all down on the ground.

Bakon was stunned. Abeland winked at him and blew the imaginary smoke off his index finger.

"Thanks for your help, whoever you are," said Abeland to the two figures emerging from the forest.

"Eg! Richy!" said Bakon.

Egelina-Marie glared at Bakon before moving her gaze to Abeland. She gestured to the soldiers. "Are there any more?"

Abeland turned to the manor. "I'm guessing probably about two dozen more. Lana sounded very mad."

"That your wife?" asked Richy.

"Ex-girlfriend, it seems," said Abeland. Egelina-Marie could see pain in his eyes, hiding behind his humor.

"You found a Pieman," said Richy. "I knew you would."

Bakon messed Richy's hair. He forced his gaze over to Egelina-Marie. His felt his throat closing, his hands getting sweaty, and his face burning.

"Shut up," said Egelina-Marie, giving him a shove and then pulling him in for a tight hug, pressing the side of her face into his chest. "You're an idiot, and you need to shut up."

Bakon closed his arms around her and whispered, "Okay."

CHAPTER TWENTY-FOUR

MOTHER'S SON

Hans stepped onto the fallen front door and looked around. "Mother, I have returned!" he yelled, once he was certain that he was alone. Stepping into the shambling remains of the kitchen, he stared at the cupboards, remembering days ago when he'd searched for food that wasn't there.

Coming back to the house had been a siren's song for him, irresistibly drawing him back. As each day had passed, he'd been less and less able to resist the idea of returning. Now, standing in the kitchen, it felt strange, disturbing, and yet—right.

In the days since he'd fought with Saul, Hans had terrorized more than a dozen small caravans as he tried to figure out what to do with himself. He'd nearly met his end by way of a retired soldier's javelin, but got the best of the old man in the end.

It didn't matter how many bodies Hans left in his wake, or how much fear he saw in the eyes of those that he let live to tell the tales of the merciless Red Hood, he still felt lost and empty. He wanted what he'd once had back so badly, but had no idea how to reclaim it.

On the way to the house, he'd visited Mother's rock-pile grave. At first, he'd felt sorrow, but it had quickly given way to rage. He'd yelled and kicked at the grave until a hand was exposed. Apologizing, and with tears streaming down his face, he'd fixed it as best he could.

Hans took in the familiar putrid smell of the house, and savored the touch of ginger in the air. He froze when he saw the floor torn up and a dozen ledgers tossed about.

"What? Oh no!" he yelled, dashing into Mother's bedroom. "No! No! No!" He knocked over the nightstand and sighed when he saw the little tan book still strapped to the bottom of it. He carefully unbuckled the book from its secret hiding place and picked it up.

As he stroked the cover, bitter and sweet memories came forward.

Hans was five years old when he'd noticed something dangling under the Ginger Lady's nightstand from the main room.

It was forbidden to go into Mother's room, and Hans had witnessed what she did to those who disobeyed, but he couldn't help himself. Something drew him in.

As Hans reached under the nightstand and carefully removed the item, he was unaware of Mother, silently standing over him.

She watched as he carefully stroked the soft brown

cover and then turned each page, marveling at the strange symbols and diagrams, muttering pretend meanings for them since he couldn't read. Her rage at having her book discovered was awkwardly at odds with a need to share her walled-off inner world.

When Hans went to put the book back, he noticed her, and was struck with absolute terror. His voice failed him and he dropped the book, trembling.

Mother carefully picked up the book and returned it to its place under the nightstand, keeping Hans glued to the spot with her gaze. She then grabbed him by the arm and dragged him outside. All the other children went quiet and watched in horror as Hans was dragged out. Saul and Gretel were away with an older child.

As the Ginger Lady strapped Hans down to the wooden blocks, Hans was silent. She could see the fear in his little light-brown eyes. For the second time in her life, she stopped and wondered what she was doing. Every other child that she had disciplined had screamed and fought, yet here was this little one that always stuck out from the others, sticking out even more. She'd found Hans clever and cruel at times, but always respectful in her presence.

Mother picked up her cane and struck him once, brutally. As she prepared for a second strike, she realized he was trying to hold in his tears. He was barely whimpering.

She lowered the cane and leaned on it. "Why aren't

you screaming?" she asked. It bothered her.

Hans glared at her with a mix of rage and fear. "I did something wrong. I'm sorry, Mother."

The Ginger Lady tapped her cane to the ground in thought. She'd only ever had one other child like this, and she missed him desperately. She glanced around to see if anyone was watching, any prying little eyes spying on them, but there was no one.

"I will make you strong," she said to him. "You will be special. But you need to remember that you must always listen to Mother."

From that day forward, though Mother was still cruel to him, she never fed him any of the Ginger. When he turned ten, she had him help prepare the meals. Without the Ginger, he felt and remembered everything, and came to love, hate, and fear her more than Saul or Gretel ever could.

As her age started to catch up with her, she became more and more dependent on him. Shortly after turning fifteen, Hans slipped some of the Ginger into her food for the first time. With her passed out, and his siblings in dazed states, Hans felt intoxicatingly powerful for the first time. When Mother realized what he'd done, she had beat him severely, but it only fueled his desire not to be caught.

As the Ginger Lady's mind had started to deteriorate, he resented when she didn't remember that he was supposed to be special to her. Deep down, he feared that he'd ruined her by giving her the Ginger so many times, and took it out on his siblings when they couldn't defend themselves.

————————

Hans carefully put the little book in a secure pocket of his red cloak. He walked over to the broken stairs that used to lead to the second floor and smiled sinisterly as he gazed up, remembering what he used to do in secret up there before he felt bold enough to do it in the open.

He stood still in the middle of the decrepit house of ginger-scented secrets, thinking. It almost felt like Mother was there, wrapping her sharp-nailed hands around him in a twisted semblance of a hug.

Hans took a deep breath, wiping the tears with his dirty sleeve. Out of the corner of his eye he caught sight of the chair he'd spent two weeks in, healing from the initial wounds given to him by Master Kutsuu, years ago.

Master Kutsuu had been hired to train the triplets to protect the Ginger Lady from her enemies, both real and imagined. She grew paranoid as she aged, and every few days she feared that the guardsmen of Mineau and Minette were going to storm her house and take away the last of her children. The trio had loved the idea of learning to fight, until they met Master Kutsuu.

He was the embodiment of vengeance, with a look and voice that could bend steel. He decided what style of fighting and what weapon Hans, Saul, and Gretel would learn. For two years, he showed up and randomly picked which one of the trio he would teach that day. His student for the day would sometimes need to be dragged out of the house, and would often return broken and bloodied. Then, without any explanation, one merciful day he stopped showing up. For a month, they feared he would jump out of a tree and take one of them to train, but it never happened.

Hans stared at the old chair. "You used to yell at us, Kutsuu, that we were locked in our shells, that we needed to break through them. We needed to discover the greatness locked inside ourselves. How many times did you say to me, as I lay there with my fingers broken or bleeding, that the pain of the past is not to be forgotten, for it is the light in the darkness of tomorrow?" Hans stopped, and scanned about as a thought hit him. "You were right. So very, very right. What better way to see my tomorrow than with a burning light?"

Later, Hans took a bite out of an apple he'd stolen and leaned back against a tree. As the Ginger Lady's house burned, he slid between laughing, sobbing, and screaming at it. Every now and then he rushed forward, wanting to put it out and apologize to someone, anyone, for what he had done. But in the end, he sat there, watching it until the rain came and finally put it out.

When he awoke in the morning, soaked to the bone, he absorbed the delicious sight of the smoldering ruins of his past. His future was his, and he knew exactly how it would start.

CHAPTER TWENTY-FIVE

CRACKED

When Tee, Elly, and Franklin discovered the smashed King's-Horses, Franklin immediately accused Christina of sabotaging them and also of stealing something from Nikolas' lab. A screaming match broke out between Franklin and Elly. Tee's silence only fueled Elly's frustration more and more.

Ignoring them, Tee covered the remains of the King's-Horses with the camouflage blanket. After telling the two of them that they needed to get to the next inn before nightfall, she started walking. Franklin and Elly calmed down and followed. A long day of traveling by foot started.

Tee decided it was best for them to stick to the forest rather than main roads, away from prying eyes. Both Tee and Elly wore their yellow-hooded cloaks.

"Shall we stop for a bit?" asked Franklin, breaking more than two hours of silence.

Elly nodded. "Tee, what do you think?"

Tee looked up at the sun. "I think we've got two or three hours of sunlight left." She pulled out the map and tried to find where they were.

Elly came and peered over Tee's shoulder. "I think we're there," said Elly, pointing right in front of Tee.

Tee grimaced. "Thanks, but we're here," she replied flatly. "I think we should be at the inn in about an hour. It's best if we keep going."

"Are you going to get us lost again?" asked Franklin, unable to help himself.

Elly glared at Franklin, but bit her lip. She'd hated being lost just as much as he had, but there was only one person allowed to yell at Tee for it, and that was her.

***

Tee thanked the innkeeper's wife once again for giving them two nice rooms and such a wonderful meal. She handed her a quickly-written note, and the old woman nodded knowingly. She could read the burdens on Tee's face, and scooped her up into a big hug of encouragement.

Tee looked at her and gave a meek smile. Slowly, she climbed the stairs and knocked on Franklin's door.

"Come in," he said.

Tee opened the door and leaned in, holding on to the handle. "Do you really know where we need to look tomorrow in Herve? I'm thinking we might be better off heading straight for Costello."

Franklin was sitting on his bed, thinking. He was happy to have a room to himself for the first time since he'd left home. He smiled at Tee. She still had the black eye and was clearly exhausted, but there was something about the way the light bounced off her long, dark hair and brown eyes. She was unlike any young woman he'd met. She was smart, courageous, driven, and quite capable in a fight. He wondered how she'd do in Ingleash society, whether she'd thrive or not.

He could feel the clouds of confusion creeping into his mind as part of him started to think about how pretty she was, and forced them out. He was not going to lose his ability to speak and think clearly all because part of him had temporarily remembered that she was, after all, a pretty girl.

"I know exactly where I left those plans," said Franklin confidently. "If we don't find them in two minutes, then we'll continue on to Costello...and see that buffoon, the Abbott."

Tee nodded and started to leave.

"Tee?"

"Yeah?" she said, hanging on the door.

"I'm sure tomorrow will be the day you deserve," he said, smiling.

"I hope so," she replied, closing the door.

She turned and stared at the door a couple of yards down the corridor. She could just feel the tension emanating from the room she was sharing with Elly. Part of her wanted to walk out the front door and head home. She slid her feet along the floor until she came to the door and slowly opened it.

Tee was relieved to see that the oil lamp on the nightstand between her and Elly's beds was turned way down, and Elly was rolled over, facing the wall. She listened intently for moment, and heard Elly's breathing rise and fall rhythmically.

She closed the door and changed into one of the long nightshirts the innkeeper's wife had provided them. Hoping that tonight would be free of dreams, Tee climbed into bed.

As she tried to drift off in the comforting glow of the light, Tee kept jolting awake as she did every night, with images of the arrow going through Pierre's chest and him lying on the ground, his life slipping away. She wished she had her mother and father to hold her, to have their parental warmth wash away all the wrongs of the world.

She thought of all the recent lessons with her father and mother about the history of the Tub, the Fare, and the purpose of Minette, along with a million other secrets and responsibilities that had made her feel like she was drowning as they poured on her shoulders. She'd argued intensely to be allowed to share some of it with Elly, until her parents finally told her why she couldn't. That night, she'd cried herself to sleep.

With a big sigh, Tee rolled over to turn off the light and found Elly glaring at her, her blankets pulled up to her chin.

"I can't take it anymore," said Elly, her voice

trembling. "I don't know who you are, I don't know where my parents are, and I have no real idea where we are going."

Tee felt cornered, and lowered her gaze. She started to roll back towards the wall when Elly yelled, "I can't take this! Don't turn away from me!"

Tee took in a big breath. Her face was drained, as if her soul had been leaking out since the beginning of the journey. She forced her gaze up to meet Elly's. It pained Tee to see her best friend's chin trembling.

"You're supposed to be my best friend," said Elly, a few tears escaping.

"I am," said Tee flatly, mentally applying all of her strength to keeping the cork on her bottled emotions. "I —"

"I nothing," said Elly, sitting up and bringing her legs in so she could hug them. "You've been lying to me—"

Tee's eyes flared and she sat up as well. "Lying? You have no idea what's been going on. I have *not* been lying to you."

"Then tell me!" yelled Elly.

Tee's jaw inched forward while she thought of how to answer. "I can't!" she said, gesturing wildly as she stood. "I can't! I'm not allowed!"

"What are you talking about?" asked Elly, standing to look at Tee eye to eye. "Where do you go in the early morning when you think I'm asleep?"

Tee felt betrayed by the remark. Not by Elly, but by her own sloppiness. "Everything. Everything has to be a secret, and I have to protect everyone! You just have to accept that!"

Elly threw her hands up. "Why? Why do I have to accept that?"

"Because that's all I'm allowed to do," said Tee, tears streaming down her flushed face. "And if you're my best friend, then you need to accept that, too! I don't have a choice."

Elly backed off for a second, returning to sit on her bed. Tee copied her. "I miss Pierre too, you know," said Elly, fishing for what was at the root of everything.

"That's not what this is even about," said Tee, deflated, hanging her head. "It just makes everything ten times worse."

There was a knock at the door. "Is everything okay in there?" asked the innkeeper's wife.

"Yes," replied the girls in unison.

"Okay, well…" said the woman, wondering what to say. "Try to keep it down."

"We will," replied Elly, glancing at the door.

Tee stared at the oil lamp's flame, trapped in its clear, curved glass cage. For all of the size and grandeur of the glass, it was unable to protect the flame from being tossed about by the wind of the outside world.

Elly felt lost seeing the distant, brooding expression

on Tee's face as Tee watched the flame. After several minutes, Elly started to cry again.

At first, she thought it was out of a sense of betrayal, and then out of a sense of loss of their friendship, but finally Elly realized it was because she felt helpless to ease the burden that was crushing Tee.

Elly thought of one of her mother's favorite phrases: I will protect you however I must, even if that means protecting you from you, when I need to. A soft, sad smile emerged.

Lost in thought for a long time, Tee came to a thought she couldn't escape. When she finally looked away from the flame, she noticed Elly was sleeping sitting up in her bed, leaning against the wall.

"Elly," whispered Tee. Elly didn't stir. Tee furrowed her brow and returned her gaze to the lamp, questioning her decision. Was she just fooling herself into thinking that what she was going to do was okay?

Tee let go of her cradled legs and stretched them out. She stared at the flame a little longer, gathering some confidence. Planting her hands on the edge of the bed, she said, "Elly."

Elly's eyes fluttered open. "Yeah?"

Tee lowered her gaze to the ground and took a deep breath, steeling herself. "Your last name is DeBoeuf."

Elly's face wrinkled as she pushed the sleep away. "No, it's not," she replied groggily.

Tee turned to the flame. "Your last name is DeBoeuf."

Elly thought for a moment. There was a weight to how Tee was saying it that Elly couldn't dismiss. She was awake enough now to know that it was impossible for Tee to be making a mistake. "What are you talking about?"

Tee chewed on her lip before meeting Elly's gaze. Elly was surprised to see none of the defenses that had been there earlier. Despite the black eye and emotional wreckage she could see in Tee's face, there was a drive and determination in Tee's eyes that filled Elly with hope.

"Your mother's real name is DeBoeuf, not Oeuf," said Tee, knowing that her parents wouldn't approve, but thinking that somehow, her Grandpapa would.

Elly shook her head incessantly. "No, no, that doesn't make any sense. We both know when a couple marries, the stronger of the family names becomes the couple's new last name. My dad's last name is Plante. Plante versus DeBoeuf would have been a no-brainer."

Tee stood up and sat beside Elly. She took Elly's hand and stared into her eyes. "Elly, your last name really is DeBoeuf."

Elly studied Tee's conviction, then how Tee was holding her hand. It reminded her of when Tee had learned of the death of Elly's dog, Chichi, and had sat Elly down to tell her before anyone else could.

She bounced her gaze around the room, her brow furrowed in a mix of emotion. "Why would my parents lie like that?" she asked slowly.

Tee let go of Elly's hand and leaned against the wall alongside her. She stared at the flame. She knew she had to be careful with what she shared, but felt there was another piece that Elly deserved to know. That Tee needed her to know. "Your mother's mother is alive."

Elly stared at the flame, too, soaking it all in. "So... Madame DeBoeuf of the Tub is my grandmother?"

Tee nodded gently. "You're more connected to the Tub than I am."

They sat there, staring at the flame in silence, each wondering about similar things.

"Did you have to betray someone to tell me that?" asked Elly.

Tee stared at the ground and shrugged. "I don't know. I don't want to think about it right now. Okay?"

Elly wasn't sure what to make of everything. She watched Tee as she crawled back into her bed. She kept wondering why she hadn't given her best friend a hug for sharing, why things still felt somewhat weird.

As Elly drifted off to sleep, she dreamt of her mother telling her, as she had many times, that noble deeds always came at a price.

———————— ⌒ ————————

As the door opened and Tee stepped through with the early morning light behind her, Franklin had a smug grin on his face. He was sitting on a chair, enjoying a cup of tea at the large oak table, with two fresh pieces of jam-covered toast on his plate.

"Planning on sneaking upstairs so you can pretend to wake up when Elly–" Franklin stopped as he saw Elly come up behind Tee. "Hmm."

Tee gave Franklin a fake smile and nabbed a piece of toast from his plate.

"My toast!" said Franklin, scrambling to get it back from Tee, but she dodged him easily.

"This? This is just bread," said Tee.

Elly closed the inn door and smirked at Franklin, who was shaking his head as Tee headed upstairs to wash.

"You guys were loud for a bit last night. What happened?" he asked, leaning forward. He could tell by the expression on Elly's face that while the gulf between them had shrunk, something was still there.

Elly glanced at the stairs, and then back to Franklin. "Tee had a nightmare. A nasty one," she said, smiling.

"A nightmare?" repeated Franklin in disbelief.

Elly nodded, her eyes going wide. "Yup. Tee dreamt you tried to kiss her." Elly made an ick face.

"Very funny," said Franklin, crossing his arms.

"Horrifying, really," said Elly, nabbing the other piece of toast and heading up the stairs.

Franklin growled. "Fine then! I'm going out for a walk. I'll be back in an hour."

"Knock yourself out," said Elly. "Please."

CHAPTER TWENTY-SIX
KARM'ING HOME

"Just over this next hill," yelled Christina to Mounira as the King's-Horse raced over the grassy plains. Even though they'd been riding the entire day, the ride kept having new thrilling moments.

They'd stopped three times to rest and check how the King's-Horse was doing. On the first stop, Mounira watched Christina do the diagnostics and tighten some of the belts and bolts. By the third time, Mounira was the one doing it, and Christina smiled with pride and took the time to answer questions until she'd completely exhausted her patience.

"What's that?" yelled Mounira as a ruined castle came into view.

Christina tilted her feet backward, slowing the King's-Horse down. "Welcome to my home. This was once the castle of the great city of Karm. Now, it's just Karm, a place long-forgotten."

"Are we in Belnia? I noticed we turned south when we bolted past that second border patrol," said Mounira, remembering the excitement.

Christina chuckled. "That was a bit fun, wasn't it? We're in the kingdom of Myke. It's quite different than its neighbors, but it's home."

Only the ruined castle remained to rise above the grassy plains of what had once been Karm. At the fringes were old forests. It gave the castle a haunted appearance.

"It looks like a giant came along and kicked down the front wall, then hit the towers with a tree. How long ago did this get smashed?" asked Mounira.

Christina brought the mechanical horse to a trot. "That battle was probably three hundred years ago or so."

"You live in a ruined castle in the middle of nowhere? There aren't even any roads to here," said Mounira, remembering the route they'd taken.

"Would you search here for a group of illegal inventors, scientists, and engineers?"

"No," said Mounira, shaking her head as she looked about.

"Exactly," said Christina, dismounting. She opened the King's-Horse's mouth and held the trigger, allowing her to pull it forward.

Mounira sniffed. There was a burned metallic scent in the air. "What's that smell?"

Christina stopped and sniffed the air, then touched the heart-panel, confirming her fear. It was red-hot. "Yig, I think we may have fried the engine." She smiled at

Mounira. "You don't know what that means, do you?"

Mounira wore a cheeky expression. "Yig? No. But you seem guilty, so I'm going to think it's a swear."

Christina shook her head. "No, not at all. It's, um—"

"You know, you're a bad liar," said Mounira. Christina went to help her off the King's-Hors. Mounira pulled away and acrobatically dismounted. "*La la!*"

"Only when I want to be," replied Christina with a half-smile. She then put her fingers to her lips and gave a shrill whistle.

Mounira tried to cover her ears, realizing for the first time that she couldn't with only one arm.

From behind overgrown shrubbery and huge stones fallen from the crumbling castle walls appeared a dozen warriors, armed with crossbows and rifles.

"Mounira, I'd like you to meet my... family," said Christina, not sure how to put it in Frelish.

"Family? I suppose," said a towering, bald man with a chest like a tree trunk. The pointy orange beard at the end of his chin made it look like his fierce face shot fire. "I'm Remy Silskin," he said, bending down on one knee and holding out his hand, palm up, towards the petite Mounira.

Mounira looked at Christina and then at him. There was a look between the two adults that told her they had some bond, but she didn't recognize it. "Um, I'm Mounira of Catalina of Augusto." She studied Remy's hand and wondered. Shrugging, she pointed at it and said, "I don't know what that means."

"Oh," said Remy, smiling and glancing up at Christina. "My palm is facing up, meaning I have nothing to hide, and my fingers are apart, meaning that I am half of the greeting. You complete the greeting."

Mounira smiled and burrowed her brown. She'd never heard of such a thing. "Where I come from, I'd usually slap it or shake it."

"Slap it?" said one of the women with a crossbow, shocked. "That'd get you shot around here, little lady."

Remy shook his tattooed head. In the blink of an eye, his fierce green eyes transformed into the gentlest Mounira had seen. "Don't mind Angelina. She's wary of strangers."

"You're all strange to me," Angelina replied, chuckling.

Mounira put her hand palm down on Remy's, and spread her fingers. Gently Remy curled his fingers up, locking them together, and they shook gently before he released her grip.

"You pick up things fast," said Christina as she slung her backpack over her shoulder and re-closed the saddlebags.

Turning to Angelina and the others, Christina asked, "Can you get this King's-Horse downstairs? Canny and Sonya are going to have a field day with it if the MCM isn't melted. Also, I left something special for them."

"MCM?" asked Remy, staring at the mechanical horse in shock.

"Mercury-copper-magnetic engine," said Mounira proudly. "It's really got some kick to it!"

Remy frowned at Mounira and then Christina. "You found one?"

Christina smiled. "Actually, I found two. The other isn't even sealed. I left it in a saddlebag."

Mounira watched Christina. It was almost as if she was a different person. The hardness that had inhabited her face and speech was missing here. Mounira could tell that Christina was among her family.

"That's… unbelievable," replied Remy. Christina leaned over and gave Remy a kiss on the cheek. He nodded in appreciation. Mounira again detected something, but wasn't sure what it was; it was something she'd not run into before. There was no romance, almost as if they were two magnets that pulled in opposite directions, but still had a bond.

Remy's high-cheekboned face went solemn. "You heard about the palace?"

"That they were bombed from the air, yes. That's why we rushed back," said Christina, very businesslike.

He turned to Mounira, thinking. "I mean no disrespect, little lady, but Christina—why did you bring her here?"

Christina paused, not ready to share why, particularly with *that* audience. "She's by herself, she's smart, and she reminds me of a young Luis." Everyone stopped and stared at Mounira.

"Because she's a Southerner?" asked a male voice in the background.

"No," snapped Christina, "because she's got that spark. She helped me assemble this rocket-cart that we flew off a cliff and used to save some friends."

"She did that?" said Remy, rubbing his chin. "Well, Little Luis, welcome."

"She has done more than that, but let's not get into it," said Christina.

Mounira saw the heads bob in acceptance, bringing a big smile to her face.

"Well," said Remy, putting his hand on Mounira's shoulder, "if you're going to follow in Luis' shoes, you're going to need bigger feet."

"Are you Christina's husband?" Mounira asked, stunning everyone and making Angelina burst into laughter.

"I love this kid!" said Angelina, doubling over.

"Ah…" said Remy, glancing at Christina, confused.

Christina rubbed her forehead. "She asks a lot of questions."

"Can I keep her?" asked Angelina.

———————— ⌒ ————————

Christina watched the members of her various teams stream into the grand hall. It had been a very busy twenty-four hours since she'd returned, and she was anxious to get the all-hands meeting over with. If she was lucky, she'd be able to catch up on some sleep before they had to leave in a few days.

Christina smiled as Mounira came into the room with Remy. Her avowed protector and her sidekick, together. It made her smile deeply for a moment. Her thoughts then turned to Tee. Christina hoped she'd judged the girl correctly, and that she'd find some way to get to Costello safely. It had been a calculated risk—one that, if it went wrong, would have far graver consequences than her personal feelings of guilt.

Christina waved to people she hadn't seen in months. It was strange. They lived in the equivalent of a small town, yet despite there only being two hundred of them, there were some people she didn't see regularly.

She'd given a lot of speeches in the grand hall over the years—some of them uplifting, some of them chilling. All of them had brought her group together more tightly.

The stone floor and high-beamed roof made the great hall feel more like a secret cavern than a place for a royal banquet. The simple pine tables had been pushed against the walls, making it a huge open space. Here they'd celebrated many vow exchanges and births, and mourned too many deaths.

Christina climbed onto the pine table behind her and waved at Mounira. "Come up here with me!" she yelled over the gentle roar of the crowd.

Mounira, surprised, made her way through the crowd and joined her on the table.

Christina paused a moment, appreciating the support from her sidekick.

Mounira offered a sheepish smile. "Don't worry, I won't ask any questions while you're talking. This is just like when one of the royal family would talk to the crowd. I know how to just listen."

Christina was relieved and put her fingers to her mouth, whistling for silence. She quickly scanned the crowd.

"Sonya, is everyone from E.L.F. here?" asked Christina, unable to find a few people.

"Yes!" yelled a brunette, some hundred people back.

"What? You have elves?" said Mounira, chuckling. She suddenly felt all the eyes in the room on her.

Christina's eyes went wide.

Remy stepped forward from the first line of the audience. "The engineering lab is located in the Lower Front. We have different work areas set up in and around, as well as under, this old castle. Each has a name. The folks from E.L.F. are often... tardy," said Remy.

"Not our fault! We're at the other end of this hulking

mess!" yelled Sonya, arriving in time to hear Remy's remark.

"Oh," said Mounira. She smiled at Christina.

"Are you done?" asked Christina, annoyed.

Mounira nodded and then suppressed her urge to ask just one more question.

"Is anyone missing?" Christina asked the crowd.

"Matt and Doug are working on something new in the back. They're running late," said a voice in the back.

Christina shook her head. "As long as nothing explodes this time, I'll be happy," she said to spurts of laughter.

"Do they blow up a lot of things?" asked Mounira, her mouth twisting cutely as she realized she was failing at not asking questions.

Christina realized she was being unfair to Mounira by asking her to act against her nature. Relenting, Christina answered, "Yes. A lot of things. They're our experts in taking something seemingly innocent and turning it into a big mess."

Mounira made a mental note to go and meet these guys. They sounded interesting.

"Okay," said Christina, clapping her hands to calm the crowd back down. "I think almost everyone has met Mounira."

"She reminds me of Luis," said someone.

"She's getting that a lot," said Christina, smiling.

"Moving on. Yesterday we returned with two King's-Horse MCM engines. We've gone from them seeming like items of myth and legend, to having two in our possession."

"Why—"

"BEFORE anyone asks," said Christina, cutting off the question, "the plan was to make our way here with both unused. Then I got this note and it changed everything." She took out a piece of paper from her green vest pocket, and her expression darkened.

A door slammed shut in the back and the room turned to stare at the latecomer. The man's face was covered in black powder, and his hair looked like it had tried to explode away from his face.

"Matt, where's Douglas?" asked Sonya disapprovingly.

"Um... he's not dead, if that's what you're asking... well?" he paused, pretending to think about what had happened. "No, no, I'm sure he's fine. He'll be here soon. We had a little... accident. He's just cleaning up, I think. But, carry on!" said Matt, pointing at Christina.

Mounira smiled. It really did feel like a family. Everyone she'd met so far reminded her of a mix of Anciano Klaus and his wife: some were the explorers of knowledge, and some helped the explorers plan and focus. They were all cogs in a machine they'd built, each helping the other. They were passionate people and full of ideas and opinions. Mounira loved the mealtimes, when they'd gather in large numbers and laugh and fight as much as eat or discuss food. It reminded her a lot of home.

Christina waved the note in her hand. "The castle in Panad has been destroyed. It was attacked from the air, according to the report."

The crowd immediately roared with chatter.

"What... what... what do you mean, destroyed?" said Cantrell, a balding man of modest height and belly. He took off his goggles and put his spectacles on. "Please, don't exaggerate—"

Mounira noticed something in the way he reacted—something just a touch off.

"Canny, I do mean *destroyed*," continued Christina. "Apparently the castle and the city around it are in ruins, and there were few survivors. They were attacked by something that reportedly looked like air balloons."

Cantrell folded his arms, unfolded them, and then folded them again nervously. "That—that makes no sense. Who has that? We don't have that. If we don't have things like that, then... are they coming for us?"

Christina took a deep breath, knowing the weight of what she was about to reveal. "This report came from Piper before she died."

Canny dropped his gaze. Christina and Remy had told him a few hours ago about Pietra Piper's death, but had said they would need to share the details with everyone at the same time.

"Pietra's dead?" whispered voices in the crowd.

"Reports I've received this morning say that the entire royal family of Myke is gone. Given the military action I saw in Freland, I suspect that someone is trying to tighten their grip... and I believe it might not be the Pieman's Fare."

The room hushed, trying to think of what this meant. They'd been focused on crazy royals, the Tub, and Marcus Pieman's Fare as their only enemies for decades, but now there was suddenly a new, and potentially more dangerous, player.

"The few details of the strike make it sound to me like a test of some sort. Something to create *rumor*."

Christina felt for Cantrell, who was still staring at the floor, a red-haired woman rubbing his arm to console him. Christina had known him for about ten years, meeting him when she'd rescued him from a prison camp for Abominators.

Cantrell finally looked up, and Christina continued. "From the second report, which we got this morning, Piper followed the air balloons to a small village called Bodear where she thought they were going to land, but instead they devastated that village. Piper died shortly after giving her report to a courier."

The noise level in the room rose to a dull roar. Christina whistled everyone to silence once again.

"I'm not done. Marcus Pieman has abducted Nikolas

Klaus, and the steam engine plans are still in play."

Someone in the crowd screamed, "We're doomed!"

"No! We're not!" boomed Christina with such decisive force that it silenced the crowd. She pointed at members of the crowd. "Canny, Matt, ELF'ies, I just told you that we have a new enemy and they have airships! What do you have to say to that?"

Mounira smiled at Christina with admiration.

"We… learn to fly," said Cantrell.

"Louder, Canny," yelled Christina.

"We learn to fly!" Canny roared

The crowd went wild.

CHAPTER TWENTY-SEVEN
CRUMBLED GINGER

The Hound had been lost in his agony and failure for days. It felt like an eternity since he'd been wearing Simon St. Malo's shock-gloves, standing on the battlefield with Richelle and the Red Hoods against the Yellow Hoods. For weeks, he'd felt like he mattered, and then in the blink of an eye it had all been taken away. All of the gains he'd made had been wiped out, and now he saw himself as less than nothing.

His sleep was constantly disrupted by pain, but now there was something new—something oddly pleasant. It was like he could somehow push back the demons of agony more easily. He opened an eye to see what force could be so powerful as to do that. He saw Saul across the room in a chair, sleeping, a foot bandaged up. As the Hound started to close his eye, the sensation came again. He summoned up the energy to move his head and saw Gretel. She removed the cloth from his back and dunked it in a bucket of water. She then wrung it out and applied some jellied salve to it before rubbing the lotion onto his back, making the sensation come again. He'd never felt such mercy.

Gretel noticed the Hound gazing at her, and paused for a moment. Over the past several days, she'd gently shaved his face and head, and tended to his wounds with vinegar and pulpy salves. She'd seen his eyes go from showing a hollowed-out soul, to having a glimmer of something when he looked at her. She took comfort in that, feeling that somehow, maybe, she was making amends for all the evil she'd previously done. When she thought of her past actions, they seemed alien to her.

The Hound stared at her, trying to understand how the ruthless archer had changed. He wondered if this was all part of an elaborate trick; he could imagine Hans doing such a thing. As he stared at Gretel, wondering about the dark rings around her eyes, a gentle smile crept across her face.

For Gretel, the nightmares of a yellow-hooded fury seeking revenge had been replaced with blurs of violence and a familiar-seeming figure. It felt like a fog was lifting from her mind, and try as she might, she couldn't get the fog to stay. Each day the nightmares became more vivid. The only thing that gave her any solace was tending to the Hound.

Gretel leaned forward and stroked the Hound's face, calming herself. The Hound tensed up, feeling that in some way she was mocking him in his sorry state.

"Does it feel better when I use the cloth?" Gretel asked softly. There was a hint of approval-seeking in her tone.

The Hound turned his head to the wall and closed his eyes.

Her shoulders dropped.

Then, the dry, gravelly voice of the Hound whispered, "Thank you."

Gretel smiled and fought back the fledgling tears. She looked at everything and nodded to herself, satisfied. She'd done as the medicine lady in the nearby village had instructed her to.

———

Saul watched his sister as she slept outside the doorway, leaning against the cabin. His foot was feeling better, and he was thankful that Gretel had been able to prevent it from getting infected. She had a gentle face, framed by her blond hair. Most of the time, she'd been kind to him, defending him from Hans when needed. Sometimes she was the sense of reason of their trio, and sometimes the instigator of trouble.

Sitting down next to her, he wondered about what Hans had said, and stared at Gretel again. He'd always known that they weren't really triplets, and the more he thought about it, the more he was certain that Gretel had always known, yet she had never treated him any differently.

Gretel started muttering and twitching. Saul recognized the signs of another nightmare. He gently put his hand on his sleeping sister's shoulder. "Gretel, it's okay," he said, hoping to soothe her soul.

Gretel sprang forward, screaming, stumbling around as she shifted from being asleep to being awake. She fell to her knees on the ground and turned around to glare at Saul, rubbing where he had touched her as if it was dirt that wouldn't come off.

"Sorry!" yelled Saul, his hands in the air. "Everything's okay. You were having another nightmare."

She scanned around the clearing and nodded. She pulled her arms in as if she was cold. "The man is getting clearer in my dreams."

"Do you think he's real?" asked Saul.

Gretel's chin trembled and she stared at the ground, nodding.

"Everything is going to be—"

"Don't say that!" screamed Gretel, pointing sharply at Saul. "Stop, please..." she begged. "The man in my nightmare keeps saying that."

Saul's face fell. Though he was only a yard away, he felt a million miles from her. They seemed to be falling apart, as if Mother was the glue that had bound them.

After a couple of minutes of listening to the wind play with the trees, Gretel asked, "Saul, why do I want to just cry?"

Saul tried to answer twice, stopping each time to think. He, too, was having confusing emotions arise; nightmares that felt like strange memories, but when he'd tried to talk to her about it, she'd demanded he stop. Finally, defeated, he said, "I don't know."

Sniffling, Gretel asked, "Can you make me gingerbread cookies, like Hans used to? They always made me feel better."

"I'm sorry," said Saul, staring at the ground. "I don't know how."

Gretel pulled her legs in and put her head on her knees. "I understand. I just want to stay here for a while, okay?"

"Okay," said Saul, standing up with a limp. "I'll check in on the Hound."

As he was about to close the door, he glanced back at Gretel. She wasn't the twenty-year-old fierce warrior he'd known. She was a scared little girl battling the monsters from under her bed.

CHAPTER TWENTY-EIGHT

BADGE OF THE CONVENTIONEER

Nikolas scratched his short, salt-and-pepper beard as he gazed out at the countryside racing by. He'd been impressed with the Neumatic Tube, and the laugh he'd shared with Marcus about Isabella had reminded him of how Marcus used to be when they'd first met.

Nikolas had been fifteen, and on the streets of Teutork, the capital of Teuton, for nearly a year. It had taken him months to flee his homeland after the death of his family. He'd found going from a life of privilege to fighting for scraps horribly difficult. Without even paper and ink, he'd found himself needing to use rocks to scratch out the designs and ideas that built up inside him —ideas that threatened to overpower his young mind. Each time, with the design done, he'd have to destroy it to make sure that he wasn't arrested or killed.

After being robbed and beaten up a few times, he'd learned to throw a punch just well enough to give some bullies and thugs pause. He'd learned more about the nature of humanity over the past two years than he'd ever found in the philosophy books he'd consumed over the years.

Then he'd seen a baker swearing and cursing over a broken wheel for his empty cart and had approached him, asking for some bread in exchange for fixing the wheel. The baker had laughed at Nikolas, seeing his shaggy hair and tattered clothing, but figured why not. "If you get it done before noon, I'll give you ten loaves!"

Rummaging through the crude tools he kept wrapped up in an old cloth bearing a noble crest, Nikolas thought through how to just repair the wheel without making it better. He'd learned that doing otherwise could be dangerous. He needed to fix it just enough so that the merchant would be happy, but not enough to get himself noticed.

As Nikolas reached over to grab a tool, he noticed a pair of polished black boots with silver buckles walking towards him. Sitting on the ground, the young Nikolas Klaus looked way up at the nobleman standing before him.

"Doing some repairs today?" asked the tall man as he crouched down. He had long brown hair done in a ponytail and a clean-shaven face. He wore a blue jerkin and white pantaloons, covered by a black cloak that was pinned to his left shoulder with a gold brooch.

Nikolas immediately recognized the gold brooch. "You're a Conventioneer," said Nikolas nervously. Most of them were not satisfied just to have their scientific endeavors protected by the crown. They also actively hunted down others who were not so protected and turned them in. He trembled.

Marcus nodded and smiled. "Yes, and I can see by the expression on your face that you have heard stories or had some bad experiences with other ones. I'm not like any of them."

Nikolas peeked around the stranger at the three people standing around him, all dressed with frills and in bright colors.

"Those are my assistants," said Marcus. "I can see that makes you more nervous."

"You must be important," said Nikolas.

"In the eyes of some, yes," said Marcus.

"Sir Pieman, we don't have time for this," said one of the aids. "There are street rats everywhere. Why talk to this one? Or any of them for that matter?"

The thirty-year-old Marcus glanced over his shoulder at the man, and then at the one beside him. "Joshua, you are now my secretary." He turned to look at the first man. "Warren, I relieve you of your responsibilities and salary."

As the two men argued behind him, Marcus turned back to look at the frozen teenager. "What's your name?"

Nikolas' eyes were glued to the gold brooch.

"They call it the Badge of the Conventioneer. It

protects you, but means you are committed to upholding clean thinking and improvements for society, and eliminating deviant behavior. Have you heard of Abominators?" asked Marcus.

The boy nodded nervously.

"Has anyone ever called you one?"

Nikolas stared blankly at Marcus, unsure of how to respond.

"In this kingdom of Teuton," said Marcus, gesturing to everything around them, "I am the right hand of the High Conventioneer." Marcus then changed languages. "Am I right in guessing you are from Brunne?"

The boy frowned. "You speak Tyroli? Why didn't you speak Brunnif? And you knew this, how?"

"Little things," said Marcus, smiling. "Everyone of noble birth speaks Tyroli as well as at least Brunnif. The wrench you have in your little set of tools—it's got a curve in it. I assume you made it, but that curve is a Brunne artifact. If you made it, and given your age, it means you are tied to that land." Marcus smiled.

The boy smiled. Then it evaporated just as quickly. "You've done a trick on me, yes? You are going to arrest me now?" he asked, his eyes filling with fear.

Marcus shook his head. "No. I have been looking for you, however. There are friends of mine who noticed you in recent weeks. Your family is dead, I assume."

"Yes," said Nikolas, glancing at the men behind

Marcus and passersby, who were shaking their heads.

Marcus read every twitch and move of Nikolas' face, and then gave him a compassionate smile. "My family were killed. This badge," he said in Tyroli, tapping it, "I hate it. But I *will* change the world and never let this happen again. Would you like to help me?"

For the first time in a long time, the young Nikolas felt hope.

"Come, you're part of my household now," said Marcus, standing, his hand outstretched.

Nikolas stared at it, thinking. Taking a leap of faith, he shook Marcus' hand.

"Do you have a family?" asked Nikolas.

Marcus nodded as they started walking. "Yes, I do. I have two little boys and a lovely wife. I won't treat you as a son though. From this moment on, you are my long-lost little brother."

Nikolas smiled at that idea.

———————

Four years later, Nikolas beamed with pride alongside Marcus' wife Richelle and their sons, as the King finished his speech and declared Marcus an official King's-Men and High Conventioneer.

Marcus smiled at being given the odd title. He had a running joke with Nikolas about it. They found it silly that it was considered plural yet used for singular appointments, how it was still hyphenated as if the term was new, yet it had been around for hundreds of years.

To Marcus, it was one more element of society that made no sense and needed to be remolded by reason and vision.

He turned to wave at the large crowd of applauding friends, admirers, and political enemies. The attempts to trip him up or take him down had failed. Marcus had proven himself to be as much a genius in the realm of people as in the realm of chemistry and devices.

As the music started and the celebration got underway, Richelle and their sons came to congratulate him. Hugging his family, Marcus noticed Nikolas standing at a distance. He waved him over and gave Nikolas a very public handshake before addressing anyone else. He was sending a clear message to all that touching Nikolas would have the same consequences as coming after him. Until that point, Marcus had avoided such public displays, although their close friendship wasn't a secret.

A few years later, Nikolas had been walking the streets of Teutork, his well-worn Badge of the Conventioneer visible on his green vest. With his maroon shirt and brown pants, Nikolas reminded many that Conventioneers were not known for dressing particularly well. He'd gotten better, according to Isabella, who was finding it less and less necessary to walk Nikolas home to change before they were allowed to start their dates. Twice he'd absentmindedly shown up in a blacksmith's apron and goggles, for which Isabella had gotten teased by her friends and family.

To many, the brooch marked Nikolas as a dangerous beast who, though leashed by the monarchy, was still to be watched carefully. Despite Marcus' successes in strengthening the laws protecting Conventioneers and working to humanize them in the eyes of people, many still dared to throw rocks, tomatoes, or worse. This would land those individuals in prison, and their family homes would be demolished. Nikolas had thought the practice extreme until he'd narrowly survived a mob attack that killed three of his Conventioneer friends. It happened with disturbing regularity.

Marcus was locked in a political war, trying to position himself as the regent for the ailing, heirless King. He and Nikolas had to be extra careful. Instead of the brainstorming sessions they'd held together, Nikolas had taken to walking the streets whenever he needed to design something. It allowed him to build the illegal contraptions in his imagination where they were safe from prying eyes.

Under Marcus' leadership, the Conventioneers had provided significant improvements in sanitation and other simple areas of urban life. Those that risked investigating where all the money and resources went, trying to determine if Marcus actually did have the rumored secret laboratories spread throughout the kingdom, often went missing or found themselves jailed for treason. It was one of the many things that Nikolas tried to ignore, as Isabella advised he should.

Out of the corner of his eye, Nikolas caught sight of someone running into an alley, quickly followed by two big, drunken hooligans.

Nikolas scanned around the deserted street. He hadn't been paying attention to where he was walking. He'd managed to get all the way over to the poor, rough eastern edge of the capital. Nikolas wasn't much of a fighter, but as with many things, Marcus had required him to learn at least the fundamentals.

Turning into the mouth of the dirty alley, Nikolas saw a white-haired man about his age, dressed in rags, with fresh blood dripping from his face. He was on his knees, one arm protecting his face and the other trying to wave off the hooligans.

"Please, leave me alone. You've had your fun," said the man desperately. Nikolas recognized the man's accent as being from Tyrol, the neighboring kingdom to the east of Brunne.

The taller of the two thugs laughed and tightened his grip on a wooden club, while the other man wound up to deliver a kick.

Nervously pushing his spectacles up on his nose, Nikolas said, "You now start leaving him alone, yes?" His voice was more like a loud whisper than a booming command like Marcus issued, and his words were more jumbled than usual.

The kicker stopped and gave Nikolas a confused frown, as if a flea had spoken. In a slurred, drunken voice, he yelled, "Hello there, professor! Oh, look, you've even got a shiny bit on you! I think I'll have that." He started walking over to Nikolas, who quickly started fussing with something up his puffy sleeves.

"Give me your shiny thing and leave, and maybe I won't beat you senseless," said the thug, towering over Nikolas by a good four inches. He tapped the Conventioneer's brooch.

"No," said Nikolas firmly.

The hooligan chuckled, then noticed Nikolas had something wooden in his hands. "What do you have there?"

Nikolas closed his eyes. "Please, do not make me hurt you, yes?"

"Hey, this guy's threatening me with three little planks of wood."

"Make him eat them," said the other hooligan.

"Oh, I like that idea," said the tall hooligan, smiling down on Nikolas.

Nikolas opened his eyes and thrust his hands forward. As he did so, the compressed springs keeping the three wooden panels together released their energy, and expanded so quickly into the face of the thug that it knocked him clean off his feet.

Nikolas yelped in pain as the mechanism in his sleeve

twisted unexpectedly. "Well, it's field-tested now," Nikolas said to himself as he hastily tried to take it off.

The remaining hooligan gestured in disbelief at Nikolas. "What did you just do?! You're... you're an another Abomy! You're a freaking Abominator!" He tightened his grip on his club as he moved towards Nikolas.

His fear gone, Nikolas saw the man's bouncy lunge in as if in slow motion. Nikolas ran at him, timing his tackle perfectly and catching the huge man off guard and off balance.

"There!" yelled a woman at the mouth of the alley, as Nikolas got to his feet.

He sighed heavily and tensed up as he saw five guards enter the alley, and then was surprised to find that the woman's voice he'd heard had been Isabella's.

Helping the stranger up, Nikolas noticed something in his eyes. He leaned close to the man and whispered in Tyroli, "Are you one of the hunted, as I was?"

The man stared at his hero in disbelief. He'd never seen a man do what this one had done—never mind someone who was clearly like himself—sticking his neck out for a stranger. He nodded nervously.

Nikolas hastily removed his Badge of the Conventioneer and pinned it on the man.

The stranger looked at Nikolas in wide-eyed confusion.

"What's going on here?" the lead guard asked Nikolas and the stranger, as the other guards restrained the thugs.

"This man is a Conventioneer," said Nikolas, sweating as he tried to sound confident. Lying was not in his blood, but it was another survival skill that he'd learned from Marcus.

The lead guard looked over the raggedy and bloody man.

"You don't look like one," said the guard, tapping on the brooch to check it was genuine.

"They did this to me," said the man, pointing at the hooligans.

"He's an Abomy! A freaking Abomy!" yelled the recently-tackled hooligan, pointing in the general direction of Nikolas and the stranger.

"I guess he means you," said the guard to the stranger.

"Sir, I found this," said one of the guards, carrying Nikolas' arm-brace and expanded wooden panels.

"Is this yours?" the lead guard asked the stranger.

"Yes," said the stranger.

"What is it?"

Nikolas interrupted. "It is a jack-in-the-box trick. That is all; see the wood and the springs. He was going to... an important birthday party. He used it to surprise one of those men, yes?" He kicked himself as his words stumbled.

The lead guard held up the apparatus. "That seem like an Abominator thing to you?" he asked the other guard.

"If it is, it's not one worth explaining to the captain," he replied.

"It's a weapon!" yelled one of the hooligans. "He broke my friend's jaw!"

"Yeah, he broke my jaw! It's all broken and stuff!"

"Take them away," said the lead guard. "And who are you?" he asked Nikolas.

"I can vouch for that man. He's my fiancé and well known to Lord Marcus Pieman, High Conventioneer," said Isabella in a commanding voice.

Nikolas' eyes went wide. *Fiancé?*

The lead guard looked at her, then back at Nikolas. "Sorry, sir. Shouldn't you have a brooch on? It's illegal to be out without one, if you're a Conventioneer."

"Him? A Conventioneer? He's a librarian," said Isabella, wrapping her arm around him. "Notice the bookish, boyish expression?"

Nikolas smiled and pushed his glasses up.

The guard nodded at them and walked off.

Isabella kissed Nikolas on the cheek and said, "I accept your engagement proposal." She gave him a devilish smile before turning to the other man. "What's your name?"

The man blinked twice and smiled at the nobly-dressed young woman, and then at his own blood-stained, tattered clothing. "My name is Christophe," he said proudly, straightening up. "Christophe Creangle."

"Well, given that you will be keeping that badge if Nikolas has anything to say about it, you better get used to adding your title at the end, Conventioneer," whispered Isabella.

The man winced at the designation. Nikolas recognized the expression. It told him that the stranger had been through a lot, likely by trying to escape those who sought to turn him in for being an Abominator, or blackmail him for it.

"Christophe Creangle, Conventioneer," Nikolas said, smiling appreciatively.

CHAPTER TWENTY-NINE

GRIMY ROOF

Abeland had fallen asleep much faster than he'd expected to. The foursome had fled south, stopping at a little roadside inn near the Laros Republic border town of Wosa. The journey had been quick, as they'd managed to borrow some horses and a cart from one of his neighbors on a promise of future payment. He had a plan, but had only shared the smallest of pieces to Bakon and the others, just enough to get them to agree to go along.

A floorboard creaked, and he instantly ascended from the deepest sleep to fully awake. He scanned around the dark room and silently rolled out of bed onto his hands and feet. He could hear boots moving about and muffled voices; then he heard someone curse.

"He bit me!" yelled someone.

"Abeland!" warned Richy from the adjacent room.

Two soldiers kicked in Abeland's bedroom door and rushed in, lanterns and pistols in hand. After a quick glance about the empty room, one of them checked under the bed.

The captain worked his way through the hallway full

of soldiers and into the room.

"He's not here, sir," said Grimes.

Snapping his fingers, the captain pointed. "The window's open, you lunker. He went out the window," he said, shoving Grimes at it.

Abeland scrambled to the top of the inn's peaked roof, and scouted about. He watched as Richy, Bakon, and Egelina-Marie were brought out of the inn and led towards a red-hooded woman on horseback. She had a dozen soldiers on horses, and another dozen on foot, spread out around the small inn. They'd come prepared.

"Freeze!" yelled Grimes, climbing onto the roof. He was hunched over, clearly terrified.

The sudden boost of adrenaline made Abeland feel more sure-footed than he'd been in a while. "Not in this weather. I'm fine, actually. How about you?" he asked the nervous, pistol-holding soldier.

Grimes was confused. "What? I'm... I'm fine," he replied, stumbling. "But that's not what I meant."

Like a cat leaping upon a mouse, Abeland tackled him, sending the man screaming and rolling to the edge of the roof. Abeland quickly picked up the pistol and watched the lantern roll off and shatter below. "It's not that far of a drop. You'll be fine-ish."

"Abeland," came a booming female voice, surprising him. "I know you're up there."

"Help!" yelled Grimes.

"Please, we're trying to have a conversation. How can I hear the woman if you're interrupting like that?" said Abeland, scowling at Grimes. "You've got at least two minutes before your arms give out. Come on, man, buck up."

Grimes nodded, not sure what he was expected to do.

Abeland walked over to the west edge of the roof. "So, it's the red-hooded woman," he said to himself, seeing her raise a speaking-trumpet to her lips, its bronze shining in all the lantern-light.

"I will have my men shoot your friends if you are not down in a minute, starting with this one," she said, pointing at Bakon.

Abeland studied the pistol in his possession for a moment. "Hey, Dangler! What's the reliable range on this?"

"Are you seriously asking me?" said Grimes.

"Sorry, did it sound humorous? I was being serious," he replied.

"About fifty yards. Why am I answering you?"

"I was afraid of that," said Abeland, staring at the pistol. He sighed with disappointment as he determined the distance to be too great. "And you're answering because,"—Abeland reached down and offered a hand —"good behavior is often rewarded."

"Thank you," said Grimes, grabbing Abeland's hand.

"Not this time, though," he added, smacking Grimes

in the head with the pistol.

Immediately, several soldiers ran to try to catch their colleague.

Abeland quickly climbed down, returning to his room. Just then, he heard a sound he was all too familiar with, as the bottom floor whooshed ablaze. He bolted down the stairs and jumped out a window.

By the time he got to his feet, the red-hooded woman and her entourage were upon him.

"I don't think we've had the pleasure," said Abeland, brushing himself off and handing over the pistol to the soldier stepping forward for it.

"Oh, we have, actually," said the hooded woman. "Mind you, it doesn't matter. I really should thank you, on behalf of your father and all your collective work, for laying all the groundwork for our grand return."

Abeland furrowed his eyebrows. There was something distinct and familiar about her voice. He studied the gold embroidery on the edges of her cloak. "Fair enough, I suppose?"

"Hmm, funny," she replied with sharp disdain. "You know, I was prepared for your antics, though to be honest, I'm surprised you're still doing them at *your* age. Now, to the business of shooting your friends and bringing you for a very public trial. See, I remember how you like an audience."

Abeland waved for her to stop talking, surprising everyone with his audacity. "They're not my friends, and to be more specific, you wouldn't want to shoot the one you're pointing at."

The woman cocked her head to the side. "Now why would that be?"

Abeland smiled. "Because, Cat, he's your son."

CHAPTER THIRTY

WOLF IN SHEEP'S CLOTHING

Despite a good morning workout together, things remained awkward between Elly and Tee. Elly resisted the urge to bombard Tee with questions, but found herself unable to simply accept things as they were; she needed answers. Part of her feared that Tee wouldn't give them to her, and that the gulf between them would remain forever. Elly was also wracked with guilt for having made Tee tell her what she had.

Tee's mind was clouded with the implications of the decision she'd made. Had she done it for Elly or for herself? Had she done the right thing, or had she taken the easy route?

"Shall we stop for a bit?" asked Elly.

Tee nodded.

"I'll be back in a couple of minutes. I want to explore around a bit. You two rest," said Franklin.

Once he was out of sight, Tee took out the map and

asked Elly to come over.

"Are we lost again?" asked Elly, concerned. "Because Franklin's going to have a field day if we are."

"No, we're fine. I wanted to show you something," said Tee, her gut twisting with apprehension for what she was about to do.

Elly plunked herself down on the forest floor beside the yellow-hooded Tee. "Hello, crazy map."

Tee made a funny, scrunched up face at her. "Hello, Elly," she said in a funny voice.

"Hi, Map!" said Elly, pretending to be an excited little kid.

"I have a secret to tell you," said Tee, shaking the map back and forth as if it was dancing.

"Really, Mister Map? What is it?" said Elly.

Tee paused for a moment. Elly glanced at her, wondering what she was thinking. Tee said, in her regular voice, "You can read it."

Elly was about to respond, but stopped as she noticed Tee wasn't joking.

Tee dropped her hands and nodded. "You can read this."

Elly picked up the map and shook her head. "I can't make any sense of this. It's just mumble jumble."

"Well, you don't read it that way," said Tee.

"What are you talking about?" asked Elly, studying it again.

Tee took a deep breath, trying to settle her nerves. "Read it like it's in a mirror."

Shaking her head, Elly shrugged. "It still doesn't make any sense."

"Pretend you're looking in a mirror, and think of the Yoyo code we've been using since we were little."

Elly gave Tee a serious stare, as Tee sighed and stared at the ground. Elly was scared to look at the map now. Her sense of guilt mounted as she forced her eyes on it. Elly mouthed the letters as she translated each character. "That… why?" she said, unable to get a clear thought out as she realized she could read the words, though very slowly.

Tee choked up. "I… ah… I couldn't leave you behind."

"But this goes back—"

"To when we were little, I know."

"But we still use this," said Elly. She stared at the ground, holding on to her emotions. "But…" she wasn't able to complete the thought.

"Enough gabbing, ladies, let's get a move on!" yelled Franklin. "There's a shortcut to Herve from here."

<hr>

Tee had never been in the forests near the northern coast of Freland. The leafy canopy was even higher than in the Red Forest, and there were some tree species she'd only ever heard about from her mother. The part of Tee that would have normally been curious to examine them didn't even hint at being present.

Today, everything seemed to remind her of her parents, and she kept imagining different versions of the discussion that would one day happen regarding what she'd revealed to Elly. Tee went up to the widest tree she could find and gave it a knock, carrying on a Baker family superstition that the vibrations would make their way to her parents to let them know she was okay.

"This seems as good a place as any for a break," said Franklin as they entered a sunken clearing. It looked as if a giant had scooped up some land with both hands, leaving brush all around it.

Elly frowned at the circle of stones making a fire pit in the middle of the clearing. "That's convenient."

"It happens. Though," said Tee, scanning around, "I haven't seen one in a sunken area before." There was something about it that bothered her.

Remembering one of the important lessons Pierre de Montagne had given them, Elly went and checked the ashes. She pushed them around with a stick, then felt some with her hand. "There's dampness. No one's been here in a couple of days, I think."

"See," said Franklin, smiling, "we're safe. Anyway, I'm hungry." Franklin opened the small sack holding his food and sat down by the fire pit.

Elly followed suit. "Tee?" she asked, hesitating to take her first bite.

Tee gradually brought her eyes to focus on Elly. "I'm

just… I'm just tired, I guess," she said, walking over and joining them.

Franklin finished first, having devoured his sandwich, and stood up excitedly. "Elly, let's get some fresh water. There's a creek just about two minutes from here."

Elly was only halfway through her sandwich. "In a minute."

"No, come on. You can finish it as we go," urged Franklin.

Concerned, Elly looked at Tee for her approval.

Tee shrugged. "I'll be fine."

"Come on, Elly," said Franklin, gesturing. "It'll give Miss Gloomy Gus here a moment to herself."

Unable to find a reason why not, Elly wrapped her sandwich back up. "I'm not that hungry, anyway. I don't know about you, Tee, but I'm going through my water faster than I'd thought."

"It's okay," said Tee, "go. I could use the rest."

"Okay," said Elly hesitantly. "We'll be back in five minutes, tops."

"Tops," repeated Franklin, showing a hint of a grin.

After Elly and Franklin left, Tee went to grab an apple from her backpack when she noticed the two pairs of shock-sticks still in there. Tee kicked herself for forgetting to give Elly hers.

Tee paced around the stones, the two sets of shock-sticks in her hands, trying to figure out which way they'd gone. Giving up, she put the shock-sticks into the secret pouches in her cloak, figuring that they'd be back soon enough. She closed up her backpack and picked up the apple she'd dropped.

Just as Tee was about to take a bite of her apple, something in the brush caught her eye. Tee pulled down her hood and crouched, closing her cloak around her arms.

"It's been far too long, Mademoiselle Tee, or should I call you 'The Little Yellow Hood'?" said the smooth and hauntingly familiar voice. "Your cloak must be new. I don't remember it shining in the light like that."

Tee's eyes darted around the brush line as she heard branches snapping all around. "Care to reveal yourself?"

"Oh, I will. Give me a moment, I don't move as well as I used to. Mind you, I have you to thank for that, now don't I?"

A chill ran through Tee. "LeLoup?"

Two rough-looking bandits stepped out of the brush, pistols pointing at Tee. They started slowly walking down the edges of the bowl-shaped clearing towards her.

With his men in place, LeLoup stepped out of the brush. It took Tee a moment to recognize him, given he was well-dressed with a triple-barreled pistol resting against his shoulder. "Ah, you know, it is so nice to be remembered," he said, grinning sinisterly from ear to ear.

"You've got some new clothes," said Tee awkwardly.

LeLoup gave her a disapproving look. "Really?" He gestured to his men. "That's not the retort I expected. I was expecting something more like…" LeLoup started to pace a bit, staying more than five yards from Tee. "Like 'Oh, LeLoup, I almost killed you last time and this time I'll finish the job.' Or maybe something like…" He tapped his pistol to his lips. "I don't know, I can't think of everything. I've been looking forward to this so much. But *that* line? You're already ruining it."

Shaking his head at Tee, he sighed and continued. "I'd like to introduce you to the Liar. That's the name of this little toy of mine. Remember me telling you how I wanted to introduce you to it? Well, here it is. State of the art in modern firearms. It'll kill you very well—very well indeed."

"Franklin," said Tee, with defeat in her voice.

LeLoup frowned at her. "That was rude. I was introducing you to the Liar, and you changed the subject."

"Franklin did this," said Tee, frustrated.

"Who?" asked LeLoup, frowning at his men playfully. "Oh, the Watt boy. The one who is going to give me the steam engine plans that I will take to Simon St. Malo and complete the mission I was originally given? That boy has a real future. He might even be better than Klaus ever was, who knows? But what am I saying. I have no idea who you're talking about," said LeLoup, chuckling menacingly.

Tee glanced at the two henchmen standing a yard behind her, one on each side.

"Now, mademoiselle, if you'd be so kind as to stand up and drop those sticks that I know are in your hands. I don't care if Franklin said that you don't have any. I know you're more resourceful than that." LeLoup pointed his pistol at Tee. "This," —he waved the gun at Tee—"this feels like old times, doesn't it?"

Tee stood, but did nothing else.

LeLoup growled. "You're going to make this difficult, aren't you? Allow me to show you what the Liar can do." He pointed it at a tree and blew a huge chunk out of it. He then pointed at another tree and blew a chunk out of it. "Repeating pistol, rotating its barrels. Two shots per barrel. Lovely little thing. Has a bit of a kick, but when you have a temper like that, what can you expect?"

At the sound of the shots, Elly dropped her wineskin in the creek and started running. "Tee!"

Franklin ran after her, tackling her. "She's going to be okay! He's just going to put a scare in her."

Rolling over, Elly kicked Franklin squarely in the left eye. Franklin screamed as Elly got back to her feet.

"You have no idea what you've done!" she yelled, running. Elly already felt guilty for not trusting her instincts and for forcing Tee to tell her things. Now she was adding to it with the knowledge that she had abandoned Tee when she knew that Tee wasn't at her best.

As Elly got to the brush-edge of the clearing, she saw Tee standing with her hands in the air and what appeared to be shock-sticks at her feet.

"LeLoup!" whispered Elly, turning to see Franklin only a couple of yards away and closing quickly. "Do you have any idea what you did?"

One of the henchmen glanced up at the bushes.

"Don't get distracted," LeLoup told his henchmen. "The Watt boy knows the deal. He'll take care of the other Hood."

"So Tee— oh, how rude of me; may I call you Tee?" LeLoup asked.

Tee shrugged.

"Stop that! Stop it!" he yelled, firing into the air. "Are you even her?" he growled. "Maybe I should just skip all of this, kill you, and see whether or not I've spoiled my fun. You sound like Tee, but you aren't acting like her."

Franklin glared at Elly, rubbing his eye. "He works for my father! He's going to take us to him after we get the plans. He just wants to put a scare into Tee. He said he owed her, and frankly, I think she deserves it."

Tears of rage streamed down Elly's face. "You are the world's biggest idiot! He's going to kill her!"

Franklin scoffed, reaching for Elly.

"Stop right there, or so help me, I'll make your black eye the best-looking part of you," said Elly, her fists at the ready.

"You stop and look at them," said Franklin, pointing. "He's just scaring her." Part of him felt for Elly and wondered if he'd done the right thing, but he knew he was in too deep to change anything.

Tee glanced up at the moving brush and caught a glimpse of Elly's yellow cloak. Hesitating for a moment, she pulled her hood back.

"It... it is you," said LeLoup, surprised and disappointed. "You... you look terrible. What happened to you?"

Tee dropped her gaze to the ground. She seemed completely defeated. "Do what you're going to do, as long as you let my friend live."

LeLoup rubbed his free hand into his forehead angrily. "This isn't... this isn't how it's supposed to go! You were supposed to fight, and then with the last shot, I would win with the Liar." He glared at Tee. "Put your hood back up! I can't stand looking at that face." He nodded to one of his henchmen. "Ruffo, pick up those sticks."

Tee raised her hood back up and dropped her hands to her sides quickly, the cloak swallowing them from sight.

"Oh no," whispered Elly to herself. The guilt in her head pounded as she saw Tee's shoulders slump and her head bow slightly. "She's not going to fight back. She's going to let him kill her."

"She's fine," said Franklin to Elly, making a grab for

her.

Elly bolted out of the brush, screaming, "Tee!"

Tee and Elly instantly locked eyes. Elly saw the wolf that was hiding in Tee's sheepish appearance.

Without a thought, LeLoup turned and fired repeatedly.

One shot hit soil, one hit a tree, and then blood flew and Elly went spinning in the air, crumbling to the ground in a soundless heap.

Tee screamed like a vengeful god awakened in pain. She flipped over the shock-sticks on the ground, picked them up, and broke one of Ruffo's ribs as she hit him in the chest, shocking him. She threw the other shock-stick, hitting the remaining henchman squarely in the jaw, dropping him as well.

LeLoup laughed maniacally. "THAT's the Tee I was looking—" LeLoup leveled the Liar at Tee, and stopped as her brown eyes drilled fear directly into his soul. He took a step back, trying to reaffirm his grip on the Liar as his hands became slick with sweat.

Tee reached into her cloak and pulled out the other two shock-sticks, her predatory eyes locked on LeLoup. She yelled as she ran at him.

LeLoup backed up more and more. He tried firing at Tee, but nothing happened. He was out of bullets.

Franklin ran down and glanced at Elly in horror. Instantly his mind was filled with terrible regret. "This is going all wrong. She's… she's going to kill him!" His eyes welling up with tears, he stared at Tee. He remembered seeing how she'd lost control after Pierre's death, and hearing about what happened in Elly's house. Running as fast as he could for Tee, Franklin screamed, "Stop! Tee, stop!"

LeLoup pulled back on the Liar's lever to get the secret, extra bullet, and it jammed. Tee smacked the pistol out of LeLoup's hands.

"Stop, Tee!" repeated Franklin, only a few yards away and closing fast.

Tee whipped a shock-stick at Franklin, sending him skidding to the ground, flailing about as electricity coursed through his body. She turned her fiery gaze on LeLoup. He was whimpering, clutching his broken hand. She wasn't anything like he'd remembered or imagined. *Had she been so fierce during our first encounter? Had she been holding back?* he wondered.

Tee walked over and picked up the Liar, pulling back hard on the lever and hearing the click of the bullet finding its home. She pointed it at LeLoup, her head a swirl of noise and rage, with images of Pierre's death and Elly's tumble through the air seared in her mind's eye.

"No!" screamed LeLoup, trying to scramble backward. "Please!" He felt whatever it was that had broken inside him on their first encounter break a little more.

Tears streamed down Tee's face as she steadied the

pistol with her other hand. "You just took everything from me!" she screamed.

"Tee," whispered Elly, her voice cutting through everything and grabbing Tee's attention. Tee whacked LeLoup in the head, and fired the pistol at a tree, before dashing to Elly's side, repeating her name.

Elly was face down, curled into a tight ball. Her yellow-hooded cloak was splattered with red and dirt. "It hurts so much, Tee," whispered Elly.

Tee stuttered as she tried to clear her head. She wanted to scream and cry and yell and laugh, all at the same time. Seeing Elly's clenched jaw and tightly-closed eyes gave Tee focus. "I—I need to examine your wound. I need to roll you over," she said, trying to remember the brief medical lessons that her Granddad, Samuel Baker, had once given her.

"I don't know if I can do that, Tee," cried Elly, grabbing Tee's hand, nearly crushing it.

Tee wiped Elly's tears with her free hand. "You can do this. We're going to do this, okay? We still have that no dying rule, remember?"

"Oh yeah," said Elly, wincing. "The no dying rule."

Tee surveyed Elly, trying to figure out the optimal movement. "I'm going to help you," said Tee, placing her hands on Elly. "When you're ready."

Elly took a pained breath and steeled herself. "Okay, now."

Tee carefully rolled Elly over onto her back and straightened out her legs. Elly did her best to suppress her screams.

Peeling back the yellow cloak, Tee saw that Elly's blouse was blood-soaked. It was clear the bullet had gone through her left side. Tee stopped herself from touching it. "I'll be right back," she said, darting over to her backpack and bringing it to Elly's side.

Tee took out the small block of soap from the mobile medical kit she'd taken from the lab, and used the water from her wineskin to wash her hands properly. She then took out the vinegar and rubbed her hands in some.

"I… I know what to do," said Tee, her hands trembling as she reached for the blouse. "I can fix this. I'll save you. Please don't die, Elly."

"I should have—" said Elly, sobbing.

Tee shushed her. "Stop. Don't say that. Whatever it was, don't say it, okay? Let's just talk about stupid stuff, okay?"

CHAPTER THIRTY-ONE
LOOSE ENDS

Simon walked into the library, yawning. The two large cups of black tea that he'd had at breakfast had yet to make their presence known. He wished he could drink something stronger, but his stomach couldn't handle it.

"Sir," said Cleeves, greeting Simon at the entrance. "There's a letter."

Simon glared at Cleeves, expecting to see it on a silver dish. "Well, where is it?"

Cleeves hesitated. "It's in your study, sir." He pointed with an old, crooked finger.

"Why did you put it there?" asked Simon, annoyed. He prepared to march over and retrieve it when Cleeves motioned for him to stop.

"I didn't, sir. I…" Cleeves pointed at the study's inner office. "I found it there."

Simon knew his servant to be many things, but liar or joker wasn't among them. He looked up at the skylights, then over at the front double doors.

"Were they locked when you got in this morning?"

"Yes, sir," replied Cleeves. "And I locked them properly when I left last night, as always."

Simon scanned around, trying to see something out of the ordinary. A chill ran through him as he started to slowly make his way to the office doors.

No one had *ever* breached his library. In addition to the official guards, he had secret guards. Added to that, he had devices and contraptions designed to detain, or even maim, anyone who tried to break in.

As he turned the corner, he noticed that the ornate white door to the office was halfway ajar. He turned to Cleeves, who put his white-gloved hands up.

"I didn't touch it. I closed the doors last night when I left, and locked them. When I came in this morning, it was like that. I was able to just barely get my head through and see that there was a letter on your desk. I then waited for you to arrive."

Simon sighed and nodded. "You did the right thing, Cleeves. I'll be back."

When Simon reappeared a minute later, he was carrying a long, thin piece of wood. He carefully shoved the thick door open with it. Stepping in, he studied every detail. There was not a single thing he could detect out of place. The only thing different was the letter on his desk, leaning against two books that had been there the day before.

Simon carefully walked around his desk, scrutinizing every detail of the floor. He then started examining the walls and ceiling. Finally, he went in front of the letter and bent down so that he was eye level with it. Even the dust on his desk appeared to have been undisturbed. Seeing his full and proper name spelled out sent a shiver down his spine, as not even Marcus knew it.

Taking a deep breath, he gently removed the letter and broke the blank seal on the back.

"Are you not afraid it's poisoned, sir?" asked Cleeves nervously, standing at the door.

Simon paused as he was about to remove the letter. "If—" Simon stopped, deciding not to say her name. "If the red-hooded woman or a member of the real Fare wanted me dead, I'd be dead already."

"If I may, sir, do you suspect that I put the letter there?" asked Cleeves, afraid of Simon's wrath.

Simon gave him a half-smile. "No. At the end of the day, Cleeves, you are family. Love you or hate you, you're here because I solemnly believe that ultimately, you have my best interests at heart."

The old, sickly-looking man stood a bit more proudly. He couldn't remember getting a compliment from Simon before. It was in that moment that he realized just how scared Simon truly was.

Simon leaned against the front of his desk and read the letter. He straightened up and took a step forward. "They have Abeland and some of his friends in prison, including one of Klaus' little Yellow Hoods. Apparently, they believe they've killed Richelle." He stopped and held the letter to his chest. "That's interesting," he said to himself, thinking of the red-hooded woman. "I doubt it, anyway. That whole family is extremely difficult to kill."

"Can they truly have become so powerful that they could capture and kill Piemans?" asked Cleeves, closing the door out of fear of being overheard.

Simon turned his gaze to the old man. "I guess they've walked in Marcus' shadow long enough. Now they are ready to strike. I thought it dangerous of them to have me hire LeLoup and send him after Klaus. We were lucky to have survived *that* catastrophe. I'm guessing they are tying things up, making their big moves now. We're going to need to be extra careful." Simon moved to the next page of the letter.

As he moved to the final page, Simon's face flushed and he crumpled the letter after finishing it. He gazed angrily at a spot on the floor.

Cleeves fidgeted as he waited for the explosion Simon always had after such expressions. "What is it, sir?" he asked, unable to take the burning silence.

Simon yanked his gaze up from the floor and locked it on Cleeves. "They know things, Cleeves. They know things that they shouldn't know, and are asking too much of me. If there's one thing I will do before I die, I will get them for this.

"I'm going to need you to take a letter to Marcus."

CHAPTER THIRTY-TWO

THE GREAT ESCAPE

Nikolas, Christophe, and Marcus knew it would be only a matter of time before the King or one of the other Conventioneers noticed that the second batch of King's-Horses that had been made weren't the same as the first. Once they'd delivered them, the trio had started planning their escape from the kingdom.

Nikolas clutched Isabella's hand and reaffirmed his grip on the brown sack containing their meager belongings. He stared at Marcus nervously. "Where's Christophe?" he asked, squinting in the moonlight. The plan had been for them to meet outside of the eastern castle wall at two in the morning. Nikolas glanced at his pocket watch; Christophe was fifteen minutes late. Christophe had never been late for anything since becoming a Conventioneer.

Marcus held the secret door in the castle wall open, a hooded lantern in his other hand. "You two need to go. I'll find him and send him out another way."

"But what about you?" asked Nikolas.

"He'll be fine," said Isabella knowingly.

Marcus nodded. "Now go. You have the map to that new mountaintop village of Minette. I have friends there who will help you establish a new life. Go, you'll be safe there." He handed Nikolas the lantern and disappeared, closing the secret door behind him.

Marcus stood on the other side of the castle wall, wondering if the big bet he was making by sending Nikolas to the west coast would work. Only time would tell.

"Lord Pieman!" yelled a soldier, running up to him.

"How did you know to look for me here?" asked Marcus.

"Conventioneer Stimple thought you might be around here," he replied. "Sorry, my lord, but there are two Conventioneers missing and it is past curfew."

"Oh, that is of concern. Who are they?" asked Marcus, walking with the soldier away from the secret door.

"Nikolas Klaus and Christophe Creangle," replied the soldier. "Stimple did the inspection himself."

"Hmm," said Marcus, rolling his eyes at Simon, once again, trying to intervene in plans where he was not invited to participate. "I'm afraid Conventioneer Klaus has drowned. I saw the body myself only a few minutes ago. I will tend to it, but Creangle..." Marcus rubbed his clean-shaven chin in thought. Despite the clearly close relationship between Nikolas and Christophe, Marcus had a very different relationship with Creangle. Christophe was always suspicious of Marcus and his ultimate intentions. "Check outside the northern castle wall. If I was Creangle, that's how I'd try to escape. He'll likely be heading eastwards.

"Now, get me Creangle, alive!" commanded Marcus. "If you need me, I'll be having a word with Conventioneer Stimple." Marcus was determined to keep a tighter leash on Simon.

———————

Nikolas and Isabella moved swiftly on the moonlit forest path, guided by Nikolas' mental map of the area and the hooded lantern's yellow light.

"Why are we stopping here?" asked Isabella, looking about.

Nikolas grabbed a camouflaged blanket and revealed an original King's-Horse.

"I thought they were all destroyed," said Isabella, confused. "Did you lie to me?"

Nikolas reached into his brown bag for a shiny copper cube. After unlocking the heart-panel, he placed it into the King's-Horse and attached the cables.

"I did not lie, but I will admit to… shaping the truth," said Nikolas, wincing. "Marcus couldn't know that we had built eight of these, four of them… like this one."

Isabella laughed. "Hmm, there's hope for you yet," she said to her husband. "Why didn't you tell Marcus?"

"The man is my brother, yes? He is a wonderful man layered over a very determined one. Some things he has done, he has tried to shield me from. I still learned of some of these things. For the King's-Horses, Christophe insisted we keep these just between us, and I think him correct, yes? Marcus isn't escaping, is he?"

Isabella smiled sadly at Nikolas as he did his final checks. She loved how his words often tumbled together, bumping into each other on the way out of his head, and she appreciated how he never asked about her relationship with Marcus. "No, he isn't," she replied.

Nikolas stopped and gazed upon Isabella, her moonlit beauty momentarily distracting him. "A man such as he cannot untangle himself. He told me the story he needed me to believe. With his family and everything, he would never flee. He has never backed down from a battle in his life. He will thrive now, with no need to worry about me."

Isabella nodded. "Nikolas?"

He smiled at her, wondering what he'd forgotten.

"Get on the King's-Horse. You've checked everything ten times."

"I know, it's just that I want to make sure—"

"Nikolas?" she said sweetly.

She was right. She had the wonderful ability to clear the fog of complication from his thinking and remove worry. Things just became simple and clear when she spoke.

"Of course," he said, helping her on the King's-Horse and then getting on himself. Nikolas then started it, and

Isabella let out a startled scream. The mechanical horse vibrated, its eyes glowing like lanterns, clicks and whirls emanating from various parts.

"Have you used it before?" she asked.

"Um… you would not be comfortable with the answer," he replied sheepishly.

"Yes," said Isabella, giving his hands a squeeze as he held the reins. "This is a lot more exciting than I expected."

"Next, Minette."

"Well, maybe," said Isabella mischievously. "All I promised Marcus is that we'd end up there. Let's see where the road takes us."

CHAPTER THIRTY-THREE

BITE MARKS

Tee couldn't stop her body from shaking with adrenaline as she dragged the two long, thick branches back to Elly. She'd carefully cut away Elly's blouse from around the wound, cleaned the wound with the vinegar, and bandaged her up with a fresh cloth.

Tee had ripped off her sleeves and tied them around Elly's waist to apply pressure. Every time she remembered Elly's cries of pain, Tee's eyes welled up.

As she approached Elly, who was wrapped in both of their yellow-hooded cloaks, she noticed that LeLoup, Franklin, the henchmen, and the Liar were gone. She glanced around nervously. Tee felt her mind circling the edge of despair. She didn't know how much more she could take.

Elly's pain-filled groan bolstered Tee's determination. Dropping the branches to the ground, Tee dug into her backpack and pulled out thick black cables she'd taken from her grandfather's lab. For a moment, she thought of when the same type of cable had saved her life from LeLoup; now she hoped it would save Elly's from him.

Tee diligently wove it back and forth between the branches.

"Elly, are you still with me?" asked Tee, steeling herself for the next task.

"Huh? Tee?" Elly replied sleepily.

"I'm going to have to move you onto the stretcher. It's going to hurt." Tee hesitated for a moment, and then tried to do it as quickly as she could. Elly's screams shredded Tee's soul.

With Elly properly on the stretcher, Tee kneeled down on the forest floor and leaned forward, letting some of her bottled-up emotions out.

Tee felt a touch and turned, surprised to see Elly reaching out to her. "You're my hero, Tee. I love you," said Elly, very slowly, her eyes barely open.

Taking Elly's hand carefully and tucking it back in, Tee searched the forest for any sign as to which direction she should go.

The dirty, sleeveless Tee shook her head. "At least don't rain," she whispered. She put on her backpack, leaving her two charged shock-sticks peeking out the top and putting the other two between Elly and the stretcher, just in case.

Talking to herself to keep herself focused, Tee said, "All you have to do now is pick up the ends and drag Elly to the road. It's… that way." Tee pointed herself in an arbitrary direction. "You can do this. You have to do this."

Tee nodded to herself and picked up the branches.

Five feet later, Tee fell, cutting her hand on the improvised handle of the stretcher. She was discouraged by how heavy it was. "You have to do this," she repeated to herself. "Just think, think." Tee reached into her backpack for a knife, and cut off her pant legs. After wrapping them around her palms, she grabbed hold of the branches again and ordered herself forward. "One more step, Tee. You can do this."

———————

Tee growled as she saw the road come into view. "Another step, Tee. Another step. Don't let the pain win," she said to herself, exhausted. She was swaying back and forth as she pulled the stretcher forward.

As Tee's foot touched the road, she put down the stretcher carefully. Her arms were decorated with cuts, her hands with blisters. She bent down, her hands on her knees, a heavy mix of emotions coming out as laughter and tears.

"Elly, we made it," said Tee, peering back at her friend. "Elly?"

Her face was pale, her lips bluish. Tee's chin trembled as she waited anxiously for Elly to take a painful breath. Tee nodded. "Good, you remember the no dying rule. You had me scared, Elly."

Tee stood up and prepared to pick up the branches when she heard a heartwarming clip-clopping sound. Watching eagerly, Tee finally saw a horse and cart come around the bend.

She took off her backpack, removing one shock-stick and holding it behind her back.

The driver brought his horse to a gradual stop beside Tee and looked her up and down. He was greasy-looking, with two days of growth on his face and dark hair that was gray at the temples. His belly stuck out half way to his knees.

He glanced at Elly and assessed their situation. Pushing up his three-point hat with a sausage-thick finger, he gave Tee a smile that made her shiver with discomfort.

"Hello, pretty girl. It looks like you need some help."

Tee stared at the man, thinking.

He looked Tee over again. "I could be nice to you, if you'd be nice to me."

Tee glanced at Elly, a million thoughts going through her head. She'd already calculated twice that unless she got her friend to Costello within the next couple of hours, Elly would die for certain.

Returning her gaze to the cart driver, Tee asked herself: how far was she willing to go to save Elly's life?

The driver's grin widened, chilling Tee.

"So are we going to help each other?" he asked.

Tee dropped her gaze to the ground. *How far are you willing to go to save her, Tee?* Her hands started shaking and Tee stared at the man. "I need your horse and cart," she said softly.

He slid over on his bench. "I know. Why don't you come up here and we can figure things out?" he said, patting the spot beside him.

Tee repeated, this time louder and with bite in her voice, "I need your horse and cart." She revealed the shock-stick from behind her back.

He chuckled. "That's a nice piece of metal you have there. Now why don't you put it down, and come keep me company up here. You want me to help your friend, don't you?"

Tee growled as her eyes pierced the driver. "I need your horse and cart!" she yelled, leaping forward.

CHAPTER THIRTY-FOUR

Fare Warning

Nikolas stared at the grand entrance, with its cathedral ceiling and stained glass. Marcus' presidential mansion was almost too much for him to take in, having been away from such opulence for so long.

Marcus glanced up and around. "Rather extraordinary, isn't it? It was designed to make visitors feel small, to give the queen a political advantage immediately upon greeting them. Supposedly, Queen Pastora Willard designed it herself, over two hundred and forty years ago.

"I had the entranceway restored to its original glory eight or nine years ago. I find it quite breathtaking."

Nikolas turned his gaze to the ten-foot-tall paintings, and then the servants in white, who moved about almost invisibly in the background.

"The paintings, and the servant uniforms, are original as well. She had the most successful reign of any monarch in this part of the continent."

Nikolas felt one of the several marble columns with his rough hands. The coolness and smoothness reminded him of the ones in his adolescent home. "You are the president for life here in Teuton, yes?"

Marcus nodded. "Of the Republic of Teuton, yes. There was a royal rebellion in the southeast when I was asked to become president. The royals didn't have enough power to win, but had enough to make life difficult if we wanted to reclaim their stronghold, so I gave them what they wanted."

Nikolas folded his arms. That didn't sound like Marcus at all.

Marcus smiled. "I gave them free rein over their lands, but I prevented their merchants from coming into Teuton or traveling into Parush. They were boxed in, and when they tried to levy taxes on the peasants they had rallied, it imploded. When the royals fell, I opened the borders. There have been serious talks about reunification going on for quite some time. It's for my successor to worry about, not me."

In all the years Nikolas had known Marcus, he'd never heard him acknowledge his mortality. Marcus' personality and ambitions sometimes seemed like they could hold back the realities of life until a moment of his choosing.

Marcus finished talking with a servant and turned to Nikolas. "Come, let's go to the main study."

As they walked, Nikolas took in the detail. He appreciated the artistry of those that had put such a place together, but cringed at the excess. He hadn't realized until just now how much his perspective had changed over time.

"That's Gilbert's Horror," remarked Nikolas, pointing to a famous painting denoting the beginning of the Era of Abominators.

Marcus stopped beside the chilling painting. "I found it in a small village called Bodear. I can't remember why I was there, but I learned they had protected our kind from the beginning. When the elders of the village learned who I was, they gave it to me. They asked me to hang it so that I would see it every day.

"I've returned to that village often. They are wonderful people. They seem very simple, but they understand a lot about physics and mathematics on a philosophical level. Whenever I go, it feels like a cleansing of the mind. I do some of my best work there. They help keep me grounded. Well, as grounded as I can be," he said with a smile.

Nikolas nodded, studying the painting. He turned to Marcus in wonder. "Did you do all the reforms you'd hoped?" he asked.

Marcus frowned. "In Teuton, I've been able to enact most of them, but it will take a generation or two for the reforms and educational changes to really have the needed effect. Old habits and mindsets are difficult to change. Elsewhere, I've had less success. In Freland, it went better than in the inexplicably disintegrating southern kingdoms. My intuition tells me it's related to

Abeland. He hasn't written to me in quite some time.

"The greatest lesson I've learned is that you have to make it more painful, more difficult, to stay with how things are, than to move to the new way things need to be. People are actually the hardest problem to solve, but I believe I have a solution."

Nikolas felt a chill at Marcus' statement.

Marcus continued. "I'm coming to believe people need something dramatic to motivate them. Otherwise, the many always feel threatened by granting the same rights and privileges to the few that they have long denied us."

Everything Marcus said was a more experienced, nuanced echo of what he'd said in the earliest days Nikolas had known him.

They walked down beautiful corridors lit with clock-work lanterns of Marcus' design until they came to a statue and the study. Marcus entered the cozy study while Nikolas stopped and stared in shock at the statue just outside.

To almost everyone, the figure would have appeared to be a remarkable statue of a horse kicking at the air, but Nikolas was certain it was an actual King's-Horse. A wooden face and mane had been added, but he could see the shiny gears and belts through the small holes intended to allow heat to exhaust. Then his eye caught the heart-panel, and he got nervous for the first time since being in Marcus' presence.

Nikolas scrutinized the details without touching the King's-Horse. It was definitely an original King's-Horse, but quick mental math accounted for all the ones that he and Christophe had built. He couldn't understand where it had come from. He stared at the heart-panel, trying to remember if they had somehow mistakenly created any more than the four he could think of that had it. He adjusted his spectacles and leaned in, making sure that the heart-panel was indeed a door. He rubbed his chin as his eyes darted around, his memory trying to figure out how this was possible. Questions ran through his mind: *If Marcus has this, what else does he have? What else has he been hiding? Does he know about the MCM engine? Or worse, does he have the plans?*

He knew better than to test the polite charade that he and Marcus had going on. Nikolas knew he was a prisoner, but as long as he didn't give Marcus any reason to make that apparent, he would be allowed to roam around and glean whatever information he could from whatever sources were available.

"Nikolas, come. The tea's ready," said Marcus.

Nikolas reached over the side of the high-armed, red velvet chair, and laid the book he'd been reading for the past two hours on the floor. He gathered the notes he'd been writing off and on for the past few days, and gazed at the tables and side tables. He still didn't want to connect his work with anything associated with Marcus' endeavor, so he placed them on the floor in a pile once again. He knew it was silly, but it was the only form of rebellion he felt he could do unnoticed. He pulled off his spectacles and rubbed between his eyes.

The tea they'd had in the study by the King's-Horse had been cut short the other day, and ever since, Nikolas had hardly seen Marcus. Whenever he'd caught a glimpse of Marcus, he'd had an intense look.

The guards allowed Nikolas to wander around the mansion and to go into the gardens, but only if accompanied. There were areas that he was politely asked to not go, and Nikolas understood all too well.

Nikolas rested his head on the high back of the chair and put his spectacles back on. He gazed in thought at the stained glass ceiling some sixty feet above him. It was a gilded cage, and he wondered what exactly Marcus' intentions were for him.

He stood up and stretched, then glanced at the catwalks and ladders that decorated the towering bookcases. Ever intrigued by the huge glass wall at the east end of the library, Nikolas made his way over to it.

He gazed down from its second floor height at the gardens below and the white stone towers that defined its boundaries.

Putting his hands in his pockets, Nikolas watched the servants and soldiers traveling between the white towers. He'd been unsuccessful in trying to glean much information about the towers, but he could tell they were significant somehow. He noticed food occasionally going in or coming out, and figured that meant they housed important prisoners of some kind—but who?

Nikolas leaned against the glass, resting his head against an arm. He casually gazed down at the massive garden. Its bushes and flowers formed wonderful patterns. Nikolas enjoyed the gardens and wondered about possibly taking lunch there.

Something caught Nikolas' imagination and started to pull him back from his thoughts. There was something about the garden, the flower arrangement in particular. He frowned and sighed as he tried to grasp the fleeting idea. What was it?

Standing back, folding his arms and tugging on his beard, he studied the towers and then the garden as a whole again, and it hit him. The void between the flowers and the shrubbery made the symbol of the old Fare, facing north. Nikolas took a step back and looked at it again to be certain. A cold sweat came over him.

Nikolas knew his history well enough to know that the Fare had first risen to prominence in the shadows of others, and had left signs of their growing boldness everywhere. What if Marcus had not replaced the Fare, taking all of its broken pieces and using it in his new puzzle, but instead been an instrument of the Fare's will all along? Had they been behind some of his more ambitious successes, and were they now behind his limited ones?

For a brief moment, Nikolas wondered if Marcus had done this intentionally. It didn't seem like something Marcus would do, given how he felt about the original Fare, but he didn't know for certain.

"Nikolas!" boomed Marcus, making him nearly jump out of his skin. Marcus was wearing his signature black long coat and vest, the gold chain of a pocket watch visible from a lower pocket. His right eye was covered in a black eye patch.

"Sorry," said Marcus. "I didn't realize you were deep in thought. Was it anything interesting? I could use a good distraction."

Nikolas glanced at the garden before focusing back on Marcus. "The garden. Has it always been like this?"

Marcus frowned and walked over to look at it. "No... is there something of particular interest? Recently the head gardener proposed some changes and I was too busy to be involved. He has a disfigured woman helping him, I've heard." Marcus looked at the garden, squinting. "It seems pleasant enough."

Nikolas nodded as he absorbed the statement.

"Are you free?" asked Marcus, turning to Nikolas and gesturing for him to follow.

"Let me gather my things," said Nikolas, picking up his papers.

Marcus smiled. "Good. I apologize for being such a bad host these past few days. Some sacrifices had to be made to stop the ambitious and the opportunistic."

"Where are we going?" asked Nikolas as they headed out of the study.

"To my principal office, in the main building. I have a couple of things I'd like to discuss with you, a few things to show you, and then we can have lunch in the garden."

Nikolas stopped, deciding that he could no longer hold off asking the question. "How long do you plan for me to be *here*?"

Marcus smiled uncomfortably. "I think—" he paused. "I think things will be clear by this evening."

CHAPTER THIRTY-FIVE

A BARGAIN MADE

Angelic voices and music wove their way into Elly's dreams, until finally she opened her eyes. Before her, on the ceiling, was a beautiful painting. It showed people leaping off a cliff and becoming birds as they flew towards the sun, then coming back, changing from birds into people again and getting in line for their next turn. Elly had never seen anything like it. She felt at peace gazing upon it.

Eventually, she moved her eyes around the room. Elly noticed two large, open windows with morning light pouring in. They had thick red-and-gold curtains drawn aside. She couldn't remember what time of day it was when she'd been shot.

She was about to close her eyes and drift off to sleep again when she realized that beside the curtains was a man kneeling, dressed identically in red-and-gold robes. He was bald and had a thin, clean-shaven face. He was muttering to himself, rocking back and forth on his knees, with his eyes closed. When Elly's eyes landed on him, he ceased moving and smiled at her, revealing his gentle eyes.

He stood, bowed, and silently left the room.

She returned to staring at the ceiling until she heard the hint of a familiar sound. Her excitement built, until finally Tee burst through the open doorway, sliding on the marble floor. Elly winced in pain as she thought about trying to move.

Tee's eyes were tear-filled, her face hopeful and pained. She leapt to Elly's low bedside, a blur of red cloth and black hair. She buried her head in the side of Elly's pillow, her left arm wrapping around her bedridden best friend.

With a choked-up voice, Tee asked, "How... ah... how are you feeling?" Tears of relief were rolling down Tee's face, wetting Elly's ear.

"I'm okay," she said weakly. "Good thing we have the no dying rule, right?"

Tee chuckled, but the river of tears continued.

Elly carefully wrapped her arms around Tee, wincing in pain as she did so. "You saved me. We're okay now." Tee's tears accelerated and she hugged Elly harder.

Elly couldn't remember ever seeing such a display from Tee. She took a deep breath and rubbed Tee's back gently. "I'm okay, you saved me," she repeated, failing to console her. As the seconds passed, Elly's anxiety crept up. "Tee? Are we okay?" she asked nervously.

Inexplicably, Elly felt her gaze drawn to the doorway. She could sense a presence there, just out of view.

"Tee? What happened?"

CHAPTER THIRTY-SIX
THE GINGERBREAD MAN

Gretel sat on the grass, gently stroking the white petals of the wild Black-eyed Susans she'd picked off the fence's vines. The afternoon light made the hearts of the flowers look bruised to Gretel. She stared at them until a rush of emotion made her crumple them and drop them to the ground.

She pulled in her legs and rocked herself back and forth as she tried to expel the images that had started invading her waking hours, no longer happy to simply be nightmares. Each day, she wanted more and more to get out of her skin and away from the increasing flood of emotions. She wondered if somehow Mother had cursed her. Had she heard the relief in Gretel's voice at her passing? Was this her revenge?

"Hi, Gretel," said Hans.

Gretel's gaze jumped from the ground to her brother. He was smiling and appeared peaceful, dressed in a new brown jerkin and darker brown pantaloons. He had a new white shirt with puffy sleeves and black, shiny boots.

"How many people did you kill to pay for all that?" asked Gretel hostilely.

Hans frowned and put his hands up, keeping a small box tucked under his arm. "I actually paid for this out of my share of our little treasure pile. A treasure pile, I will point out, that you raided quite unfairly to pay for food and other stuff to tend to your... hobby."

"And our brother," said Gretel.

Hans gnashed his teeth, his eyes narrowed. "You know," he said, "I came to try and make things how they used to be."

"I'm sorry," said Gretel, letting out an uneasy breath.

"I didn't want to talk about him. To be honest, I'd prefer if we never talked about him or that pet of yours again," said Hans.

Gretel glared at him.

"Allow me to start again?" asked Hans, sitting down a few feet away. "I have just spoken with Saul. We have squared away our differences. He will take care of the Hound, and you and I are free to go wherever we will."

"But Saul's—"

Hans grimaced as he interrupted. "Nothing to us. You know it's a lie as much as I do. Mother must have told you, and if she didn't, then you must have figured it out," said Hans. "I gave him what he deserved of the treasure as well." He gazed down at the simple wooden box in his lap.

Gretel released her legs so she could sit more comfortably. "You shouldn't have hurt Saul."

Hans wobbled his head back and forth in thought. "Maybe… maybe not. Maybe he deserved it for getting between us. Things have been… very different since Mother left."

"Like the nightmares," said Gretel, staring at the grass, wanting the ground to swallow her up.

"Yes," said Hans, sounding sympathetic, "the nightmares. What ones are you having?"

Gretel's eyes welled up as she tried to talk.

Hans moved beside her and rubbed her back. "It's okay, shh, never mind. Look, I made you something," he said, opening the box.

"Gingerbread?" said Gretel in happy astonishment.

"I will admit," said Hans coyly, "that I didn't make any for the Hound or Saul. This is just for you. Though in fairness, I did give them another type of treat."

Gretel smiled at him as she reached for the large cookie. After a few small bites, Gretel felt a small wave of calm hit her.

Hans closed the lid. "I just want things to be how they were, but better," he said. "You and me and the world. I want all of it." He stood and offered Gretel his hand.

Gretel stopped and sniffed the air for a moment. "Do you smell something?"

Hans sniffed. "It's probably some wood smoke from the campers I saw nearby. I was going to rob them, but I thought the last thing you needed to see were signs of a fight on my new clothes. I wanted to look nice for you, to make this reunion special."

Gretel munched on her cookie as they walked and chatted about old times.

"We should go back," said Gretel, glancing around, trying to figure out which way it was to the cabin. "I need to make sure that Saul is really okay with everything. That the Hound—"

"No," said Hans, grabbing her hand.

Gretel tried to pull her hand away, and stumbled. Hans caught her by the elbows.

"Hans, I don't... I don't feel right," said Gretel, worried.

He stroked the back of Gretel's hands with his thumbs. "Everything is going to be wonderfully fine," he said with a deeply sinister smile. "It's going to be like it used to be."

Gretel's eyes went wide with horror. "That's what the man says in my nightmares."

"Oh, you remember that, do you? I wasn't sure how quickly the Ginger would affect your mind; apparently not as quickly as I expected," said Hans. A giggle quickly grew into a maniacal laugh as he let go of Gretel and enjoyed the terror in her eyes. "I was so disappointed at how you changed as your steady diet of Ginger wore off.

Saul lost focus, but you... you changed into this crying mess. I had no idea that your mind would remember all those wonderful times we spent together, and bring them back as nightmares. You know, it actually pains me to know that *you* have replaced my sweet, cruel Gretel."

Gretel stumbled. "That's... that's why you never ate the cookies," she stammered, recoiling and nearly falling over.

"The cookies were always my way of preparing you for our special moments together." Hans sprang forward and pushed Gretel back as she tried to regain her footing. "It's nasty stuff, that Ginger. When I was sixteen, I made a batch so strong I was able to knock out a horse for three days. I felt so... powerful that day," said Hans, his hands out.

He twitched as he saw the anger and disgust in Gretel's eyes, and turned his gaze to the sky. "Mother loved me, you know. Through everything she did to me, or had done to me, I believe she was always trying to make me stronger. And as long as I was a good boy, she'd let me do anything." Hans' eyes pierced Gretel. "Anything."

Gretel got up and took a clumsy swing at Hans. He easily stepped out of the way and pushed her to the ground again. As she landed, the world started to spin.

Hans chewed on his lip for a moment, his eyes dancing with malevolent joy. "Sorry about the nightmares, but I have to tell you, it honestly delights me.

It means I wasn't alone in those moments. I sometimes felt like I could have set fire to the house and no one would have noticed, no one would have moved a muscle. I'm getting quite good at that, by the way."

Gretel forced herself up and started running, staggering back and forth.

Hans laughed hard. "Running back to your Beast, or just running away? Come on then, run!" Hans mocked her as she ran like a drunk in the dark. "Go on! Run, Gretel, run!" He yelled at her, his tone twisting. "Run, run, as fast as you can, you can't outrun me... I'm the Gingerbread Man."

Gretel's soul-splitting scream traveled down the forest path, into the burning cabin, and snapped the Hound's eyes open. He felt an intensity of purpose fill his veins like never before. Suddenly there was no pain, no self-pity. There was only one thought: Gretel.

CHAPTER THIRTY-SEVEN

ARMED AND DANGEROUS

Mounira awoke to a knock at her door in the middle of the night. A hunched-over old man stepped out of view just as she opened the door. For a few minutes, she followed him through the stone corridors of the ruined castle, wondering who he was and if he had indeed awoken her.

"Who are you?" she asked, not wanting to take another step until she had some sense of where she was being taken. She didn't recognize this part of the castle.

"Ah," said the old man, turning and allowing Mounira her first real look at him. He had a long white beard and crazy, bushy white hair. His brilliant blue eyes twinkled in the white light emanating from the top of his cane.

"That light... that's like Anciano Klaus' light in his study," said Mounira. "Do you know him?"

The old man seemed disoriented for a moment, almost surprised to see Mounira standing there a few yards away. "There are lots of things," he said, glancing around at the walls, "lots of things I know, lots of people I've met, and some of them were even real." He scratched his head. "Are you real?"

Mounira narrowed her eyes, wondering what the stranger was talking about. "I am. Are you?"

"I hope so, otherwise I'm a ghost who forgot to shed his mortal coil," he said. He tapped his forehead with his fingers while shushing, almost as if trying to quiet voices inside.

"You have coils?" asked Mounira, not sure exactly what he meant. His Frelish was heavily accented, more so than Nikolas', but similar.

A sweet smile spread across the old man's face. "Christina was not exaggerating when she said you are a fountain of questions. She didn't know I was listening, but I was. I was there. I was listening."

Mounira smiled uncomfortably. She could tell that something wasn't right about the man, like his soul was stuck in a broken machine. It dawned on her that he'd not been wandering aimlessly, but rather had brought her to a part of the castle that she hadn't explored.

"Have you enjoyed your week here? Are the people nice?" he asked, resting both hands on the cane. "I don't know them. I stay in my room. I look at my wall. Sometimes I write on her. I like my wall."

Mounira walked up to the man, studying his face as she did. "You brought me here. Did you want to show me something?" she asked, guessing.

The man nodded and sighed with relief.

She gently took his hand and he jumped.

"Who are you?" he asked, startled.

A memory from long ago flashed before Mounira and tears came to her eyes. She remembered the last days of her great-grandmother, before she passed.

"My name is Mounira. I'm a friend. You were going to show me something. What's your name?"

The man glanced all around fearfully. "My name is Christophe the Con…?"

"Hello, Christophe," said Mounira soothingly. She held his hand, and he gazed down at it and sighed heavily. "Are you feeling okay now?"

Christophe nodded. "I feel better, yes. You remind me of Luis. Did you know him?"

"No," replied Mounira, curious. "What happened to him?"

"Brilliant boy. He drowned. So sad," said Christophe, staring off in the distance.

"Oh." Mounira thought for a moment. "How come I haven't met you yet? I've been here for a week."

"Christina was not exaggerating when she said you are a fountain of questions. She didn't know I was listening, but I was. I was there. I was listening," said Christophe, exactly as he had before.

"I know Anciano… I mean, I know Nikolas Klaus. Do

you know him? He's a very nice man."

The old man nodded. "Yes, I know Nikolas. I haven't seen him in a long time. Is he okay?"

Mounira frowned, and bit her lip in thought for a moment. "He's fine. Everything is fine. Do you leave your wall very often?"

"No," muttered Christophe. "I like my wall. She's very good to me. I get to write all my ideas on her when I have to get them out of my head." He gazed down at Mounira, her brown eyes shining in the light. "Oh! I wanted to show you something. I make it when I sneak out at night. The lock they have on my room, it's not very good. They think I'm not all there, but I am! I am!"

Mounira wondered if it was such a good idea to be out with this man. "Okay then, why don't you show me?"

"Yes, yes it's right..." Christophe glanced around. "It's this way!"

———— ⟋ ————

Christina knocked on Mounira's bedroom door and gently pushed it open. She'd tended to all of her morning duties, and had been surprised to hear that Mounira had returned to her room after a quick breakfast.

Mounira was staring out the window at the grassy lands surrounding the ruined castle. It was so different from her homeland. She had her yellow cloak on, the hood up.

"Good morning," said Christina. "Everything okay?"

Mounira nodded.

"Well, we're going to meet up with Tee and Elly this morning. I promised Nikolas I'd keep an eye on them."

Still staring out the window, Mounira asked, "I met him last night. Did you know he wanders the halls sometimes at night?"

"Who are you talking about?" asked Christina, leaning on the doorframe.

"Your father. Christophe."

Christina stiffened and straightened up. "What are you talking about? He's dead to the world, a body with no soul anymore."

Mounira shook her head. "He heard you talk about me. He said you said I ask a lot of questions."

"This isn't funny," said Christina, a tremor of emotion in her voice. "My father—"

As Mounira turned to face her, Christina caught sight of a lump on her back, almost like she had a backpack underneath her cloak.

"I met him last night. He was wandering the halls. He had something to show me," said Mounira, a strange smile spreading over her face.

"What are you talking about?" asked Christina, stepping into the room and closing the door behind her.

Mounira pulled her cloak aside, jerked her head back, and moved her stump. Christina watched as pieces of metal rotated and clicked into place.

Raising her mechanical arm, Mounira moved its two fingers and thumb.

Christina's chin trembled. "He made that?" she whispered, trying to keep everything in.

Mounira nodded, a tear rolling down her cheek.

Sliding down the door to sit on the floor, Christina stared at the marvel as Mounira walked up to her. "He hasn't done anything other than write nonsense or stare at that wall for years. I talk to him every day that I'm here, and he just stares blankly at that wall."

"He heard you talk about me. Is that why he made this?" Mounira asked.

Christina shrugged, sniffling and rubbing her nose with her hand. "I... I don't know," she said, working around the lump in her throat. She grabbed Mounira and hugged her tightly. "You have no idea how much this means to me. I'd thought the arm had been lost, I thought he'd been lost... now, we need to get Tee and Elly before they are lost."

CHAPTER THIRTY-EIGHT

HUMPTY DUMPTY

As Marcus and Nikolas walked out of the library building and started to cross the garden towards the presidential manor, a young male servant ran up to them.

"Lord Pieman," he said, then waited for Marcus to acknowledge him.

"Yes, what is it?" said Marcus, annoyed.

"You have an unexpected visitor. He says that you know him and that he works for Simon St. Malo."

Marcus thought for a moment. Simon had never sent anyone with a message before. "Is this an old man?"

"Yes, and he has a sickly look about him."

He rubbed his stubbly chin. "Thank you. I'll see to the visitor," he said, dismissing the boy. After the servant left, he said, "Simon treats Arthur horribly, always has. Even though the man is his only family."

Nikolas was taken aback. "Family? But—"

Marcus started walking. "He's Simon's uncle. He appeared about ten years after you left. Arthur saw Simon walking in the streets of Relna and walked up to him. He recognized the man, even in his beggar robes. Arthur was to be arrested when he begged Simon for forgiveness and offered anything to make it up to him. The rest is history."

"What was the apology for?" asked Nikolas, unable to hold back his curiosity.

"For trading the lives of Simon's family for a small bag of gold."

————————

Marcus smiled and extended his hand. He was suspicious of Arthur's arrival, as no one had ever visited any of Marcus' residences uninvited. "Arthur, this is quite a surprise. Is Simon with you?"

Arthur smiled nervously. "No. He sent me alone, said he had some very pressing matters to attend to." He paused, wondering if he should share some of his concerns—particularly Simon's emotional state when he left—but figured it was unbecoming of his role. "I'm sorry to disturb you, Lord Pieman—"

Marcus raised an eyebrow.

"Marcus." Arthur glanced past him to the slightly familiar-looking, bald, bearded man. It took him a minute before he realized the man was the one from the painting Simon had recently put back up in the hallway leading to his study. They exchanged nods.

"Now, Arthur," said Marcus, motioning for Cleeves to follow him, "don't take this the wrong way, as you are always welcome, but why are you here?"

Cleeves tapped his vest, handing his long coat to a servant. "Simon had a letter he needed me to give you in person. He was quite... insistent on it."

"Why didn't he send it by Neumatic Tube?" asked Nikolas, grabbing their attention. It was clear from Cleeves' reaction that the same question was on both of their minds.

"Well?" asked Marcus, folding his arms.

Cleeves glanced at the nearly invisible servants about. "If we could discuss all of this in private, I'd feel more comfortable."

"Come," said Marcus, leading the way.

His balcony office was a beautifully decorated large room, with bookcases along the left wall, and pictures and shelves with objects of art on the right. There was a beautiful, yet clearly unused, drawing table, a mahogany desk, and a sitting area for six with high-backed chairs by a fireplace. Huge windows framed a set of double doors that led to a massive raised balcony overlooking the central garden.

"Would you mind opening those, Nikolas? The air in here is a bit stuffy," said Marcus. He rarely used the office for anything other than formal meetings.

Nikolas opened the balcony doors and a chill ran down his spin as he caught a glimpse of the old Fare symbol etched into the grand garden. He leaned against one of the large windowpanes and returned his attention to Marcus and Cleeves.

Marcus' charm melted away, leaving a stern face and a palpable, intimidating presence. "Arthur," he said sharply, "you still haven't told me why you are here. I understand there's a letter, and I appreciate you confirming that Simon's been out and about while pretending to be at home, but I don't understand why you have been sent."

Arthur reached into his red vest's breast pocket. "Simon insisted that I deliver this to you personally. He said it was a matter of life and death. He wanted to ensure there was no opportunity for anyone to intercept it. That's why he didn't want to send the message by tube or anyone else."

Marcus glared at Arthur suspiciously as he held out the beige envelope with its blue stamped seal. Marcus picked up a small bronze knife off his desk, ready to take and open the letter, and then stopped. He crossed his arms and leaned back against his desk. The tension in the room went up a notch.

"Oh, it doesn't require a blade," said Cleeves. "He's using a rather weak wax these days." He held out the letter again.

Marcus stared at the letter, several feet away. He found it odd that Arthur was so afraid that he seemed to be rooted to the spot. He seemed neither curious about what the letter said, nor comfortable being there. Marcus was surprised that Cleeves wasn't taking any enjoyment from being away from Simon or his usual confines.

"Cleeves, I don't have my monocle on me. Would you mind opening it and reading it to me? You can trust Nikolas here."

Nikolas hid his reaction by glancing out the window. He knew very well that Marcus could read without his monocle. "I hope this isn't more pointless news about the Staaten royalty," sniped Marcus.

Arthur nervously stared at Nikolas and then at Marcus. "Um, are you aware that there's a new regent in Staaten, and that she has annexed Elizabetina?"

"What?" yelled Marcus, standing up. "When did this happen?"

"Several days ago," said Arthur, each word petering out more quietly than the previous one.

Marcus was about to reach out and snatch the letter from Arthur's hand in rage, when he caught Nikolas' subtle gesture to calm down. Leaning against his desk once again, Marcus rubbed his face and folded his arms. "Read it please, Arthur," he commanded. "I'm in no mood."

Arthur cracked the letter's seal and gave the papers inside, which appeared to be stuck, a tug. White powder flew into the air and all over Cleeves' face.

Marcus' eyes went wide. Without thinking, he tackled Nikolas onto the balcony. Nikolas' head hit the stone balcony floor with a wet thud. Marcus scrambled to his feet and glanced back at Arthur.

The old man was on the ground, grabbing his throat,

his eyes shut tight. Marcus watched helplessly as Arthur gasped his last breaths.

Suddenly one of the white towers exploded at its base, followed by another explosion, and then a third. Marcus shielded himself and Nikolas from the small pieces of rocks that showered down. Marcus could hear the screams of servants coming from everywhere as more explosions followed.

A minute later, his ears ringing, Marcus wiped the dust from his face and peered through the haze. The sun sliced through with red afternoon light upon the scene of destruction. He dragged his gaze, absorbing everything, until he came upon Nikolas laying there, unconscious. Marcus tapped his face gently. "Nikolas, wake up." After a couple of gentle shakes, he shook his old friend vigorously. "Nikolas, wake up! Wake up! Nikolas!"

CHAPTER THIRTY-NINE

FAITH IN FAMILY

Amami slid off the emerald-blue, armored, mechanical warhorse. She opened its mouth, reached in, and flipped a switch. With a series of sharp jerks and grinding clicks, it stopped vibrating and became silent, its head bowing as it shut down. As was tradition, she gave it a pat and thanked it for its service.

Removing a gauntlet, she felt the heart-panel for heat and nodded, satisfied. She then took off her other gauntlet and her helmet, and hung them on small hooks on the back of her King's-Horse.

Straightening up, Amami took a deep breath, steeling herself for the task ahead. She hadn't been home in two years, and she knew that her mother would disapprove of her visit just as much as she had on the previous occasions.

She turned her gaze to her run-down family home. There was still some bamboo growing around the small, one-level house. It had once been a huge home, a lush oasis on the arid plains in the foothills of the Eastern Mountains. As hope and purpose had been lost and rooms had fallen into disrepair, they had been amputated, until there remained only the one room. The mechanisms that had brilliantly fed the flora from springs deep below the surface had all but ceased working. It always looked worse than Amami imagined.

She gently pushed the door open, revealing the ten-foot-by-fifteen-foot room behind it. Amami quietly took off her boots and carefully placed her rifle and sword on the floor beside them. She nudged them until they were in perfectly alignment, allowing her to breathe more easily.

An old woman rocked in the far corner, staring out the sole window at the distant mountains. She glanced at Amami momentarily, her wispy white hair and sunken face showing how unkind the past two years had been, before returning to the window.

The Eastern Mountains were captivating, even to Amami, who had grown up at their feet. She'd heard tales about what it was like on the other side, and the incredible journey her mother had taken, crossing them. She'd intended to return after repairing her flying machine, but then she'd met Amami's father and life had changed, and then changed again.

Amami noticed the bowl of food with chopsticks on the top of it and a clay mug for cold tea on a table near her mother. She was thankful that the people from the nearby village were continuing to check in on the old woman.

The irrigation systems her mother had built for them long ago still worked as well as the day she'd made them, and they now took care of her as she had once them. Amami had fond childhood memories of her mother working on it and other things.

Silently, Amami shuffled over to the small jute rug beside her mother's rocking chair, and knelt down. She sat there, her head bowed, waiting.

After an eternity, her mother turned and whispered in a dry, cracked voice, "It is good to see you, Amami. I had wished to say goodbye."

She smiled and took her mother's hand, tears in her eyes. "There is no need to say goodbye, mother. I have brought important news." She looked at her mother's thin, pale face. Amami knew how her ancestors thought starving one's self to death cleansed the soul of sins, but she hated the idea, as her father had.

Her mother's face turned sour and she snapped her hand back. She returned her gaze to the peaceful mountains. "Important news… you always say that when you are about to throw away your life and chase after another rumor, a lie someone has said to make you feel there is hope. There is no hope," rebuked her mother.

Amami's expression hardened as she took her mother's hand again. "I have heard that a warrior boy from over the mountains is in a prison to the west."

"Again? You lost your position with the Tyrol army over such a lie once. You threw away an engagement to a good merchant's son for another. You have thrown away things that *matter*, and now, after rebuilding your life again, you seek to throw it all away once more. Each time you return from such foolery, you are more broken than before. I want nothing of it."

"But mother—"

Snapping at her daughter, she said, "We are not the only ones from over the mountain!"

"But I am told he has blue eyes," said Amami firmly.

The skeletal woman turned her stony, pained gaze on her twenty-year-old daughter. "You want to travel the world again to find out that there is no end to the rainbow? Your brother is gone. I built what they demanded. I built them a new Hotaru and they could have sailed over the mountains, all so that they could return him, but they didn't. They lied. He is dead. He has been dead a long time. Let it go. You deserve to be happy and have peace."

Amami shook her head. "This comes from someone I trust deeply. This is true."

"It cannot be!"

"But we never buried him! We never got his body back. He is still out there," pleaded Amami.

"Your father used to say that, and he died for it. You have thrown away more chances at a happy life than I can count. It was my failing, and mine alone. Do me proud and lead an honorable, happy life. Let his memory live through your life," she said sorrowfully. She was too worn out, too dehydrated, and too scarred inside to cry anymore.

Amami stood up angrily and glared at the broken, old woman. "I came here to ask, as foolish as it seemed, if you wanted to join me in finding him. But if you prefer to die, then do so. Die in shame rather than live in redemption!"

"You are a fool and will die a fool's death, Amami. Leave me to my peace." The old woman peeked out of the corner of her eye as her daughter reclaimed her boots and weapons. She was secretly proud of her daughter, but she feared Amami would drive herself off the ends of Eorthe for her mother's sins.

With her hand on the door, Amami turned back to her mother, who was staring out the window once again, and said, "I will never stop until I find Riichi. He is my only family now."

THANK YOU
FOR READING THIS BOOK

Please write a review!
Your reviews are vital in helping other readers learn about the book and series. Every little bit helps. We suggest reviewing the book at your retailer's website and **GoodReads.com!**

The story continues in Book 4 - Beauties of the Beast! And don't miss Snappy & Dashing - A Yellow Hoods Companion Tale, the novelette that follows Richelle Pieman after book 2!

Did you miss book 1 or 2? Pick them up today at your favorite bookstore or if your bookstore doesn't have them, get them to email us at:
GetTheBooks@ADZOPublishing.com

Take a moment and join our newsletter at **TheYellowHoods.com/newsletter**! We'd love to keep you in the loop and share a sneak peek of what's to come.

TheYellowHoods.com

ABOUT THE AUTHOR

In 2014, Adam burst onto the indie author scene, putting an end to over 25 years of writing short stories that few ever saw. The Yellow Hoods series quickly became a best seller. In 2015, he became a full-time author and put aside his 20-year-long career as a software architect.

Adam enjoys engaging with readers and students, whether at events or online. You can follow him on Twitter **@adamdreece**, or on his blog at **AdamDreece.com**.

He lives in Calgary, Alberta, Canada with his awesome wife, amazing kids, and a lot of sticky-notes.